BOY CRAZY

BOY CRAZY
The Secret Life of a 1950s Girl

"February 5, 1957: I've never been so popular all at once.
I don't know why, but I love every moment of it!"

Angela Weiss

iUniverse®

BOY CRAZY
The Secret Life of a 1950s Girl

This is a work of fiction. All of the characters, names, incidents, organizations, and dialogue in this novel are either the products of the author's imagination or are used fictitiously.

iUniverse books may be ordered through booksellers or by contacting:

iUniverse
1663 Liberty Drive
Bloomington, IN 47403
www.iuniverse.com
1-800-Authors (1-800-288-4677)

ISBN: 978-1-4917-6157-1 (sc)
ISBN: 978-1-4917-6109-0 (hc)
ISBN: 978-1-4917-6158-8 (e)

Library of Congress Control Number: 2015903020

Print information available on the last page.

iUniverse rev. date: 07/01/2015

Dedication

For Aunt Sara, Mom, and Dad

Wherever You May Be

Contents

Pre-Diary Memories

1949

Saturday Night, New Year's Eve 1949: Nightmare

"Mommy! Daddy!" I want my mommy and daddy. I'm frightened! I keep calling, but no one comes. Where are they? "Daddy! Mommy!" I had a scary dream. I hear the wind howling outside. The tree branches are slapping the window. "Mommy! Daddy!" I'm alone in a giant bed. I can see through the thin white curtains. It's nighttime outside. It's dark in this big room. I can hardly see the pretty flowered wallpaper. I'm in Grandma C's upstairs guest room. I've never slept here before. I'm a big girl. I'm almost five. But I'm afraid! "Daddy! Mommy!" It seems as if days go by before I hear footsteps. The door opens. I see Grandma with the hall light behind her. She's wearing a long, white flannel nightgown. She is shorter than Mommy and Daddy and the other grown-ups. She has a gray braid of hair. It goes almost down to her tushy. Yesterday I told Mommy, "Your mommy is really old."

Mommy laughed and said, "She's only seventy. It's not that old."

Grandma commands, "Gay schluffen! Gay schluffen!" She speaks only Yiddish. Though I don't know Yiddish, I remember this means, "Go to sleep!" But I'm afraid. I want my parents or even my brown bear to hug. Grandma doesn't hug me. She doesn't come near me. She's in the doorway, a dark shape against the light. Over and over, I hear, "Gay schluffen!"

"Daddy! Mommy!" I keep crying for my parents. At home in Albany, I don't cry. In our apartment, I'm not afraid. I stay with sitters when my parents go out. I sleep in a daybed in the living room. Here in Gloversville, I'm many miles from home. I haven't been alone with Grandma before. I don't know whether I like her. Even though I need a hug, I'm not sure I want her to hug me. She doesn't smell good. "Mommy! Daddy!" I become more upset. I keep calling them. Grandma never comes into the room.

1

Finally, after more orders of "Gay schluffen," she closes the door and leaves. I'm scared. I'm all alone again. It's very dark. As her footsteps go down the hall, the floor creaks. Then I hear only the storm outside. I see a white thing on the arm chair by the window. It's my rabbit-fur muff! Aunt Sara gave it to me on my birthday. I love it! If I touch it, I might feel better. But it's dark. I'm afraid to get out of bed.

"Mommy! Daddy!" Nothing happens. Why don't they come? Oh! I remember. They got all dressed up.

Daddy said, "We're going to the Jewish Community Center with Uncle Abner and Aunt Myrna."

I asked Mommy, "Why aren't Aunt Sara and Uncle Jules here?"

Mommy said, "They live too far away. Spring Valley is near NYC."

"Daddy! Mommy!" I'm still alone in the dark. I try to get out of bed. But it's too cold and scary. I yell their names more. I cry louder and faster. After a long time of fearful crying, the door opens. Did Grandma call my parents? I see them in their party clothes! "Mommy! Daddy!" I hug them. I stop crying. Mommy's face is sad. I feel bad. I say, "Is your New Year's Eve party over? I'm sorry."

Daddy says, "It's okay, Angela. Happy New Year!" With Daddy and Mommy nearby, I calm down and fall asleep. Being alone with Grandma was too much.

Fern and Angela in 1945

Herm and Angela in 1947

Grandma C around 1949

1950

Saturday, January 7, 1950: Birthday Shoes
After vacation, I'm back in kindergarten and in tap and ballet class. I'm five today! I got patent leather tap shoes! They tie with a ribbon. I like to click the silver taps on the floor. I wear soft black slippers to do the five ballet positions. I love to dance!

Friday, February 3, 1950: Stars
Pretty Miss Bridges gave me my report card. Mommy said, "Angela, you got yeses on almost everything. Very good! I'm putting a giant gold star on your chart." I like stars! I get them when I do something good. I have red stars for telling time. I have little gold stars for tying my shoe laces in a bow. If I am really good, maybe I will get a sister or brother.

Sunday, March 5, 1950: Flower Girl
I am happy. Daddy, Mommy, and I took the train to NYC. It made a lot of noise. My new plaid taffeta dress is so pretty! The collar has ruffles and lace. I was the flower girl. Cousin Justine was the bride. Her handsome husband has blue eyes. Nice Grandma W and Daddy's sisters hugged me. My uncles were quiet. I had fun with my cousins Ron and Hal. I asked, "What's a honeymoon?"
    Mommy said, "It's like a vacation."

Justine's wedding, back row, left to right: Herm, Fern, Aunt Lila, the groom, the bride, Grandma W, Aunt Hannah, Uncle Cal; front row: Hal, Angela, Ron

Sunday, March 12, 1950: Tad

Tad lives down the hall. He has blue eyes and is five. I told him about my cousin's wedding. He got down on his knee. "Angela, will you marry me?"

I laughed and said yes. I was excited. Mommy helped me dress up in a pretend long dress made of scarves. My veil was a scarf. Mommy and I cut red, orange, and yellow paper flowers for a bouquet. All the kids in the three apartment buildings came to our wedding. Tad looked nice in his suit.

First Tad said, "I do."

Then I said, "I do." Tad put a ring on my finger. He kissed me. Tad's pretty mommy gave everyone punch and cookies. Tad and I danced. Our wedding was fun. He's my husband now. We don't get a honeymoon.

Angela, *bride* of Tad

Monday, April 3, 1950: School

Daddy read my report card out loud:

Angela has learned to listen quietly. She is well mannered.

Angela is a very fine pupil. She is interested in everything.

I like my nice teacher and Hudson School.

Sunday, April 16, 1950: The Funnies

I like Sunday. Daddy's home from work! I unlocked our front door and picked up the heavy newspaper. I opened the bedroom door. Daddy and Mommy were asleep and woke up. Mommy looked unhappy. She put on her robe and went to make breakfast. Daddy is always happy to see me. I jumped into bed and listened to Daddy read the funnies. Dagwood and Blondie are the best. We laughed at the jokes. Daddy let me jump up and down on the bed. I love Daddy.

Tuesday, April 25, 1950: Get Busy

I heard Mommy tell Daddy, "The dermatologist suggested that I get a job or do something similar. My rashes should go away if I'm too busy to worry."

Sunday, May 28, 1950: Toys

Mommy drove Daddy and me from Albany toward Schenectady. We stopped to look at an empty store. Mommy said, "It is small, but will keep me busy. Any profits will help us buy a house. Angela, I'll drop you at first grade in Colonie before opening the store. We'll sell clothes, home supplies, and things they have at five-and-ten-cent stores."

I asked, "Will we sell toys?"

Daddy said yes. I like the store. I can get more toys. Dolls are the best.

Sunday, June 11, 1950: Ranger

I shot my two cap guns and played cowboys with my friends. I liked wearing my dungarees, cowgirl shirt, chaps, tie, big hat, and holster. The Lone Ranger is my favorite cowboy. Roy Rogers and Dale Evans are next best. I don't like Gene Autry and Hopalong Cassidy much.

Angela, ready for *Annie Get Your Gun*

Friday, June 23, 1950: Well-Adjusted
Mommy read my report card out loud:

> Angela works and plays very well with others. She always obeys promptly and cheerfully. She always answers in complete sentences. She counts from one to a hundred. Angela is well-adjusted emotionally.

I asked what well-adjusted means.

> Daddy said, "It's good!" I'm happy! It's vacation!

Tuesday, June 27, 1950: The Store
Mommy and I go to Fern's Cleaners and Variety Center every day except Sunday. Stores are closed on Sunday. I love looking at the toys and clothes in our store, but can't have them. We have to sell them for money. On white cardboard from the inside of shirts, Mommy painted fancy signs in big letters of different colors. "Angela, I learned to make signs in art school. Soon you'll learn to read this flyer telling people in the housing development that we're open. It lists specials: plastic tablecloths, sixty-nine cents; salt and pepper shakers, four cents; nylon hose, $1.09; and fifteen cents to launder a man's shirt. We'll use Albany dry cleaners."

> I said, "Our new phone number is 8-8044."
> Mommy said, "You have a good memory, Angela."

Friday, June 30, 1950: Separation
Tad is lucky. He has a baby brother and moved to a bigger house. I'm sorry I can't see him anymore.

Tuesday, July 11, 1950: Chief Helper
Daddy sells clothes at the Surplus Store on South Pearl Street in Albany. After work, he brings vegetables and kosher meat on the bus to Colonie. In the back of the store, Mommy cooks dinner. We eat between customers. The store has no hot water. At nine o'clock, we put the dirty dishes in the car. Mommy drives us home. If Daddy tells a story, we get home faster than thirty minutes. I like to hear how Chief Helper gets people out of trouble. Angie Indian, a girl like me, helps the Chief, like Tonto helping the Lone Ranger.

Monday, July 17, 1950: Pray

Mommy said, "Angela, your job's important. Watch the kids and tell me if they steal anything in the store."

I answered, "If I do my job, can I have a sister?" Mommy looked kind of funny. Daddy and Mommy looked at each other.

Daddy said, "After Rowena was born dead, the doctor said, 'No more babies.' God answered our prayers and sent you."

I asked, "Can't we pray again?"

Daddy answered, "The doctor said it's dangerous for Mommy." If I am good and pray maybe God will change his mind.

Monday, August 14, 1950: College

Mommy rang up a sale on the cash register. I whispered to her, "The boy put two toy cars in his pocket."

When the boy's mommy paid for clothes, my mommy said, "The total is $8.50, including the toy cars."

The mommy looked at the boy. "What cars?"

My mommy said, "In his pocket." The boy's face got red.

His mommy pulled out the cars and spanked his tushy hard. "Put these back, Johnny. Haven't I told you not to take anything in stores?"

After they left, Mommy smiled and said, "Good job, Angela."

At dinner, Daddy said, "Dolly, I'm putting two dollars, instead of one, in your college savings account. You've saved us money by watching customers." Daddy calls me "Dolly" when he's happy.

I asked, "What's college?"

Daddy said, "An important school, which costs money, after high school."

Mommy said, "The Depression kept Daddy and me from finishing college."

I asked, "What's the Depression?"

Daddy answered, "A bad time. People lost jobs and couldn't buy food." I hope it doesn't come back.

Sunday, September 3, 1950: Coincidence

We took the train to NYC. Uncle Bert drove us to the Belle Harbor summer house of my aunts and uncles. Nice Grandma W hugged me. I had fun on the beach with Ron! When Daddy and

I came out of the ocean, we both said, "Ouch!" Under my foot was a green metal bed for a doll house. Under Daddy's foot was a green metal truck. No one came for the toys, so I kept them. I wonder why Daddy stepped on a big boy toy when I stepped on a little girl toy.

Sunday, September 10, 1950: Ledge
Mommy and Daddy cleaned our apartment and did the laundry. I had fun playing ledge with my friends. The ledge is a stone shelf around our red brick building. We threw our pink rubber balls onto the ledge. We liked the popping sound of the balls bouncing out high from the back of the ledge.

Wednesday, September 20, 1950: Big Girl
Wearing dungarees, I played ledge with a friend. Mommy and Daddy were all dressed up. Mommy said, "We're walking to the synagogue for *Kol Nidre*. Come along. It's too late to change."

I asked, "Can I stay and play?"

Mommy answered, "Okay. We'll return in an hour."

I played until my friend's mommy said, "Time for supper." It was no fun alone. The sun was going down. I looked down the street. I couldn't see Mommy and Daddy. I played more. The sky was darker. I felt afraid. Our apartment was locked. I thought: if I don't talk to strangers, even if they have candy, I can run to the synagogue. Hoping scary Annie wasn't out, I started down our street. The long block had junky row houses. Negro men in white undershirts sat on the stoops and drank from dark bottles. At the corner, I looked both ways and saw no cars. I ran across the street and down another long block with old houses attached to one another. With Daddy and Mommy, it didn't seem this far. I felt scared of getting lost. My heart pounded. I breathed hard and wished I'd stayed near our building. I hoped Mommy and Daddy would be proud of me if I found them. I turned left and crossed the empty street. I ran a short block to the corner. I didn't know where to go. Facing right, I crossed the street and raced to the next corner. When I looked to the right and saw the synagogue, I stopped holding my breath. I let out a big sigh about not seeing scary Annie. In the empty hall, I heard loud voices chanting prayers. I wanted to sit with Daddy in the good seats downstairs. I climbed to the ladies' balcony, hoping to find Mommy. I was afraid to go home alone in the dark. I tiptoed down the aisle behind the seats. I was glad to see Mommy's black felt hat with the feather! I ran to Mommy. I usually don't hug her, but this time I did. Looking surprised, she whispered, "Did you come by yourself?"

I nodded yes.

Later, Daddy said to Mommy, "Angela found the synagogue, like a homing pigeon. She had to make three turns and cross streets." I let out my breath because they weren't mad.

Thursday, November 16, 1950: Schoolhouse
My two-room schoolhouse is on a country road. Our first grade is across the hall from second grade. Woods with ferns are in the back. It's hard to write on the junky desks because kids carved things in the wood. I can read my book about Dick, Jane, and Spot now!

Monday, December 4, 1950: Crazy
After we lit Hanukkah candles, Mommy told Daddy, "Jules had Sara committed as crazy. My brothers are getting her out of the private, locked sanatorium."

I asked, "Is she crazy?" I felt worried.

I'm happy that Mommy shook her head no and said, "Jules is a conventional businessman without imagination. He can't understand Sara's artistic temperament. He became a tyrant when she wasn't a housewife with his dinner ready every night."

Sunday, December 24, 1950: Divorce
Mommy told Daddy, "Sara called. Thank goodness she's free. Poor Sara! Another divorce!"

I asked, "What's divorce?"

Daddy answered, "They'll stop being married. Fern, at least Jules was fun. George had no sense of humor. Remember our 1942 camping weekend at Lake George?"

Mommy nodded yes and answered, "But George supported Sara when she was publishing her three music books."

Daddy said, "True. He used his attorney contacts to get her on the Albany Symphony Board." I don't remember Uncle George.

At their fancy house in Spring Valley, tall Uncle Jules smiled and said, "You look like Sara." He looked handsome with wavy blond hair.

I smiled and said, "Thank you." Mommy wants me to look like her and Daddy. Aunt Sara took me for a fun ride with the top down. Uncle Jules took our picture in the convertible. It's in our album. I'm sorry he was mean to my best aunt. He was my nicest uncle.

Back row: Aunt Sara, Uncle George; middle row: Aunt
Faith, Uncle Peter with son Nick in front, around 1940

Aunt Sara and Angela in the convertible

1951

Friday, April 27, 1951: Scream
At school, my friend and I screamed at a snake crawling on the floor near our desks. Scared, I jumped on my chair. After taking the snake outside on a broom handle in a bag, our teacher said, "Settle down, class. It's a harmless garter snake." Instead of listening to the lesson, I kept looking at the floor for snakes. Ugh!

Sunday, May 13, 1951: Mothers and Daughters
My doll, Molly, and I wore the aqua mother and daughter hats and sweaters Mommy knitted. I told Mommy, "Molly wants a sister. I'll take a sister or brother." Mommy smiled, but didn't say anything. When we went to Grandma C's, Mommy and I wore our matching navy dresses, which Mommy sewed.

She asked, "Do you like your silk shantung dress, Angela?"

I nodded and said, "Thank you." Mine's smaller.

Dear mama
you know

There's extra special love, Dear Mom,
In every wish that goes your way
To hope you'll find a world of joy
In store for you on Mother's Day.

I love you

Mother's Day card

Mother and daughter dresses

Sunday, June 24, 1951: Perfect

In Albany, I played hopscotch. On the sidewalk, we drew ten chalk squares with a number in each. I threw a stone into square one. After hopping around the empty squares in order and hopping back, I stood on one foot while picking up the stone. I threw the stone into the second square and kept going until I stepped into the square with the stone by mistake. I said, "Oh, no!" and lost my turn.

One friend said, "Darn!" when both feet got in one square. She lost her turn.

Another friend missed a square. She laughed and said, "I'm out."

I lost my second turn when a friend said, "Your foot's on the line."

I told Mommy, "Hopscotch is fun. I want to do all ten squares without mistakes."

She said, "As with reading, practice makes perfect." I'll try to be perfect.

Monday, July 9, 1951: Wendell

Wendell is staying with his Grandma Meade. She owns the grocery store and gas station next to our store. Wendell's too young, only four. But he's the only kid around. We walked past the trailers behind the stores. He said, "I have to pee." Wendell took down his pants and held his penis. Yellow water came out and wet the dirt. He had no toilet paper. He shook his penis dry and pulled up his pants. I can't believe he did it in front of a girl. I would never go outside where people can see or let a boy watch.

Sunday, August 19, 1951: Pony

Mommy and Daddy took me for a pony ride. Like a real cowgirl, I wore my tan vest and cowgirl skirt with brown fringe. When I sat on the brown pony, the owner said, "Giddy up!" The pony galloped instead of walking around the ring.

Mommy yelled, "Hang on tight, Angela." I held the saddle horn and tried to keep my feet in the stirrups. The bad pony tried to throw me off. He bobbed up and down. I was glad to get back to the start. The owner grabbed the pony and helped me off. Mommy and Daddy looked worried.

Daddy asked, "Are you okay, Dolly?"

I said yes. Cowgirls are brave, so I didn't say I was afraid. They might think: she's a baby who's too young for pony rides and other exciting things.

Angela on the pony

Sunday, October 14, 1951: Snake

My best friend at Sunday school in the synagogue is Tara. We sit together and talk. She's lucky to have a big sister. Our teacher tells us Bible stories. Eve wasn't afraid when she met a snake and it talked to her.

Wednesday, December 19, 1951: Blond Desk

Our brand new Mayfield School is open! It's beautiful with green, instead of black, chalkboards. I love the blond wood desks with smooth tops. Mrs. L wrote on my report card:

> Angela is a polite and courteous girl. She is always neat and clean. She works and plays well in a group. She does very good work in all her subjects. She is a very good reader. Angela is very cooperative and helpful.

Mommy and Daddy would be mad if I got in trouble.

Sunday, December 23, 1951: Haiti

In Gloversville for Hanukkah, Aunt Sara talked about her exciting trip to learn folk songs. Cousins Lydia and Ella and I love the pretty Haitian beads and dolls she gave us. Each doll has a different print dress. My red-and-gray beads look good with my gray pullover sweater. I'm happy I got to keep Aunt Sara's postcard. It has a map of Haiti, the Dominican Republic, and the Caribbean Sea. I want to go there when I grow up.

Ella, Angela, Aunt Sara, and Lydia

The Childhood Diary

1952

Monday, January 7, 1952: Student Council
Our class elected Tommy and me to the student council! I like his blond hair and blue eyes. He gets good marks. We're in the bluebird group. We read harder words than the eagles, robins, and owls. Today is my birthday. Tommy sat next to me at the student council meeting. He smiled and sang *Happy Birthday.*

I smiled back and said, "Thank you!" When he told me about his brother and sister, I said, "You're lucky. I wish I had one."

First row, left to right: Angela and Tommy at the meeting

Thursday, February 14, 1952: Valentine's Card
Mommy likes the card Daddy helped me buy. I wrote "Dearest Mommy" above the poem:

Throughout the wide world from one end to the other
No one can compare with my own darling mother
And since I will love you forever, I'll say
Here's all my love on St. Valentine's Day.

I like the rime (*sic*).

Saturday, February 16, 1952: To Grandma
I wrote to Grandma W in NYC:

Dear Grandma,
I am feeling fine. I love Brownies. I have new roller skates. I was practicing this afternoon with them. Hope you feel fine. Write me soon.
Love, Angela
P.S. When is your birthday?

Sunday, March 23, 1952: Rat
A rat or mouse ran across the living room floor near me. I screamed and jumped on top of my daybed. When Mommy came, I felt less afraid. We both hate mice and rats.

Wednesday, April 9, 1952: Jewish Bunny
At school, I drew purple flowers, orange flowers, a green tree, and a pink bunny on my card. I wrote:

Happy Easter to a sweet mother!

Mommy didn't look happy. She said, "Jewish people don't celebrate Easter."

Angela's Easter card

Wednesday, April 30, 1952: Dolls

Daddy read my report card:

Angela's score on the reading test was very high. She does excellent work in numbers and spelling. Her work in language and social studies is excellent. Her desire for neatness and order is strong.

When Daddy patted my back, I asked, "May I please have a doll with blond hair I can comb?"

Mommy said, "What's wrong with your five dolls? I never had any. I had to cut paper dolls from magazines."

I answered, "Robin's the best, but I can't comb brown rubber hair. You can have one of my dolls, Mommy."

Mommy said, "Thanks, but I'm too old for a doll."

Daddy said, "The dolls in the store are to sell for money to buy a house where you'll have your own room."

Wednesday, September 24, 1952: Baby

Tommy said to me, "I like learning about growing food, like wheat and corn, in social studies." He told our third-grade class about his new sister. I still like Tommy.

Sunday, November 16, 1952: Autograph Book

Aunt Sara came on the train today! I liked her black-and-white full skirt. Her black sweater looked good with her reddish-brown hair. We all played gin rummy. My aunt gave me a big smile and hug. "Here's your Hanukkah present. Open it now and enjoy it." It's an autograph book! She signed:

To my lovely, beautiful niece, good luck!

Love and kisses, Aunt Sara

I gave her a hug and kiss and said, "Thank you!" I love her and the red book with pink, blue, and yellow pages!

Tuesday, November 18, 1952: Everyone Can Sign

My friends have autograph books. Now I can get famous people to sign. Mommy said, "People sign even if they're not famous." She wrote:

Roses are red. Violets are blue. Sugar is sweet. And so are you. From your own mommy

31

Daddy wrote:
> To a sweet little girl named Angela
> With love, Daddy

Wednesday, November 19, 1952: Teachers

My nice teachers wrote autographs in pretty handwriting:
> Best wishes and good luck to Angela!
> Sincerely,
> Helen Meehan, third grade

> The best of luck to you always!
> Mrs. Lindsey, second grade

> Dear Angela, I wonder whether you will remember our
> pleasant times together at Lisha Kill when we had to go
> to school there before Mayfield was finished.
> Sincerely yours,
> Frieda Hanner, first grade

Sunday, November 23, 1952: Autographs

We pretended today is Thanksgiving. I liked riding on the train
to NYC, even though it has soot. I got autographs:
> To my darling Angela!
> Love and kisses from Grandma Weiss

> To Angela,
> Stay as sweet as you are always.
> Love from Aunt Hannah and Uncle Cal

> Dear Angela,
> Best wishes and love from Hal

> Dear Angela,
> I love you, Angela.
> Ron

Dear Angela,
Your future lies before you, like a drift of driven snow.
Be careful how you tread it, for every mark will show.
Love and kisses from Aunt Lila

Friday, December 5, 1952: Mistakes

I'm glad that my report card is good:

Angela is doing excellent work in third grade. She reads with expression and understands the content of the material. Her arithmetic work is good. Sometimes, however, she has tried to do her work too quickly and has made mistakes. In the past few weeks, she has shown improvement.

I'm trying to get everything right.

New Year's Eve, 1952: Flacons

I sat on the double bed watching Mommy dress for a party. I love the perfume bottles on top of her dresser. One is black glass with a clear stopper. A white flower sticks out on the front. The light green bottle is square and goes in at the top. Mommy calls them 1930s flacons.

1953

Tuesday, January 20, 1953: Eisenhower
Our teacher said, "Eisenhower was inaugurdreed (*sic*) as president today." We saw him on a TV at a hotel last summer. He's tall and bald. Mommy and Daddy don't like him. They voted for Stevenson.

Tuesday, March 3, 1953: *Howdy Doody*
After school, I went to my friend's house and laughed at a kids' TV show. Howdy Doody is a cute marionette. We don't have TV.

Friday, March 20, 1953: Jesus
In the school lunch room, a stupid girl in my class said, "You killed Jesus."

I got mad and said, "I did not." But the other kids looked at me funny. I'm the only Jewish kid at Mayfield.

Monday, March 23, 1953: Our Lord
A mean sixth grader yelled at me, "Father Patrick said you killed our lord Jesus." He beat me up. I tried to get away, but he was big and strong. He punched and kicked me all over. I was afraid and cried. The nurse put bandages on my face, arms, and legs. She gave me aspirin and drove me to our store. Mommy and Daddy were upset. What a bad day!

Tuesday, March 24, 1953: Hurt
Kids at school looked at me funny. I didn't say anything. The nurse put on new bandages. Everything still hurts. Mommy said, "Daddy called the rabbi."

Thursday, March 26, 1953: Rabbi
I got new bandages. Daddy said, "The rabbi said that the Catholic priest agreed to explain to the Sunday school class that Jesus died two thousand years ago and that people today are not at fault." I hope it helps.

Monday, March 30, 1953: Romans

My heart pounded when the sixth-grade bully came into our store with his parents.

He said, "I'm sorry I hit you." I looked down and didn't say anything.

His parents said, "We're very sorry for what our son did. He's been punished and it will never happen again."

Mommy said, "We accept your apology. Please tell everyone at your church that Jesus was a Jew, killed by Romans. The lie about Jews has hurt us for two thousand years." They nodded and bought clothes.

Later, Daddy said, "I'm glad they bought a lot, but nothing compensates for the attack on Angela."

Monday, May 11, 1953: Bankquit

Mommy and I went to a nice bankquit (*sic*) for mothers and daughters at the synagogue.

Wednesday, May 13, 1953: The Best

After my teacher called, Mommy looked happy and whispered to Daddy. He wears a hearing aid and said, "What?"

When Mommy talked louder, I heard, "Angela got 138 on her IQ test." Isn't one hundred the best? I can't ask because kids can't know IQ scores.

Wednesday, May 27, 1953: Concert

Daddy came to our concert and liked my new school. I played violin and felt excited hearing people clap. We practiced at school because we can't take violins home. Mommy stayed in the store to sell clothes to good customers. Afterwards, she said, "Daddy played drums in his trio."

Daddy said, "We'll save for a violin."

I said, "I want to play the piano, like Aunt Sara."

Mommy said, "At your age, she played the violin."

Daddy said, "I'll look for a used piano." I love Daddy!

Aunt Sara around 1927

Thursday, June 18, 1953: Haste
My teacher wrote:
> Angela enjoys reading many library books. Angela has learned her multiplication tables through fives. She is striving to become more accurate. She works with too much haste. Her work in spelling and writing is excellent.
> It has been a pleasure to work with Angela this year.

I'm glad my report card is good.

Friday, June 19, 1953: Moving
I wish Tommy wasn't moving away. I still like him.

Wednesday, July 8, 1953: Bike
I finally got a two-wheeler! Daddy found a blue girls' Schwinn on sale at Sears. It's twenty-four inches. I love it! Mommy said, "You got it because you've made change, worked the cash register, and watched customers."

Daddy added, "We're sorry you must sleep in the living room."

I asked, "When we buy a house, may I please have ballerina wallpaper?" I was happy when Mommy nodded.

Tuesday, July 28, 1953: War and Waves
Daddy said, "The war in Korea is over!" I'm glad it wasn't in America. War is bad. We're on vacation in Rockaway Beach. We're staying with Grandma C's sister and her husband in their apartment. Mommy's aunt speaks more English and is nicer than Grandma. I saw lots of kids and grown-ups at the beach. I loved playing in the warm sand with my pail and shovel. The air smelled good. I don't know how to swim. Daddy and I bobbed up and down with each wave before it broke. When a wave broke on me, I didn't like salt water up my nose. I liked the crashing sound of the waves.

Sunday, August 2, 1953: Hospital
Cousin Justine had a baby boy! Mommy and Daddy visited them in the hospital. I wanted to see them, but kids have to stay in the lobby. Darn!

Angela Weiss

Tuesday, August 11, 1953: Eggplant
In front of our store, I waited for all the cars to whiz past. I crossed all four lanes of the Albany-Schenectady Road to visit Mrs. T's farm. She took me up and down the rows of vegetables. She gave me green peppers and eggplant! Why is it called egg? It tasted much better. Mommy makes me eat a soft-boiled egg every week. She says, "It's good for you." I hate eggs.

Angela in front of the store with the Albany-Schenectady Road and the farm in the background

Wednesday, September 2, 1953: Billy

Mommy said, "Ma Meade's older daughter and grandson have moved into a trailer behind our stores. She's waitressing. Billy is ten and just left reform school." Cute Billy came over to play. He has blue eyes and is an only child. But he bragged, showed off, and acted mean and bossy. I have no other kids to play with. He has no bike and wanted to ride mine.

I said, "My parents won't let anyone but me ride it." I was afraid he'd break it. I rode on the best place: the blacktop circle in front of the animal hospital. It was shady and I never see cars there.

On the way home, Daddy said, "It was one hundred degrees and broke a record for this date!"

Thursday, September 3, 1953: Fire

Today was just as hot. Billy and I played in the field behind the trailers. He tried to get me to help him start a fire. I said, "No! It might kill everyone in the trailers." I ran to our store. I was scared all day. I didn't want to tattle unless Billy set a fire. He must have changed his mind. I'm afraid to play with him anymore.

Wednesday, September 16, 1953: Crash

When I got off the school bus, I saw policemen and their cars behind our store. Mommy said, "This morning, a loud motor above our roof shook the store really hard. I'm thankful everyone in the Lone Pine Trailer Camp is okay. Plane wreckage is scattered behind it. The police, investigators, and doctors used our phone." Billy wanted to see the mess, but not me. The police kept everyone out. I'm glad the dead bodies are gone. It's scary.

Thursday, September 17, 1953: Famous

Mommy's name is in the newspaper:

Mrs. Fern Weiss, proprietor of Fern's Cleaners and Variety Center, heard the plane's engines directly above her store before an explosive thump shook the small building to the core and she ran outside to investigate. Later, she said, "I will never forget the sight of the Mohawk airplane on the ground less than a hundred yards away with its nose pointing toward our store. The plane was broken into many pieces and bodies were strewn all over the ground."

Mommy isn't afraid of anything. I'm glad I was at school when the plane crashed.

Friday, September 18, 1953: Details

Daddy read a newspaper story out loud:

It was the first airline catastrophe in the Capital Region. Flight 723 was en route from Boston to Chicago. The two-engine Convair had circled for fifteen minutes waiting for fog to lift so it could land at Albany Airport, three miles from the crash scene. The pilot hit two of the Station WPTR radio towers. All twenty-eight people on the plane died.

Mommy said, "We've been swamped with customers wanting details, but not buying much."

Monday, September 21, 1953: Questions

Kids at school kept asking about the plane. Mrs. McFarland had me tell about the crash because kids were not paying attention to her lesson. People laughed when I got mixed up and called Mohawk Airlines "Slow Hawk" the way Daddy and Mommy always do.

Friday, October 23, 1953: Piano!

Daddy paid movers at our building twenty-five dollars for an upright piano in the van. I can't wait to play and wish Aunt Sara could teach me. I felt special looking at *Musical Tales*, the children's book which she dedicated to me. My favorite story is *The Sorcerer's Apprentice*.

Aunt Sara performing

Tuesday, October 27, 1953: Closed

We closed the store for good. Mommy said, "Business wasn't good. We changed our minds about building a store and house in Colonie."

Dad said, "Despite the bully's apology, we want you in an Albany school with Jewish kids. Our lot sold for enough to buy a house in Albany." I will miss my Mayfield friends. I'm afraid that Hudson School will be ahead of me. But if I get my own room, I'll be happy. I'm happy to be old enough to call Daddy "Dad" from now on.

Tuesday, November 3, 1953: Hudson

I miss Mayfield's big grass field. Hudson has recess in a small concrete yard. My pencil gets stuck in kids' carvings on my old school desk. I like my young teacher, Miss Koren. She wears glasses. She wrote on my composition:

Good work!

My Father

My father has a wonderful sense of humor. He is always trying to make me laugh He usually makes me laugh He works in the Army and Navy store on So. Pearl St. in Albany. When he goes to work in the morning He has so many friends to take him down to work that he very seldom takes the bus. He was born in New York city. He has three sisters He is the youngest and the only boy in his family. I am glad he is my father.

Angela's essay

Angela's drawing of Herm

Friday, November 13, 1953: Not Behind

Everything is different at school. I like the smartest kids: Jana, Paul, and George in my vanilla reading group. The chocolate group is next best. The worst group is strawberry. Vanilla is my favorite ice cream. I'm happy with my report card:

> Angela reads with full understanding and a clear, well-modulated voice. She is an interested listener. She writes naturally, almost as if she were talking. Her written work makes interesting reading. Angela took an immediate interest in our study of Albany. She has done excellent work in division. She has an excellent basic knowledge of music. She is friendly to everyone and made herself a good class member in a short time.

Thursday, November 19, 1953: Thankful

Nice Miss K wrote on my composition:

> Excellent thoughts! 100 percent

What I'm thankful for on Thanksgiving

On Thanksgiving I am thankful for a lot of things, but most of all my parents and my home. I don't know what I would do with out them. The next two things are my health and freedom to do what I want to do.

My home is small but I love it anyway. My parents are good to me and I couldn't ask for them to be any better. I get enough to eat and all the clothes I need and a warm bed to sleep in.

Thats what I am thankful for and I am glad that the war is over and I hope there aren't any more

Angela's Thanksgiving essay

1954

Friday, January 1, 1954: Alone
Mommy and Dad gave me New Year's Eve party hats and noisemakers from their dance. Babysitters are for little kids. It was fun to stay alone and read my Bobbsey Twins book. Bert and Nan are older twins. Flossie and Freddie are the younger twins. The American Bridge, United States Steel brown diary Dad gave me has these interesting things:

Population of Principal Cities: Albany has 134,382 people.

NY's legal interest rate is six. I wonder what it means.

A gallon of water weighs 8 1/3 pounds.

One horsepower is lifting 33,000 pounds one foot in one minute.

It's scary that artificial respiration might take three hours after an accident!

Postal Information: I know that a stamp costs three cents.

Los Alamos Canyon Highway Bridge in New Mexico is the prettiest bridge picture in the diary.

Sunday, January 3, 1954: Seventeenth Anniverery and Diary
Mommy and Dad like the anniverery (*sic*) card I made. When they got home from eating out, I said, "My diary has all the presidents. Lincoln from Kentucky is my favorite because he freed the slaves. He was fifty-two when he became president. President Eisenhower from Texas is sixty-three." On the Identification page, I wrote my name, address, phone (2-0772), birthday, height (4'10"), and weight (eighty-six).

Wednesday, January 13, 1954: Gray
I'm glad Mommy likes the birthday card I made. Mommy has some gray hair in the front. Dad, who has lots of gray hair, said, "My family turns gray young."

He laughed when I said, "I hope I don't get gray hair soon." I asked, "How come Aunt Lila has light red hair and Aunt Rhoda has blond hair?"

Dad made me laugh by answering, "Lila eats tomatoes and Rhoda likes lemons."

Friday, January 29, 1954: Grades
I'm glad I got almost all As on my report card. Arithmetic and penmanship were Bs. Hudson is harder.

Tuesday, February 2, 1954: Homeowners
Dad had a big smile on his face. "We closed the deal and own 549 Merritt Street!"

I said, "Yaay! Can we see movies, instead of looking at houses every Sunday?"

Dad said, "Not yet. We need money to renovate our flat before moving in July."

He laughed when I said, "My own room will be better than movies."

Mommy said, "Rent from the upstairs flat will help pay the mortgage. I'm starting Russell Sage College classes to be a real estate agent." I didn't say that Mommy's too old for school. She might feel bad.

Friday, February 12, 1954: Paul
I'm happy that the boy I like best left a white envelope with my name on my desk. I felt excited when I pulled out a pretty Valentine! I looked up and smiled at Paul. He was smiling at me. I felt good. Paul was born in Sicily and speaks Italian and good English. He's smart and handsome with brown hair and brown eyes. His friend said, "Paul likes you."

Monday, February 15, 1954: Jana and Curls
I hope George likes Jana, who likes him. She's thin with brown eyes and straight brown hair. Mommy curls mine. Tonight, she pulled hard. I said, "Ouch!"

She said, "If my mother had curled my hair, maybe I would have had boyfriends in school. It hurts to be beautiful." I hope she was kidding.

Friday, March 5, 1954: Achiefment
I told Mommy, "My teacher said that I got the highest mark on the fourth-grade achiefment (*sic*) test."

Mommy said, "That's good! This is Miss K's first teaching job."

I said, "She makes school fun. We wrote in ink today. I'm making Dad's birthday card with ink, which looks nicer."

Saturday, March 20, 1954: Art Class
Mommy likes to paint pictures. She took me to Albany Art Institute. Other kids and I drew in our art notebooks.

Friday, April 2, 1954: Report Card
I'm glad my report card said:
> Arithmetic: Angela has few careless errors now and shows ability to compute mentally.
> Science: asks thought-provoking questions.
> Reading: Angela reads "between the lines."

I wish I knew what it meant. Miss K wrote:
> Angela has had to learn Palmer Method penmanship. Angela strives for perfection. She was becoming a "talker" until seat changes eliminated the problem.

Jana and I are lucky that Miss K didn't mark us down for talking.

Jana

Angela Weiss

Sunday, April 18, 1954: Baseball
I've been growing my hair longer. I made braids and went to watch Paul and his older brother run around playing baseball in Lincoln Park across from school. Paul smiled at me. His handsome brother is around twelve, too old for me.

Thursday, April 22, 1954: Tap
Mommy takes me to Hamilton School, which has better kids, for tap. My friend can't go, so I taught her my favorite steps in our courtyard:
>   Buffalo: step with one foot, shuffle with the other, and
>   hop with the first foot.
>   Irish: shuffle, hop, and step with each foot.
I can't wait to be old enough for tap shoes with heels. I want a penny between the shoe and the tap for a better sound.

Thursday, April 29, 1954: No Honor
Jana said, "Being on traffic patrol this month seems more like punishment than an honor." I laughed and agreed. On the stairs, bullies got in line only because our principal was watching. Tough Hilda and Gina gave me dirty looks.

Friday, April 30, 1954: Breakup
Paul used to look and smile at me and talk to me. He's stopped paying attention. He must not like me anymore. I feel bad. Jana said, "You should stop talking to him." So I did. I wouldn't have thought of it. Jana has the best ideas.

Saturday, May 1, 1954: *Quizdown*
I was lucky to be picked for the weekly radio show *Quizdown!* The Knickerbocker News made up questions about Old Albany. Jana did well! I hit the bell first for, "Who owned Albany before the English?"

I got points for saying, "The Dutch."

I never heard of the last question: "On what corner of downtown Albany was the famous, historic elm tree?"

Paul's answer, "State Street and Pearl Street," helped Hudson win! Friends cheered for us! I like our prizes: gray ballpoint pen and mechanical pencil sets with *Quizdown 1954* in red!

Sunday, May 2, 1954: Newspaper
I'm excited that the newspaper printed our Hudson team *Quizdown* picture. Mommy sent it to relatives.

Wednesday, May 5, 1954: Beaten
After Jana turned off on Swan Street, I had to walk two more blocks alone. Gina said, "Don't ever tell us to get in line again."

I said, "It's my traffic patrol job."

Hilda said, "No one tells us what to do," before they beat me up. Mommy and Dad are mad at them. I hate them and am scared that they will do it again.

Thursday, May 6, 1954: Afraid
I'm glad that Jana and I are off traffic patrol. Mommy said, "Gina's and Hilda's parents weren't home. I warned the girls that they will get in trouble unless they leave you alone." If Paul still liked me and walked me home, I wouldn't be alone or afraid.

Friday, May 7, 1954: Jana
When Jana and I saw Gina twice, my heart beat faster and I felt scared. At my house, playing Monopoly was fun. Jana laughed when I said, "I'm surprised that my Cinderella watch still runs after it fell on the floor!"

When we played Candyland, Jana, an only child, said, "I want a sister or brother, but Mother is too old."

I replied, "I want one, but my mother can't. She said that adopting is too expensive." Jana smiled when I gave her half the flowers I picked at our new house.

Saturday, May 8, 1954: Grandma C
I'm surprised that Grandma C is visiting Albany. Mommy said, "Once we move, she'll stay with us." I hope Mommy didn't mean that Grandma will live with us. I'd be nervous.

Sunday, May 9, 1954: Mother's Day
I'm glad Mommy likes the dusting powder and homemade card I gave her. She smiled when I brought cereal, milk, and juice on a tray for breakfast in bed. Dad took her to dinner.

Monday, May 10, 1954: Boys
I'm happy that Jana came over after school. We never run out of things to say. When we stared at the rain, she said, "I'm giving up George. I don't know why he stopped talking to me."

I said, "Just like Paul."

Jana nodded and asked, "Will you stop talking to George if I stop talking to him and Paul?"

I said yes. Paul still looks at me. It's hard to ignore him.

Friday, May 14, 1954: Danger
After mean Gina said, "We might beat you up again," I felt afraid. On the way home, Jana and I were surprised to see Miss K outside school for the first time. Was she watching for bullies? At Jana's house, we started writing a mystery with a big storm and finished it at my house. I like it when Jana thinks of new things to do.

Saturday, May 15, 1954: TV
We watched Ozzie and Harriet on our first TV. The son, Ricky Nelson, is cute, like Paul's brother. The TV's in the kitchen. My parents watch it while I'm asleep on the daybed.

Sunday, May 16, 1954: Willow
In Grandma C's Gloversville backyard, I heard birds sing. Dew made me wet while I hid under the big weeping willow, which Grandpa planted when I was born. The leaves touched the ground. The big snowball flowers I like weren't out yet. We filled the rented trailer behind our car with furniture. I'm happy that my room will have Aunt Sara's old bedroom set!

Grandma's house, left to right: Grandma, Herm, Lydia, Fern, Angela, Aunt Sara, Ella

Monday, May 17, 1954: Mansion
I felt afraid when our class walked past Gina's and Hilda's row houses. On the next block of Catherine Street, we visited Schuyler Mansion. I was surprised to hear, "George Washington slept here. Philip Schuyler's daughter Betsy married the first Treasury Secretary, Alexander Hamilton, here." The furniture was fancy.

Wednesday, May 19, 1954: Jazzy
George acted nicer, so Jana and I made up with him. We dressed jazzy, but Paul wasn't at the baseball diamond. We studied the Girl Scout laws. After baths all winter, I liked my first cool shower.

Friday, May 21, 1954: Secret
After our Brownie meeting at Hamilton School, Jana, Anna, and I played at Jana's house. After Anna left, Jana said, "Anna told a girl one of our secrets. We should break up with Anna." I agreed. I can't write the secret. Someone might read this.

Saturday, May 22, 1954: Hat and Clover
I'm glad that Mommy helped me decorate her old green hat with tissue paper flowers for the art school hat contest. A nice girl won. Her pretty hat had a pink veil, silk flowers, and streamers. The party was fun. At our new house, I found my first four-leave (*sic*) clover and pressed it in a book. I'll keep it for good luck. I tried not to think about Paul when I sang the song *I'm Looking over a Four-Leave (sic) Clover*.

Sunday, May 23, 1954: Grandma's
After we drove to Grandma's Albany boarding house, Mommy translated from Yiddish, "Grandma's proud of you for getting the best mark on the Sunday school Bible test." Tara's and my favorite story is Noah. We like the animals going into the ark in pairs. I don't like the killings in the Cain and Abel, Abraham and Isaac, and Moses stories.

I said to Grandma, "Thank you for the five dollars!" On TV, Johnny Carson was on *Earn Your Vacation*. If we won this game show, we could go on any free vacation. I'd pick the beach.

Wednesday, May 26, 1954: Not Overweight
I got my last booster shot. I was happy when Dr. Cohn said, "You aren't overweight." Regular girls' clothes are tight. I'm glad that Chubbette sizes are too big.

Saturday, May 29, 1954: Across the Hudson
At the last *Quizdown* show, Jana and I saw a boy from Amsterdam win the grand prize, a bike. After I had lunch at Jana's, she came with us to our new house and across the bridge to a store in Rensselaer. We had fun looking at vinyl tile for kitchen floors. We liked the checkerboards better than those with blobs or streaks in different colors. I'm lucky Jana is my best friend. She's fun and very smart.

Monday, May 31, 1954: Holiday
Dad's store was closed. We drove a long way on New Scotland Avenue and up into the mountains. Thatcher Park was full of people at picnic tables near stone fireplaces under big trees on both sides of the road. At the George Doone area, a man helped Dad cook hot dogs and hamburgers over a fire. They smelled and tasted better than at home. I liked the view of big Albany buildings. My friend, an only child, said, "I don't want a sister or brother because I'd get fewer toys and clothes."

I was surprised and answered, "I'd rather have a sister."

I was glad when she said, "My grandfather has started the carpenter work on your new house." At Tollgate Soda Fountain in Slingerlands, the rum-raisin ice cream was yummy.

After a good movie, *How to Marry a Millionaire* with Marilyn Monroe, a blonde, Dad said, "I prefer Jane Russell."

Mommy said, "You can like Jane, because she's a brunette, like me." Dad and I laughed.

Saturday, June 5, 1954: Murph

At Rosen's Department Store, I got size 2 blue sneakers and Mommy got clothes to sell in Colonie. She said, "Selling helps pay for our new house. Ma Meade orders the most." I was surprised that our old store was still empty. Why does Ma Meade call Mommy "Murph"?

Ma Meade said to me, "Little Murph, call me Grandma." I don't want to be like her grandsons.

Sunday, June 6, 1954: Houses and Cars

After Mommy showed a house for sale to people, we had fun riding around and looking at the inside of houses for sale. I said, "Mommy sounds babyish. Can I call you Mom?" She nodded and was surprised when I named these cars on the street without reading the names:

Cadillac, Buick, Oldsmobile, Pontiac, Chevrolet

Chrysler, DeSoto, Dodge, Plymouth

Ford, Mercury, Lincoln.

Tuesday, June 8, 1954: Furniture

It's *Shavuot*, a holiday to celebrate Moses getting the Torah. After synagogue services, Mom and I had fun shopping for furniture. We loved a beautiful, expensive Heywood-Wakefield desk. It's blond maple, like our Mayfield desks, but more like satin. We both liked the charcoal Formica dinette table with wrought-iron legs. The pink vinyl padded chairs were the best. Mom said, "Above the black chair rail in the dinette, the wallpaper and matching café curtains have green trees and black and pink Paris, France, cafes on white backgrounds. Our living room will be the latest color, chartreuse green. I'll sew slipcovers and drapes from this sandalwood-and-white print material."

I said, "Sandalwood is better than brown because it's lighter and more pinkish." I love decorating.

Thursday, June 10, 1954: Shorts and Nancy Drew

After school, Jana and I felt important walking Miss K home. When cute Paul saw us on the street in shorts, we giggled. I whispered to Jana, "I wonder whether he thinks our legs look

58

good." Jana and I got good library books, including *Mystery of the Park Oak*. The detective, Nancy Drew, is better than the Bobbsey twins.

Saturday, June 12, 1954: Flying Up
We're done with ugly Brownie uniforms! At Greenfern camp, we read the laws and said the promise:

> On my honor, I will try to do my duty to God and country, to help other people at all times, and to obey the Girl Scout laws.

Instead of flying up like birds, we had wings pinned on our new green uniforms. The punch and cookies tasted good!

Monday, June 14, 1954: Recital
Dad praised my tap recital. We copied Gene Kelly's song and dance from the movie *Singin' in the Rain*. Our plastic raincoats were hot, but opening and closing umbrellas while we danced was fun.

Wednesday, June 16, 1954: Test
"I'm beat. It was so difficult that I'm sure I flunked," Mom said after the real estate test for her license. I laughed. She sounded like me after a hard test.

Saturday, June 19, 1954: Cherry
I love the *Cherry Ames* books Dad bought. Cherry attends nursing school and works in homes, hospitals, and clinics. Handsome doctor boyfriends help her solve mysteries. I want to read all the books! Cherries are my favorite fruit.

Monday, June 21, 1954: Fire and Sister
I felt grown-up staying by myself. It was hot out. A fire on Catherine Street made me afraid of our building burning down. Dad said, "Mom went to Gloversville to visit Rowena's grave on her fourteenth birthday." I wish God would answer my prayers for a sister.

Wednesday, June 23, 1954: Comics and Aunt Sara
It rained, so Jana and I had fun listening to records and reading *Looney Tunes* comic books. Mom called Aunt Sara in NYC to sing *Happy Birthday*. I wish she was here.

Thursday, June 24, 1954: Cradle of the Union
I'm happy to live in an important city. I wrote in my notebook what Miss K said:

> Congress just named Albany the Birthplace of American Union, a big honor. The recent TV special showed how Benjamin Franklin organized the First American Congress here. Today's pageant honors its two hundredth anniversary. Actors will show events leading up to the Congress. Articles of Union were adopted June 24, 1754. The 1776 Articles of Confederation came before our 1787 Constitution.

The parade was beautiful! I liked the old-style costumes.

Friday, June 25, 1954: Good-bye
I felt sorry for three kids who will repeat fourth grade. I'm happy with all As, except a B in penmanship. Miss K wrote:

> We're all disappointed that Angela won't be at Hudson next year.

I'm glad that Jana got all As. I won't see her because we're moving. I'll miss her. We kissed good-bye. My eyes got watery.

Wednesday, June 30, 1954: Moving
I'm excited that we moved at 12:30 from 90 Morton Avenue to 549 Merritt Street. Dad, who was home from work, laughed when I said, "The only thing better in our apartment was the white bathroom floor." Each small tile had six sides. They fit together with black lines in between. Our big refrigerator is much better than the old one with a separate round top. The movers brought everything in at once. We're unpacking boxes.

Thursday, July 1, 1954: My Room
I finally have my own room! My parents smiled after I said, "My bedroom set looks new with glossy white paint. The night stand

and dressing table with drawers on each side of the full-length mirror are great. I love the padded, mint-green vinyl headboard with buttons and the ballerina wallpaper behind my bed." My coral bedspread and drapes match the pink in the wallpaper. I'm happy that my clothes are neat in my own closet and dresser drawers!

Saturday, July 3, 1954: Parakeet

Aunt Sara's here! She said, "Angela was sad after her fish and turtles died. I'll buy her a parakeet. Let's find a bird breeder." On Clinton Avenue, the bird lady's hair looked like black shoe polish. Her talking parrots had bright blue, green, and red feathers. We got the prettiest turquoise parakeet with black-and-white wings. His name, Tumba, comes from *Tumbalalaika*, which Aunt Sara sings in her one-woman shows. I hope he talks. I love Aunt Sara!

Tumba

Sunday, July 11, 1954: Bookcase
Over the radiator, Dad put up three wood planks with brackets for my bookcase. I was happy to arrange my dictionary, almanac, mysteries, library books, baby book, magazines, and school books on the shelves.

Monday, July 12, 1954: Crash
We were eating canned fruit cocktail for dessert. We heard a loud crash and rushed to my room. The books, shelves, and brackets were on the floor. A bookcase was too good to be true.

Thursday, July 15, 1954: Studs
Dad's friend, Karl, laughed at my broken bookcase. "Herm, did you find the studs?"

Dad asked, "What are studs?"

Karl said, "They're vertical boards inside the wall. You attach the brackets to them." Knowing Dad, I put the books in the closet and gave up on a bookcase.

Sunday, July 25, 1954: Housewarming
Dad said to Mom, "Hon, you did a great job on our housewarming! Our relatives and friends got to see our home and we got to meet neighbors."

"Thirty-five adults signed the guest book and at least fifteen kids attended. The backyard chairs gave us room for a big crowd."

"I'm glad it didn't rain."

"Herm, we were lucky to have the sisters next door prepare low-cost snacks and drinks and provide folding chairs."

"Hon, several people said that the gray stone pillars supporting our front porch columns look impressive."

"Women liked the pink bathroom with my skirted dressing table. They complimented our peach quilted bedspread and striped taffeta drapes and dust ruffle." I had fun, but strangers looking into Tumba's cage made him quieter than usual.

Friday, July 30, 1954: Piano and Tumba
Nice young Miss Lohen said, "Angela, you have good piano hands. Your long fingers reach a full octave. Please practice scales,

chords, and your piano piece thirty minutes each day." I walked home from her house on Ontario Street, thinking that the white piano keys are easier to feel than the smaller black ones. I practiced *Good King Wenceslas*. I don't like it, but it's easy. Tumba perched on my shoulder to rest while flying around for exercise. I laughed when he chirped words I've taught him, "Sara" and "I Love You," in the middle of a long bunch of babble. I love Tumba!

Monday, August 9, 1954: Surprise
I can't believe that the beautiful Heywood-Wakefield desk is mine! Dad said, "It's to help you to keep getting good marks in school."

I smiled and said, "Thank you!" I put my papers, pencils, pens, ruler, scissors, Scotch tape, paper clips, and other stuff in the drawers. I touched the satiny wood and round corners of the desk. I told Mom, "I love my desk and room!" Mom smiled and looked happy.

Thursday, August 19, 1954: My Block
My nice Protestant neighbor, Cara, has freckles and straight brown hair. We both live in two-family houses. While we played Candyland, I was surprised to hear, "Eighty-five Catholic kids live on our block in around fifteen one-family houses. The mothers have five or six kids and stay home." Cara hates sports. I was the only girl playing baseball in the empty lot with rowdy St. Teresa's boys. Big, stupid Jimmy pitched the ball hard into the left side of my head on purpose. It knocked me down. When I cried, no one cared, so I went home. I'm not playing with these rough boys again. My head hurts.

Friday, September 10, 1954: Tara
I'm happy that smart Tara from Sunday school is in my fifth-grade class. She lives on my corner. Going to school, we walk six blocks down Quail Street and turn left. On Madison, we pass Hague Photo Studio, Michael's Coffee Shop, and Dutch Oven Bakery, which smells good. If Jana was in my class, everything would be perfect. I miss her.

Saturday, September 18, 1954: Favorite Grandma

Dad's nice mother died. He cried and is very upset. I asked Mom, "Did she die because she was old?"

Mom answered, "Grandma had heart problems and was seventy-six." We will take the train to NYC tomorrow.

Sunday, September 19, 1954: Crying

Grandma W's funeral at the Orthodox synagogue on East 85th Street was my first. The ladies' balcony was warm and sunny, but we were crying. Rabbi Lookstein said that Grandpa and Grandma started our family going to Congregation Kehilath Jeshurun over fifty years ago! I didn't understand the Hebrew prayers. I liked looking at red, blue, yellow, and green light coming through tall stained glass windows with round tops. At the cemetery, people cried and took turns shoveling dirt on top of the casket. Aunt Lila's apartment was full of people. The mirrors were covered. Ron and I went to his room, but weren't in the mood to play. I said, "Even grown-ups are crying."

He said, "My mother and Aunt Rhoda cry a lot."

I said, "My mother never cries. Dad cries at the end of movies."

Ron said, "Weisses cry more than my father's family."

I said, "You and Hal will have more room in your bedroom."

Ron said, "I'd rather have Grandma back. She was nice to us." Tears were in his eyes, so I was afraid to say more.

Monday, September 20, 1954: *Shiva*

Dad said, "For a week, I'll sit shiva with our relatives to mourn. People will visit Aunt Lila's apartment to give comfort. They'll bring food and say they're sorry that Grandma died. I'll sleep in Ron's and Hal's room, but we can't afford a hotel for you and Mom." I'm glad to be home. Funerals are awful. I'm praying that no one else dies.

Mom asked, "Remember 1948, when Dad worked in NYC in the dry cleaning store for two months while Uncle Harvey was in the hospital?" She looked surprised when I said no. Tumba cheered me up by talking a blue streak after flying around.

Monday, September 27, 1954: Scared

Tara and I are scared to death of our strict gym teacher. Mrs. Welsh has a deep voice and doesn't like mistakes. She said, "I was a sergeant in the WACs or Women's Army Corps." She marches us around like soldiers. "Forward march, left, right, left, right, column right, march! Attention!"

I laughed when Tara said, "I like 'At ease' the best."

She agreed when I said, "I'm afraid of getting on her bad side. These seafoam-green bloomer uniforms are ugly!"

Tuesday, September 28, 1954: Doreen

Near Tara and me in the middle of the gym height line is a very sweet, smart friend. Doreen lives near school and goes to our Ohav Shalom synagogue. She said, "I came here from Eastern Europe when I was four." She speaks perfect English without any accent. She has her father's fair skin and short, wavy reddish hair.

Wednesday, October 13, 1954: Marsha

Patroon School has the best kids! Marsha is smart, fun, and shorter with pretty blond hair and blue eyes. She is a Girl Scout with Tara, Doreen, and me and goes to our synagogue.

Wednesday, November 17, 1954: Progress

We got report cards. Mrs. Buck, my nice teacher, gave me good marks in reading, language, spelling, social studies, arithmetic, science, penmanship, music, art, attitudes, and work habits. Mom signed and wrote, "We are happy with Angela's progress." I love Patroon.

Wednesday, December 1, 1954: Dancing

Tara and Doreen agreed when I said, "I love our fox-trot and waltz dance class with boys!" Next are fast dances. While cleaning Tumba's cage, I often repeated, "May I have this dance?"

Thursday, December 9, 1954: *Troop 9 Favorite Recipes*

Each Girl Scout decorated her cookbook cover differently. Tara said, "I like your black oilcloth cover with the red yarn binding.

I wish I had painted my red cover. Your red, green, and gold baskets, hearts, and diamonds look good."

"Thank you! I like your candy cane cookie and Marsha's vanilla cookie recipes."

Tara replied, "I'm going to try all thirty-three recipes, starting with your oven-fried veal and potatoes and Doreen's honey cake."

Wednesday, December 15, 1954: Periods
Mom asked, "Do you have questions about the booklet I gave you about menstruation?" After I shook my head no, she said, "Your period is a normal part of being a woman and having babies." After we bought Kotex sanitary napkins and a belt to hold a napkin in place, I tried everything on. I'm ready but surprised that some ten-year-old girls can have babies! It's weird to bleed every month. I hope that my period waits to start.

Thursday, December 23, 1954: Death
I'm sorry that nice Aunt Hannah, Justine's mother, died of cancer. We took the train to NYC for another sad funeral. With tears in his eyes, Dad said, "Ten years older, Hannah was like a second mother. She looked out for me and made Lila and Rhoda stop playing mean pranks because I was the youngest."

Mom said to Dad, "Cal's taking it hard." Uncle Cal is handsome and has a European accent.

Sunday, December 26, 1954: Hanukkah
Dad is in NYC, sitting shiva again. At home, I lit Hanukkah candles and thanked Mom for a white half-slip last night and a sweater tonight. Tumba made us laugh. He looked into his mirror and said, "Pretty bird," as if it's another bird.

Angela with long hair in front of the
family's duplex and 1952 DeSoto

1955

Friday, January 7, 1955: Tenth Birthday
My parents sang *Happy Birthday* before we ate chocolate cake. Yum! I said, "Thank you for my favorite Carter's underpants. I like the pink, blue, and yellow rosebuds. This walking doll with blond, rooted hair to comb is pretty!" While I held her hand and made her legs walk, I laughed when Tumba landed on her head. I hardly ever play with dolls now, but my parents didn't have the money three years ago when I first asked.

Friday, January 14, 1955: Bolivia
I like studying South America and Mexico. We had to pick a country for a report. I told Dad, "I wrote about Bolivia, which has tin and is high in the Andes Mountains."

Wednesday, February 2, 1955: Freezing
Dad said, "Today's low of minus eighteen degrees set a new record for this date. Today's high was only six degrees above zero, another record."

I said, "I hate cold weather."

Tumba replied, "I love you, Tumba," which made us laugh.

Monday, February 14, 1955: Valentines
At school, we sent little Valentines from packages to kids we like. No one at Patroon is as cute as my boyfriend Paul.

Tuesday, February 15, 1955: Marks
I'm happy my report card has As, except for a B in science. For gym, Mrs. W wrote:

Her coordination is improving and it's fun to have her in class.

I like playing volleyball.

Friday, March 18, 1955: Test and Pet
I smiled after getting 100 percent on the Great Plains social studies test! Next is southwestern USA. A classmate said, "We

have trouble getting our green parakeet back in his cage when he's out flying."

I replied, "We're lucky. Tumba returns to his cage when we open the door. He quiets down for the night when we cover his cage in the dinette. At meals, we like hearing him talk."

Wednesday, March 23, 1955: Guard
I told Tara, "Girls' basketball is fun. As a guard, I enjoy keeping the forwards on the other team from making baskets."

I laughed when she said, "I'd rather skip gym."

Wednesday, April 20, 1955: Splendid
Mom and Dad smiled about my report card, which said my reading is "splendid." I love this word and started teaching it to Tumba.

Monday, May 2, 1955: Far-Sighted
Ugh! I need reading glasses. I must have Dad's eyes. He always wears glasses. I'm afraid it's true that boys don't make passes at girls with glasses.

Friday, June 24, 1955: School's Done
On my final report card, Mrs. Buck wrote:

Splendid. It has been a pleasure to teach Angela.

I'm glad about all As, except a B in science. Kids said, "Our teacher next fall, strict Miss Kilfoil, gets mad." We're worried.

Tumba was funny, saying, "Splendid," for the first time, but it came out as "Spended (*sic*)."

I kept repeating, "I spended (*sic*) the money," when I could stop giggling.

Angela before cutting off her long hair

Sunday, July 24, 1955: Massachusetts

On vacation with a friend and our parents, I said, "I'm excited to see new places." We drove to a small, white guest house near Boston. Bea and I slept in cots in our parents' rooms upstairs. Dad said, "We're lucky to escape to the ocean. Albany had a record heat of ninety-six for yesterday's date."

Monday, July 25, 1955: Nantasket

It's fun to have a friend here. Bea and I played on the sandy beach and jumped up and down with the waves.

Tuesday, July 26, 1955: 1620

Our handsome Plymouth guide, who wore old-fashioned clothes, said, "The Pilgrims landed here and started Thanksgiving because they were grateful to be free to practice the religion they chose." Bea and I liked the giant statue of an Indian who helped the settlers.

Left to right: Bea, Plymouth guide, Angela

Thursday, July 28, 1955: Cool Vacation
I wrote postcards to Ron, Lydia, and Ella:

>My friend Bea and I are having fun at cool, breezy Hyannis beach every day. We like the gray shingles on our new guest house. We boarded Tumba with the bird lady.

During a delicious ocean fish dinner at a restaurant, Bea's father said, "The Albany heat wave continued with another record high for yesterday's date: ninety-seven."

Dad answered, "I hope it cools for our trip home Sunday."

Monday, September 26, 1955: Pinching
We fasted for Yom Kippur to atone for our mistakes. At the synagogue, tall, bald Mr. J smiled and walked toward me. He has a fat stomach and booming voice. He's scary when he pinches my cheek so hard it hurts. He stopped smiling when he saw me enter the ladies' room before he got near me. Dad said, "He escaped from the Nazis when they killed six million Jews. He has no kids and probably doesn't realize he's hurting you." I felt sorry for him, but not enough to get pinched.

Wednesday, September 28, 1955: Afraid
In sixth grade, Miss Kilfoil is sarcastic and mean to kids who get in bad with her. I told Doreen, "I'm afraid to answer or ask questions. I'd be embarrassed if she made fun of me and everyone laughed."

Saturday, October 29, 1955: Green Apples, Green Bug
Our classmate Julia had a fun Halloween party, including playing musical chairs. My witch hat and mask made it hard to bob for apples. Julia's family has the only Volkswagen Beetle I've seen. It's like a light green giant bug. Her mother is Protestant and her Dad was born Jewish. They like the Unitarian Church.

Thursday, November 24, 1955: Aunt Faith

In Gloversville, I told Aunt Myrna, "Your Thanksgiving turkey and green apple pie were yummy!" After fun with Lydia and Ella, we visited Uncle Peter and Aunt Faith in their big house on a fancy street. I liked looking at the expensive clothes and shoes in her huge closet. I wish we saw her more. We visited her son Nick, his baby boy, and pretty green-eyed wife. I like them all.

1956

Saturday, January 7, 1956: Eleventh
I had a wonderful birthday party! Mom took Tara, Doreen, Marsha, and me to a movie at the Madison Theatre. Next door at Le Petit Paris ice cream parlor, my friends said, "Yum! These banana splits and ice cream sundaes are delicious!"

Sunday, January 8, 1956: Typewriter
Mom said, "Grandma's taking mineral waters at the Savoy in Saratoga Springs." I sent a note:
> Dear Grandma,
> Thank you very, very much for the lovely card and money!
> I put the ten dollars in my portable typewriter fund. I had fun at my party and got nice presents. Thank you again.
> Love and XXXXXXXXXXXXXXXX, Angela
> P.S. I miss you. I wish you were here.
> P.P.S. How do you take mineral waters?

Thursday, January 12, 1956: Mom's Birthday
Mom liked the beige cardboard bookmark I made and said, "Now all I need is time to read a book." I copied "token of my appreciation" from a store's card.

We laughed when Tumba said, "Fern," "I spended (*sic*) the money," and "May I have this dance?" while yakking on and on.

Angela's birthday gift

Friday, February 3, 1956: Dance

I told Tara, "I'm excited! Marcus invited me to the Boy Scout dance, my first date!" He's smart with tightly curled light hair and blue eyes. He's tall, which is good for dancing. Our faces are both broken out.

When I mentioned the dance at dinner, Tumba cracked us up with, "May I have this dance?"

Saturday, February 11, 1956: Date

Doreen called about the dance. I said, "I got dressed up, including sheer nylon stockings attached to a garter belt. Marcus looked handsome and took me there. I was happy to dance almost every time."

"Do you like him?"

"I had as much fun as I could with a boy I'm just getting to know. I like dates and hope to get asked to more dances!"

Marcus

Tuesday, February 14, 1956: Valentines
Many kids at school sent me little Valentines. Two boys in my class are okay, but not as boyfriends.

Thursday, March 22, 1956: C
Dad, unhappy, wrote:
> Angela has always received As in arithmetic.

Miss Kilfoil called it a "mistake" and changed the report card C to B. My other marks were As. I'm glad she wrote under attitudes:
> A fine girl

Miss K is nicer to me now.

Friday, March 23, 1956: Welshie
Walking home with Tara, I said, "I'm surprised to get As in gym from Welshie."

Tara said, "Remember how afraid of her we were last year?"

I nodded and asked, "Does she wear a dress, stockings, and heels when she goes out with her husband?" She laughed. No other teacher wears baggy wool skirts, loose tweed jackets, and big pullover sweaters, rather than blouses. Above her sneaks and sox, her calf muscles are gigantic! She makes us learn rules and play right. We work hard, but sports are fun, so I almost like her.

Friday, May 4, 1956: Report Card
On my report card, Welshie wrote that I've had a hard time tumbling. I finally can do forward and backward rolls the right way without landing on my head. I said to Doreen, "I'm lucky to get A minus, instead of C." I was surprised but glad about Miss K's note under attitudes:
> Happy, well-adjusted. Work is characteristic of her high mental ability. Always cooperative and dependable. Always relaxed and poised.

I laughed because I never relax with Miss K!

Mom said, "We're pleased that you got excellent or very good on everything."

Friday, June 22, 1956: Summer
Miss K made this year hard, but my final report card has all As.
I said to Marsha, "I can't wait to be more grown-up and change
classes for each subject in September."

Sunday, July 29, 1956: Vacation
Aunt Myrna said, "Our store's new manager had a heart attack,
so Uncle Abner has to work, instead of being here." Atlantic City
is wonderful! We got on the little jitney bus in front of Twin
Manor Hotel, our nice boarding house with a shady porch. We got
off at the long boardwalk, where we ate dinner. We talked about
a big ship which just sank near Cape Cod. Its name is Andrea
Doria, similar to Angela Doreen. Mom said, "Most passengers
survived, unlike the Titanic sinking in 1912." Boats are scary!

Wednesday, August 1, 1956: Fire
Last night, we treated Lydia to a tenth birthday dinner at fancy
Breakers Restaurant. At the Million Dollar Pier, Ella, seven, said,
"I can't believe that horse jumped through a fire ring into the
ocean!" I wrote a picture postcard to Doreen:
> At the big sandy beach, my cousins and I build castles, read
> mystery books, get tan, and ride the waves every day!

Saturday, August 4, 1956: Tantrum
At the Hotel Jefferson Plantation Room on Kentucky Avenue,
Dad looked ridiculous, about two years old, when his face got red
and he banged on the table. He yelled at the waitress, "We've
been waiting for almost an hour and now you bring the wrong
order. For crying out loud (his favorite expression when mad),
take this back and bring our seafood immediately!"
Even though he was right, I said to Lydia, "Let's become
invisible and crawl away."

Sunday, August 5, 1956: Atlantic City
Before getting on the bus for Albany, Dad smiled and joked, "I'll
miss being the only man with five beautiful women." We're sorry
that he gets only a week's vacation, but glad to avoid tantrums
next week. I sent Tara a picture postcard about our fun vacation:

After swimming at the beach, we eat hot dogs and ice cream on the boardwalk for lunch and play Skee-Ball. We roll the ball down a little lane to get it in a hole with a high number. We're trying for enough points for a stuffed animal.

Friday, August 10, 1956: Hackney's
The Steel Pier rides and shows are too expensive, but we enjoy fresh fish dinners in different restaurants. Tonight, we dressed up for famous Hackney's. My pink flower headband and dropped waist white dress looked good with my dark tan.

Monday, August 13, 1956: Home
I feel let down after the best vacation ever, two wonderful weeks with my cousins! Dad is cracking jokes and acting extra nice. Eating alone for a week made him miss us.

Sunday, August 19, 1956: Batted
At the synagogue picnic, Dad was at bat at the baseball diamond. I stood too close behind him. When he swung back, the bat hit me on the forehead. I felt dizzy. The emergency room doctor said, "Rest this week and use an ice pack." My head has a big bump. What's a concussion?

Tuesday, August 21, 1956: Sad Dad
Dad isn't making his usual jokes. He looks worried and sorry about hitting me. Even though he yells at Mom and me when he's mad, the accident was my fault. After two days on the wicker couch on our enclosed back porch, I feel better, but a little weird. I remembered Jimmy pitching the baseball at my head. If I keep playing baseball, I won't have any brains left.

Monday, August 27, 1956: Braces
After putting on silver braces, my orthodontist Dr. Turk said, "Straightening your teeth will take a year." As I looked up at his round glasses and grayish crew cut, tears came to my eyes. Alone in my room, I cried about smiling with my lips closed. Like Mom, I hardly ever cry.

Thursday, August 30, 1956: Thruway

Reading the paper, Dad clapped! "This weekend, we'll take the new Thruway to Gloversville. We'll reach NYC fast without excursion trains!" I love visiting my cousins.

Near Gloversville at Old Orchard Inn near
Sacandaga Reservoir, left to right: Herm,
Angela, Uncle Abner, Fern, Aunt Sara, Ella

Saturday, September 8, 1956: Bra
I'm happy to be grown-up enough for my first bra, size 30AA. Tara already wears one. I'm glad not to be the first or last to need one.

Monday, September 10, 1956: Six Teachers
Dad asked about my new teachers. I replied: "I have Welshie again for gym, Mrs. Denis for home ec, Miss Smitt for math, strict and scary Miss Stewart for social studies, nice Mrs. Bern for English, and fun Mrs. Lewis for art and science."

Thursday, October 25, 1956: Badge
I'm enjoying my Girl Scout interior decorating badge. Mom said, "Your three-dimensional, roofless house of heavy colored paper and Scotch tape looks good."

I answered, "Thanks! I like to move around the colored paper furniture, so it's not taped down."

We chuckled after Tumba chirped, "Pretty boy," and blew the furniture out of place by flying over it.

Thursday, November 22, 1956: Thanksgiving
I'm thankful to be elected treasurer of Patroon School because it's an honor. I won't have to do much because we don't have any money.

Friday, November 23, 1956: Dances
I love the Center (Jewish Community Center) casual dances for kids every other week. Mom lets me wear pink lipstick! I agreed when Doreen said, "It's better to go with friends and dance with different boys, especially good dancers, than be stuck all evening on a date with a bad dancer."

Friday, December 7, 1956: Diary
I sent a note to Aunt Rhoda and Uncle Harvey about my Hanukkah gift:

Thank you for the darling leatherette, gold-trimmed diary with a key! I love it!

The key's on a chain around my neck to keep my parents out. They don't know that smart eighth-grader Edwin likes me. He has brown hair, freckles, and a good smile. He's vice president of our school.

1957

Private Personal Diary: Seventh Grade

Tuesday, January 1, 1957: Masculine

At the rabbi's house with my parents, I felt sad. Auto accident injuries keep his poor, sweet wife from walking and caring for her three kids. I joked around with blue-eyed son Frankie, whose voice is deep and masculine. When he asked about New Year's Eve, I replied, "I had fun sleeping over at Tara's. By the way, I'm selling this stamp collection." I left out that I find stamps boring.

He said, "These Argentine stamps are cool."

I said, "Mom writes our Buenos Aires cousins in Yiddish. They sent these Israeli stamps."

Frankie said, "If I had money, I'd buy them. I'll tell guys who collect."

I said, "Thanks! I wish vacation wasn't over."

While practicing a Chopin Polonaise, which I love, on the piano and listening to radio hit songs, I thought: Frankie's kind of cute. But he smokes and is sort of wild.

Wednesday, January 2, 1957: Early Bird Frozen and Uncertain

I hate getting out of bed shivering. The thermostat's at only fifty-five at night to save money. I hope Tumba's warm enough. The house warms up only after we dress and leave for the day. Edwin asked me to watch him play basketball. To avoid hurting his feelings, I said, "Thanks, but I have homework." I'm unsure whether I like him as a boyfriend.

Thursday, January 3, 1957: Gift and Poem

I'm glad I saved my weekly twenty-five-cent allowance for four months. My parents looked surprised and happy with their $3.98 twentieth anniversary present. Dad said, "Thanks for the excellent long-playing Sarah Vaughn record album!" Today, I like Edwin after hearing the wonderful poem he wrote!

Angela

I know a girl. Her name is Angie.
Just look at her. You'll know she's dandy.
Her eyes are so bright and gay.
I think of her the livelong day.

Her personality sticks out all over.
And her smile is bigger than the Cliffs of Dover.
Her lips are as sweet as a honeysuckle.
And when she kisses you, your knees will buckle.

Her teeth are as white as a fairy's pearl.
When you're next to her, your mind will swirl.
Whenever I see Angie, her hair is shiny and bright.
I dream of that doll night after night.

Friday, January 4, 1957: Volcano and Secretary

Our teacher was explaining a math problem. Her face looked odd before her head bent forward. Our eyes bulged and mouths dropped open to see a huge gush of barf pour out of her mouth onto the floor in front of our desks. It was like a volcano eruption I saw in a science book. She hurried from the room, leaving us in shock about seeing a teacher throw up. We sat paralyzed, except for kids in front holding their noses. After a while, Principal Burnsy arrived. "Miss Smitt has gone home. When the bell rings, proceed to your next class." We stepped around the yucky vomit, which the poor janitor had to clean up.

After our school officers' meeting, Edwin said, "Congratulations on being elected recording secretary of the school traffic court!" Smiling, I thanked him before he added, "I'm glad my ring is on your neck chain. You said not to worry about that other ring, so I'm not jealous." I love the marquise-aquamarine, white-gold ring from Mom's boyfriend before Dad. Only Tara's in on the secret: it isn't from a boy.

Saturday, January 5, 1957: King Tut

I listened to the week's Top Forty radio countdown of rock-and-roll hits while washing the floor and helping Mom get ready for my twelfth birthday party. In my black-and-white-striped nylon dress, I was in a whirl of dancing, opening presents, and playing Spin the Bottle and other kissing games. My parents chaperoned in the other room. Mimicking mummies unwinding their bandages in the game King Tut, we did pretend strip teases. Everyone behaved, except Carl. I guess he had to pee because he clutched his penis through his trousers. He didn't seem to know not to grab it in public. We all died of laughter watching him.

Sunday, January 6, 1957: Thank Yous

I enjoyed picturing the party, laughing about Carl, writing thank-you notes, and putting away my lovely gifts: red leather wallet (Edwin), collar pin with hanging ballet slippers (Doreen), Western tie (Tara), autograph giraffe signed by the kids (Marsha), white Orlon sweater (Carl), gold address book with Jewish star (Myles), twelve pencils in a leather pencil holder (Udeh), china pocketbook bank with pin money (Aryeh), and more. I thanked my parents for a beautiful striped skirt in size 10 preteen, Aunt Lila for a warm sweater, Grandma for five dollars, and Ron for a travel kit. Receiving four wallets, including Aunt Rhoda's in blue leather and Aunt Sara's black wallet, made me conclude that people must think I have money.

Monday, January 7, 1957: Thumb Sucking

On the phone, after Edwin admitted sucking his thumb in secret until he was seven, I said, "I thought I was the only one."

He said, "I was ashamed of this babyish habit. Did your mom put bad-tasting stuff on your thumb?"

I answered, "Yes! It didn't work. One day, I decided to quit and did."

Tuesday, January 8, 1957: Scary

Will I be fired as the new volleyball team captain? Our Volleyettes lost. Gym class is too short for a complete game, so Welshie makes us stay after school by staring us down over her rimless glasses. Her sarcastic, gruff voice is scary. After two years of soldier drills, we are prepared for the Army. But no girl I know wants to join.

Wednesday, January 9, 1957: Hebrew
Hebrew school was a riot because of making fun of the cantor, a boring teacher who seldom smiles. I wish he'd stick with his job of chanting during services. When we all laughed at Fatso Cantor, my eyes met Aryeh's green eyes. Something clicked. No one knows that I kind of like him.

Thursday, January 10, 1957: California
Watching Edwin work the movie machine at school assembly, I felt romantic. He smiled at me during the movie. He called, pretending to be Tara so we could talk. I said, "I had a sad dream that you moved far away to California."

On Art Linkletter's *House Party* radio show, I heard, "It's seventy degrees here in sunny Los Angeles." It sounds like heaven when Albany may have snow until the May Tulip Festival.

Saturday, January 12, 1957: Fire and Love
At the Center dance, Frankie pulled fun tab books from his pocket. When he flipped the pages fast, the pictures looked like a movie. We helped Doreen after a sore bled. I was close to tears worrying after her mom said that family friends had a house fire. Wonderful Edwin and I, secretly on the phone over an hour, each said, "I love you." It was romantic! Edwin recited the poem *Angela* on the phone. I can't hear it enough.

Sunday, January 13, 1957: Movie and Aunt Sara
Tara and I saw top rock-and-roll singers (The Platters, Little Richard, and Fats Domino) in *The Girl Can't Help It*. Child actor Barry Gordon, whose family goes to our synagogue, was cute in this wonderful movie! Jayne Mansfield was the dumb blonde. Mom's birthday dinner included Aunt Sara, who has added the accordion to her shows. She said, "In places like Greensboro, North Carolina, the few Jews talk with a Southern accent. I sing Caribbean folk music and Jewish songs. People in the audience

who enjoy the performances invite me to their homes, so it's fun." After I said that her photo looked glamorous, she replied, "My boyfriend, Mort, a part-time cantor who travels to perform as a baritone, likes that dress."

Aunt Sara singing

Monday, January 14, 1957: Lucy

My favorite TV comedy, *I Love Lucy*, was hilarious! Lucy's son's heart was set on having Superman at his birthday party. When Superman canceled, Lucy, dressed as Superman, pretended she had flown onto the ledge outside their apartment. I rolled on the floor laughing with tears running down, watching Lucy stuck on the ledge in the rain. Finally, the real Superman showed up and rescued her.

Tuesday, January 15, 1957: Twenty-Four Below

After thanking Aunt Sara for the wallet and her visit, I wrote:

> I hope it's warmer in NYC. Yesterday and today set new low records for these dates. It was twenty-four and twenty degrees below zero. Mom drove me to school, but our "lemon" car broke down. A man we know dropped me off on time. We froze in the unheated gym. During lunch, Tara said, "I wish we could play hooky." I agreed, but we were good and returned to school. Schools close only during huge blizzards. I hate winter! My heavy coat and boots aren't warm enough.

The delicious pineapple upside-down cake Mom made cheered me up. She hardly ever bakes. Cooking isn't her favorite thing.

Wednesday, January 16, 1957: Brownies

I told my parents, "Tara is sweet. She used her bigger allowance to buy two delicious brownies at the Dutch Oven Bakery. She gave me one."

Mom replied, "As a lawyer for the state, her father makes a lot more than Dad at the Surplus Store."

I replied, "I know. My twenty-five-cent weekly allowance is enough."

Thursday, January 17, 1957: Cramming for Examming

On this last day before midyear exams, I was too nervous to concentrate on Welshie's lecture: Fundamentals of Women's Basketball. I crammed for over two hours for our citizenship education (formerly social studies) exam. We call it cit ed for short.

Friday, January 18, 1957: Stiff and Letting Off Steam

Nineteen-below-zero cold froze me stiff. Our exam made me scared stiff. It seemed easy. After double-checking it, I was the first to leave at 10:25. Edwin came to synagogue services with my family. We teens let off steam by teasing one another, annoying adults, and running around downstairs screaming. Carl was nervous about his *Bar Mitzvah*.

Saturday, January 19, 1957: Romance and Four Roses

I enjoyed Edwin's romantic phone conversation, including "I love you" and compliments about my looks and personality. He can't wait to kiss and do things. I'm glad he knows not to try now. I've never necked, but the parents must be afraid I will to require chaperones. Carl's party was fun with dancing, signing autograph books, and eating a chicken dinner. After Dad let me try Four Roses whiskey with ginger ale, I felt giddy, flirting with Edwin and looking into Myles' dreamy blue eyes.

Dad laughed when I said, "Four Roses tastes worse than medicine. Grape juice tastes better than wine."

Dad replied, "Jewish alcoholics are rare because alcohol isn't forbidden. Kids are used to Sabbath wine."

Sunday, January 20, 1957: *Eddie, My Love*

I woke up at 11:20 completely pooped. Was I hung over? Doreen and I were afraid to see a movie because ringworm is going around. I thought of Edwin while singing a favorite hit song, "Eddie, my love, I love you so...Please, Eddie, don't make me wait too long." At my house, Edwin, talking about our future, bored me. I'm too young to think about marriage. I changed to fun subjects. I love him less than he seems to love me.

Monday, January 21, 1957: Paintings and Exploding Cigars

Diagramming sentences helped me pass (I hope) the English grammar exam. After lunch, I painted watercolor pictures. At Hebrew, our anti-cantor club will give Fatso chocolate-covered rocks, tight shirts to choke him because his neck is too big to get fingers around, and exploding cigars. I almost wet my pants from laughing so hard. Even my parents laughed when I told them.

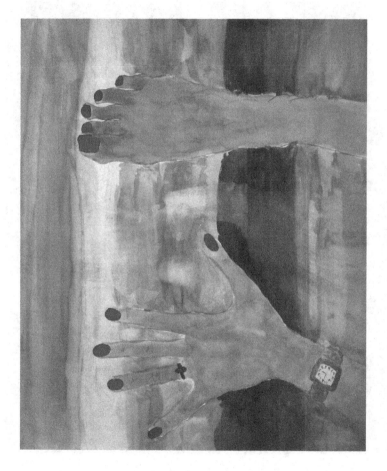

Angela's watercolor: traced hand and foot against a rainbow background

Watercolor: Studying

Tuesday, January 22, 1957: Perspective and Study

My art exam, covering perspective, color, and design, wasn't hard. Eddie annoyed me by calling several times with nothing new to say. Singing the Seven Dwarfs song, "Heigh ho, heigh ho, it's off to work I go," stopped my procrastinating and started an hour of studying.

Wednesday, January 23, 1957: Bonus Bargain Days

After my math midyear, I met Mom downtown at Wondershop for a mad rush of buying wonderful sale clothes: mint-green suit, red wool dress, and yellow tight skirt, all size 10 preteen; striped jersey, red sweater, and white boy shirt in size 12 preteen; and bedroom slippers and red flats, size 6B. Before our Chrysler had to be towed, I was feeling lucky to be average in height and weight, like Tara and Doreen. My measurements are 30-23-34. At five foot one and one hundred pounds, I can find bargains. I'm enjoying the hit records Mom bought today: *Don't Forbid Me* and *Bigelow 6-2-0-0*.

Thursday, January 24, 1957: Turkey and Sex

Turkey (my name for Dr. Turk) checked my braces. I don't like him much. He acts cheerful but seems fake. Eddie and I had a nice conversation I shouldn't have had: everything we know about sex. It was a short talk. The book Mom gave me years ago said the penis puts out sperm, like polliwogs swimming up the vagina to try to get into the egg. If a sperm makes it, a baby grows. Tadpoles swimming inside your body don't sound great, but Eddie is very interested.

Friday, January 25, 1957: Wishful Thinking and Speech

I'm falling hard for Myles, who walked me home. He loves Tara. Is it wishful thinking when I feel that he likes me? At synagogue family night, I wish he had been the one who said, "You look good enough to eat." I enjoyed wearing my red dress and shoes. People called my speech "excellent." I was sorry to miss a school dance!

Saturday, January 26, 1957: Protected
At my house, Doreen, Marsha, and I talked about boys and jitterbugged. At the Center dance, I had a wonderful time, wearing my red outfit. When I danced with Myles and Rob, Eddie got mad. I felt tied down. With Myles, I felt feminine and protected. I asked his size. His light blue eyes looked down at me. He smiled and answered in his rumbling voice, "I'm five foot eight and 120 pounds." On the way home when Tara and I took away his hat and got kind of crazy, I tickled Myles' long, lean body. She likes him only as a pal. Ooh! I love him so much! I wish the feeling was mutual. Eddie, who's wearing off, is seven inches shorter.

Sunday, January 27, 1957: Too Serious
After I read the newspaper, Marsha, Tara, and I went downtown to the Palace Theatre to see *Anastasia*, about the daughter of the last Russian tsar. Ingrid Bergman was wonderful as Anastasia. Eddie called, talking seriously when I wanted to laugh. I'm losing interest.

Tuesday, January 29, 1957: Science
I wrote to Aunt Sara:
> Second semester started at 8:50. After eight classes of forty-five minutes each in math, English, cit ed, science, spelling, music, gym, and home economics, we finish as late as 4:30. I don't know whether I like science, but Mrs. Lewis is funny! The topics sound interesting: the human machine, minerals, cells, disease with apple experiment, tests for starch and fat, seven basic food groups, fire, plants, conservation, rocks, weather with air pressure experiment, solar system, and the ear.

Wednesday, January 30, 1957: Loss, Refusal, and Idol
At the alumni volleyball game, I was sorry that the eighth-grade girls lost to the returning ninth-graders by one stupid point! Someone said, "Rob likes you," but the feeling's not mutual. He doesn't say anything interesting or make me laugh. At five foot five with brown eyes and brown hair, he needs to lose twenty

pounds. I politely refused his invitation to the synagogue dance to avoid being with him all evening. I hope others ask me to dance first. Occasional ladies' choice songs are the only times we can ask boys to dance. In *The Singing Idol* on TV, I liked Tommy Sands as a rock-and-roll star, like Elvis Presley.

Thursday, January 31, 1957: Friends and Levi's

Eddie didn't seem surprised or say much when I said, "I'm too young for a regular boyfriend. I'd like to be friends." I don't want to hurt his feelings. At Hebrew, Myles did a lovely job of annoying the cantor. I love Myles, who chatted at my house before walking around the corner to his house. When he smiles down at me, sometimes I get the feeling that he likes me. I don't blame him for mooning after sweet, smart Tara. Her mischievous streak makes her fun. Her face and figure are better than mine.

When Tara said, "I'm nervous about my piano recital Saturday," I sympathized. I wouldn't flirt if she liked Myles as a boyfriend. His tall, thin body looks good in tight Levi's! Why aren't the boys who like me the boys I go for?

Saturday, February 2, 1957: Artie

I ironed my white boy shirt to wear with my tight skirt to the synagogue dance, which Mom organized for kids our age. After cute, blond Lewis and I decorated, loads of kids danced for three hours to the 150 free hit singles Mom got a store to donate. I was thrilled to win a jitterbug contest with Myles! He, Lewis, and Artie, a new boy my age and size, competed by cutting in to dance with me. Did my yellow skirt make me popular enough to dance almost every time? I told Tara, "I really like Artie from Mohican School!"

Sunday, February 3, 1957: Oklahoma and Artie

After eleven hours of sleep, I got up at eleven. Tara, Doreen, and I saw the movie *Oklahoma* with wonderful dancing and songs like *Oh What a Beautiful Morning* and *I Can't Say No.* I said, "When dreamy Gordon MacRae sang *People Will Say We're in Love*, I pictured Artie's brown eyes, big smile, and even white teeth."

His brown hair is combed up in a pompadour in front. I like his rosy tan complexion and good body!

Monday, February 4, 1957: Home Ec
Except for laughing too much for a good mark in self-control, Tara and I followed the home ec requirements: wear apron and cap, follow directions, keep things clean and orderly, and be courteous and reliable. I'm memorizing *Recipe Abbreviations and Measurement Equivalents.* I didn't realize that food is made up of fat, protein, and vitamins. I'm looking forward to making and eating baked apples, drop biscuits, creamed tuna fish on baked potatoes, and penuche candy.

Tuesday, February 5, 1957: As and Popular
In a tizzy with butterflies in my stomach before seeing my grades, I felt relieved about five exams from 96 percent to 100 percent. Health was 90 percent. My report card has all As for the first time. At Hebrew, I smiled when Udeh said, "I gave Artie your phone number when he asked. He'll be at the Center Saturday."

I told Doreen, "I can't wait to see Artie!" Udeh, Myles, Rob, Lewis, Edwin, and Artie seem to like me. I've never been so popular all at once. I don't know why, but I love every moment of it!

Thursday, February 7, 1957: Bad
To bug the cantor after yesterday's murderous test, we dressed sloppily. My wrinkled red shirt had the collar up. I wore chalked-up black dungarees and dirty shoes. I combed my hair over my eyes in a sexy way. Before I left for Hebrew, Mom asked her usual annoying, "What will they think?"

I replied as usual, "Who are they?" I got only 67 percent because I hadn't memorized tons of new words. Hebrew doesn't count, so I goof off. It's fun to give teachers a hard time. In regular school, I'm afraid to be bad. Smart-aleck Frankie is bad everywhere. The rabbi probably killed him for joking in math and getting sent to the principal. I hope that Myles' and Aryeh's playful fighting with me means that they like me.

Saturday, February 9, 1957: Call

Home with an awful cold, I was overjoyed when Artie called for a few minutes from the noisy dance. I love him and sent a guess-who Valentine. To design fancy, old-fashioned clothes, I painted a colorful watercolor of a royal couple, watching dancing couples. Listening to Johnnie Ray's *Look Homeward, Angel,* I filed ten hit records, which Mom let me keep after the dance, with my other thirty. Liking Artie as a boyfriend, I'm fine being platonic with Myles.

Angela's colorful costume designs

Sunday, February 10, 1957: *Bat Mitzvahs*
Doreen said, "I like studying for my Bat Mitzvah, but it's hard."
I'm relieved to skip the terror of chanting in Hebrew, which I
dislike and hardly know, to tons of people. My parents agreed,
probably because parties are expensive. I'll enjoy other girls' Bat
Mitzvahs. I'm glad I'm not a boy. Bar Mitzvahs are mandatory.
Though I pray at bedtime, I go to the synagogue to flirt.

Monday, February 11, 1957: Don't Make Me Wait
While alone in orthodontist Turkey's waiting room, I quietly sang
Eddie, My Love with Artie's name, "Don't make me wait too long."
Turkey, always cracking corny jokes for a laugh, is making me
wait two months longer to get the braces off. Ugh!

Tuesday, February 12, 1957: Tab and College
At Girl Scouts, we heard, "We saw the movie star Tab Hunter
live. Ooh, what a living doll!"
    I agreed when Doreen said, "I wish we'd seen him, instead of
the movie *Westward Ho the Wagons*."
    After I gave Dad the three dollars a girl paid for my
outgrown skirt, he said, "I'll put this in your college account. If
I had finished college while working all day, I'd make more now.
You need the best grades for scholarships to finish college."
I'm happy to stop Hebrew this June to free more time for
schoolwork and socializing. When I grow up, I want to escape
from money worries and avoid a bad neighborhood with bullies
beating up people.

Thursday, February 14, 1957: Valentine's Day
The math test average was 50 percent; only four kids passed
with over 74 percent. I was happy with the only perfect math
score and forty school Valentines, more than I sent! After
waiting eagerly all day, we felt let down when our dance ended
after only five records. I bet the teachers wanted to get home.

Saturday, February 16, 1957: No Sister
At Tara's, I said, "I'm happy we'll be in the school honor class
together!" We listened to new records before a nice talk about

what sex is like. Her grown-up sister passes on dirty jokes. I wish Rowena was alive to explain this joke:

What's sixty-nine squared?

Answer: Dinner for four.

I'm stuck being an only child. Mom explained, "The doctor warned that my tipped uterus will make a baby come out too early." We looked at the uterus picture in my book.

Tuesday, February 19, 1957: Sex, Kids, and Loss

Tara dreamed about a boy she likes acting wild with a fat girl we know. I said, "People say that boys do everything with her."

Tara responded, "It's hard to believe."

I replied, "Maybe that's the only way fat girls can get boys." After eating delicious biscuits we baked in home ec, we were bored visiting kindergarten to learn about kids. My Snappy Six basketball team lost the first game of the season. Our name should be Stupid Six.

Wednesday, February 20, 1957: Surprised

I almost fell off my chair in shock. Strict, sarcastic Miss Stewart said, "Good," after my answers to two cit ed questions. Welshie, who seldom smiles, grinned and said, "Good," after my unexpected basket. I felt happier because at home Mom's obnoxious voice nags and criticizes me. Friends' parents sound easier to satisfy.

Mom was nice to buy me black peg (tapered) slacks when I said, "All the girls have 'em." After I said, "I like Tommy Sands more than Elvis," we bought Tommy's *Teenage Crush*, sung on Tennessee Ernie Ford's TV show.

Friday, February 22, 1957: Washington's Birthday

Off school, we decorated for the Girl Scout dance. Feeling excited standing on the sidelines in my salmon shirtwaist, I watched the door for cute boys. We sixteen girls were let down! Only nine average boys trickled in. They drank hardly any of the six cases of soda.

Saturday, February 23, 1957: Unpopular

At the Center dance after Albany won the basketball game, I danced only once and missed seeing Artie. Why am I popular only on some nights? Was it my bobby socks, loafers, skirt, or boy shirt?

Sunday, February 24, 1957: Jobs

Because Mom has worked hard, but sold few houses, she took the NY State job test. She said, "Being a Department of Mental Hygiene secretary is ideal because I like psychology. We're lucky to live in a state capital with good jobs."

I said, "Tara's mother is a secretary in another state department."

Tuesday, February 26, 1957: Quirky and Worst Six

After I made and gulped down my favorite sandwich, baloney with mayonnaise on rye, Quirky Turkey put elastic bands on my braces. Being unable to smile with my teeth showing may be why I'm unpopular sometimes. My Snappy Six team lost to the best girls' basketball team. At least our boys' team won yesterday. I wish Artie had been among the nineteen kids I recognized from his school.

Thursday, February 28, 1957: Teaching and Nursing

I'm glad I spent over an hour on my American Revolution composition because I got an A. I told Mom, "Miss Stewart read it to cit ed class."

Mom asked, "Why not be a teacher? It pays better than the state and you get summers off."

I answered, "Talking to kids all day sounds boring."

Mom said, "I'd love to teach. Nursing was my first choice. My uniforms were packed for Syracuse University when my father stopped me, saying that no daughter of his was going to clean bedpans." Grandpa's pictures in our album look nice, but he was mean to Mom. When I'm sick, Mom takes good care of me. Aunt Myrna and two cousins were nurses before marriage. Working with sick people sounds worse than teaching.

Friday, March 1, 1957: Camping

After crossing the Hudson River to Rensselaer, we drove slowly on icy country roads to East Greenbush. The untouched snow on big hills was prettier than Albany's dirty stuff. Jumping up and down with excitement, Doreen and I agreed that Camp Is-Sho-Da looks like pictures of Abraham Lincoln's log cabin. Our Girl Scout birthday party included jitterbugging and games. I got the First Aid badge I earned. A friend sneaked over to talk with Doreen and me in the corner bunk. I love Is-Sho-Da.

Saturday, March 2, 1957: Break-In and Artie

Last night, noise scared and woke us. Mrs. Bruins yelled at and chased away drunk teenagers trying to break into Is-Sho-Da, which is far from houses. Teens don't scare a mother of nine kids. We laughed and went back to sleep. After washing breakfast dishes and making bedrolls, we enjoyed a toboggan ride into a big bush. No one was hurt. Our snowballs knocked off loads of snow weighing down evergreen branches. Mom arrived and got mad that we might get scarlet fever from a girl who went home sick. I was too dead tired to attend the synagogue dance. I was sad to miss seeing Artie, who asked for me.

Sunday, March 3, 1957: Better Than Nothing

Mom led our first meeting for Jewish teens. After we danced the Israeli hora in a circle, Tara asked, "Is Young Judaea less fun with your mother here?"

I nodded. "But she's the only parent willing to lead."

Tara said, "She seems too busy to notice you." I laughed, relieved to flirt freely.

Monday, March 4, 1957: Worried

Doreen was signing my slam notebook when our teacher took it, read bad things kids have written about some teachers, and kept it! My heart pounded with fear and embarrassment. I've tried never to get in trouble at school. I'm upset!

Tuesday, March 5, 1957: Tough Day

My face felt really hot and red when Miss Stewart discussed the slam book in class. I was dying until she changed the subject. In the cold nurse's office, we froze undressing for our annual physicals. Our Snappy Six, who haven't won one measly game, lost. The only good thing was my *American Girl* magazine coming in the mail.

Thursday, March 7, 1957: Muscles

At the junior high city championship game, we lost 20-17, but I adored seeing new boys' cute muscular bodies in basketball uniforms. Screaming and cheering loudly made my throat too sore to swallow.

Saturday, March 9, 1957: Sick

After Doreen and I were home sick yesterday, my sore throat woke me every time I swallowed after 4 a.m. The doctor brought tonsillitis medicine, which has started working. I finished a wonderful teen novel, *Sweet 16*. Dad laughed at the birthday card I made! I'm happy that Artie called to ask, "Will Angela be at the Center dance tonight?"

Mom said, "She wants to go, but is still sick." I miss Artie and haven't danced for two weeks.

Monday, March 11, 1957: Good as Men

I did cheerleading jumps while watching the TV quiz show *Twenty One*. A beautiful, smart woman lawyer won! Blond, thirty-year-old Vivienne Nearing, who has a perfect figure, beat cute Charles Van Doren. He won the most ever on a TV show: $129,000. Charles previously beat her husband, so she must be smarter than her husband. I'm glad Vivienne proved that women are as good as men and can combine brains and good looks!

Tuesday, March 12, 1957: A Penny Saved Gets a Bracelet

Gym was a riot with an auction of cheap jewelry and junk that kids have left in the locker room. We laughed at Welshie saying, "This fine bracelet is going, going, gone to the lady in the green gym bloomers for three cents."

Wednesday, March 13, 1957: Cheered and Brainless

Today's warm weather and Udeh's comment before Hebrew cheered me: "Artie worried about you when you were sick and still likes you." The cantor sent Edwin home for sassing. Boys' squirt guns drenched me.

The cantor announced, "We're splitting Hebrew class in half to facilitate learning."

Frankie whispered, "To make us behave!"

I murmured, "They can't kick us all out. Hasn't the cantor been a good egg lately?"

Myles mumbled, "Less annoying and boring."

Frankie muttered, "We're just used to him. What did you get on the tests?"

I whispered, "History 91 percent and 78 percent in Bible." My Hebrew grades are too low for anyone to call me a brain, an unfeminine label I hate!

Thursday, March 14, 1957: Holidays and Politics

On a beautiful seventy-degree day, we were cooped up watching a St. Patrick's Day program. Almost everyone wore green. I pretended to like the Irish songs we had to sing. I whispered to Doreen, "Irish boys are cute, but I feel left out on St. Patrick's Day. It's wrong for schools to celebrate Irish holidays and not Jewish ones."

She nodded. "Mohican, Iroquois, and Patroon Schools have more Jewish than Irish kids."

Later, Dad explained, "The Irish dominate because Dan O'Connell's Democratic political machine runs Albany."

Mom said, "If we don't register Democrat, our property taxes increase."

I replied, "That's unfair!"

Sunday, March 17, 1957: Heroine

At the synagogue reading of the *Book of Esther*, I told Doreen, "Purim's a good holiday because it's for a female! Jewish heroes are usually men."

She agreed. "I'm glad that Queen Esther was beautiful and smart." After screaming against the wicked villain Haman, I'm discouraged about another sore throat.

Saturday, March 23, 1957: Rabbi
After synagogue services, Tara, looking her best in a cherry red sweater and charcoal gray skirt, said, "The rabbi gives interesting sermons."

I agreed. "Other rabbis put me to sleep."

Doreen, dressed in a cute navy dress with a flared skirt, said, "His ideas help me handle everyday situations." My friends take religion seriously, so I was afraid to say that I'd rather skip the repetitious prayers and listen only to the sermons. Maybe if God had sent a sister or even a brother, I'd be like my friends. I've prayed every night, always done all my homework, gotten the best grades, and helped around the house. No matter how good I've been, I'm still an only child, which I really dislike.

Tuesday, March 26, 1957: Women's Careers
I'm happy, but puzzled about my classmates clapping after hearing my English composition. It wasn't that good, except for the quotation I found. Thomas Huxley, a nineteenth-century scientist, said:

> I am at a loss to understand on what grounds of justice
> or public policy a career, which is open to the weakest and
> most foolish of the male sex, should be forcibly closed to
> women of vigor and capacity.

I'm irritated about girls getting pushed into nursing and teaching. Working on my Girl Scout badge, I said to Tara, "I'd like to work in art. I enjoy drawing and loved my interior decorating badge."

She replied, "You also liked your dance badge."

I nodded and asked, "Which badge is your favorite?"

She replied, "The First Aid badge skills let me help injured people. I loved the Music badge."

I said, "You play piano well! My music grade went down to B. If it wasn't the slam book, it's because I can't carry a tune."

Tara laughed and thanked me before confiding. "I might need a blood test because I can't get rid of my sore throat." I felt worried about her.

Wednesday, March 27, 1957: Beating Frankie
The rowdiest boys were put in the other Hebrew class. Our class behaves, except for pest Frankie making fun of me. After I warned him to stop, he said, "What are you going to do about it?" I ripped a button off his old, wrinkled blue shirt. Before he could grab my books, I ran off laughing as he shouted, "I'm telling everyone you're a fuck." Does it mean fast? I hope he's kidding. Does he tease me because he likes me? He has blue eyes, my favorite color, but I'm unsure if his new brush cut looks better. I didn't mind that Mom made me sew on his button. Ripping it off was fun and we feel sorry that his sweet mom is still an invalid.

Thursday, March 28, 1957: Long, Lean Bodies
In a wonderful dream, Myles and I, wearing tight black swimsuits, lay on a sandy beach hugging and kissing a lot. His body felt good. He asked, "Will you marry me?"

I said yes and we got engaged! I wish I had these exciting dreams every night! Myles and handsome Ari both have tall, thin bodies. Ari, an Israeli medical student, substituted for the cantor tonight. After class, I flirted with him, smiling while I looked into his dark eyes. When I teased and flattered him, he smiled and looked into my eyes.

When Doreen commented, "Too many girlfriends must make him conceited," I nodded agreement.

Friday, March 29, 1957: Strength and Underwear
Tara said, "Buddy is cute with a beautiful build."

I added, "He came in first on the school strength tests!"

She replied, "Imagine if we girls had to do pull-ups and push-ups."

After laughing and rolling my eyes, I said, "Two eighth-grade girls already go for Buddy."

She said, "Code names Dub and Dubby will keep our crushes secret."

We laughed after I added, "And Rub a Dub." In study hall, Tara and I couldn't stop giggling after pulling up the back of a new boy's tweed jacket and seeing his white underwear through a hole in his dark pants. Because he's cute with green eyes, we teased him and scattered his books around the room.

Saturday, March 30, 1957: Doreen
Seeing the wonderful movie *The King and I* put Doreen and me in good moods. Marsha came to Doreen's for a pajama party. After eating and listening to radio hit songs, we lay in bed talking and telling dirty jokes. I can't figure out this one:
What do you call a Roman with hair in his teeth?
Answer: Gladiator.

Sunday, March 31, 1957: Girls' Basketball
After memorizing a poem for English, I rewarded myself by shooting my basketball into our garage hoop in the warm sun. I smiled, remembering what Welshie said: "You guarded well, preventing some baskets."

Later, I told Tara, "I wish girl guards could cross the center line and shoot."

I agreed after she replied, "They think girls are too feeble to run the length of the court."

Monday, April 1, 1957: April Fools
I asked kids, "Did you study for the math test today?"

Each one looked alarmed and said, "What test? I didn't know and haven't studied."

I smiled and replied, "April Fool's joke!" Glad there was no test, everyone laughed. Similar pranks made it a funny day.

Tuesday, April 2, 1957: Biggest
Walking from school in the lovely spring weather, Tara and I had our usual fun, discussing fourteen-year-old Dubby, the biggest boy in school at five foot nine and 150 pounds. She said, "His brown hair looks good with a wavy pompadour in the front."

I nodded. "Don't forget his big brown eyes and long eyebrows."

She said, "He has a handsome smile and is a sharp dresser." We've fallen for our star basketball player. I imagined slow dancing with him. Feeling his big, strong muscles, I felt protected. His kiss was perfect.

Wednesday, April 3, 1957: Dubby
During a movie in assembly, Tara and I sat ahead of Dubby and looked back to see him. Can he tell we have crushes? Walking home, I told Tara a daydream: "You, Ben, Dub, and I double-dated for the prom."

She chuckled, "You hogged Dub as your date."

I laughed and continued. "The boys said we looked pretty and gave us rose corsages. Your corsage and pretty dress were white."

Tara commented, "I bet yours was pink."

I nodded, laughing. "We danced, ate out, and had fun. Dub kissed me goodnight and said that he really liked me!"

Tara smiled. "At least I got to date Ben. Dub hardly knows we exist. In only two months, he'll graduate."

We giggled after I said, "Because he's too popular to date me, his lack of brains won't bore me."

Wednesday, April 10, 1957: Lives
On TV's *This Is Your Life*, I enjoyed learning that Tommy Sands was a Houston, Texas, disc jockey at my age! He learned to play guitar at age seven. Now, at twenty, he sings hits and stars in TV shows. While off school for business education day (whatever that is), Doreen, Marsha, and I loved all four hours of the magnificent movie *This Is Your Life, Moses*, my name for *The Ten Commandments*. People's lives are interesting!

Saturday, April 13, 1957: I Love Artie
I was overjoyed that Artie called yesterday to say, "I'll meet you at the Center dance." It was heavenly! I danced almost every time with Artie, with Myles and Udeh cutting in. I love Artie!! Myles may like me. I came home with my head in the clouds. Artie's a living doll and smarter than Dub!

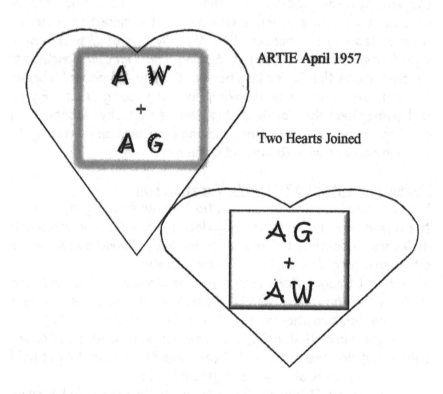

ARTIE April 1957

Two Hearts Joined

Angela's and Artie's doodled initials

Monday, April 15, 1957: Seder

I rushed madly for hours, helping Mom clean the house and change the milk and the meat dishes for Passover. My feet felt dead. A customer at the store made Dad late, as usual. At the Levines' Seder, sweet Robin, eleven and the youngest, asked the four questions in phonetic Hebrew. In English, I know only:

Why is this night different from all other nights?

Evelyn's chicken was tastier than Mom's. The walnut-apple-wine mixture I helped make was delish. I dislike the required hard-boiled egg and horseradish. My tiny sips of Manischewitz wine tasted sickeningly sweet. Seeing *The Ten Commandments* recently made the Seder less boring. Singing *Dayenu* in Hebrew, I read the English words, thanking God for freeing Jews in Egypt and giving them the Torah. *Artza Alinu* is a catchy Hebrew song about planting crops in Israel. Playing checkers and listening to popular records with Robin and Oren were fun.

Wednesday, April 17, 1957: Vacation Fun

We girls are happy to be on vacation! After synagogue, we took the bus in roasting heat to shop downtown. After we ate lunch at Myers Department Store, Marsha said, "*Round and Round* is a favorite song. I'm buying this sheet music."

When I bought *Rehearsal for Love, Promise of Delight*, and *A Secret in the Daisy*, Doreen, wearing a new turquoise top and matching Jamaica shorts, said, "They look like fun novels."

At the library, Marsha, a cat owner, looked at the Cornell College catalog and murmured, "Vet school is for me. I'll get paid to be with animals all day!" She giggled happily.

I whispered, "I love books and reading, but the only librarian program nearby is at Albany State. I want to leave home for college."

The librarian stamped the due date on each book's card and returned it to the inside cover holder. Doreen whispered, "How did you get ten more books than our limit of three?"

Smiling, I mumbled, "Mom loaned me her adult card."

Saturday, April 20, 1957: *Funny Face* and Wallflowers

After *Funny Face*, the Fred Astaire movie about modeling, I said to Tara, "I'm going to collect fashion magazine pictures. I'd love to look and be like slim Audrey Hepburn, my favorite actress."

Tara replied, "She's beautiful and sweet!"

After standing around most of the evening at the Center dance, I agreed when Marsha said, "Everyone must be away on vacation."

I said, "It's just as well that Artie's gone. My hair didn't come out right."

Sunday, April 21, 1957: Gloversville

Easter was warm enough to wear my green suit to Grandma's lovely white clapboard, two-story house. As usual, Grandma smiled with her gold tooth showing when Dad clapped after finishing her barley soup, roast chicken, and vegetable-fruit juice. I thanked Grandma for a locket and money. I got bored listening to Yiddish I don't understand. After reading in the cheery sunroom, I walked down the street to talk about boys and laugh about parents with Lydia and Ella. On the drive home, I woke from dozing when Mom said to Dad, "My mother keeps giving money to Sara whose music teaching and performing don't pay enough to cover travel, dresses, and NYC rent. Abner, Peter, and I are married and independent. Sara needs to remarry or find a job that pays more to stop burdening Ma." I felt like saying that Sara's better and more fun than anyone in our family.

Wednesday, April 24, 1957: Mothers

I'm glad we're back to leavened food after Passover. I called Doreen to say, "After a tooth extraction, Mom's home from work and in a bad mood."

She replied, "My mother isn't too moody."

I said, "You're lucky! My older mom's got the change of life. I dread my parents ganging up on me at tonight's family meeting. I wish I had a sister."

She sympathized. "Mom does many chores. I do only half of what's left."

Thursday, April 25, 1957: Tired and Shorn

I looked better with my ponytail, but needed a change. Short is easier, but I dislike looking worse in the mirror. I was tired all day after the dreadful family meeting kept me from my usual sleeping like a log. Mean Mom added hedge cutting to my chores, though I said, "I always do all my homework on time and get the best grades. I already wash all the dishes, clean my bedroom, iron my clothes, help do the laundry, vacuum and dust the house every week, help make dinner, weed the yard, take care of Tumba, and clean the kitchen floor." When I grow up, I'll hire a cleaning lady to avoid boring housework. After studying, I went to bed early at 9:30.

Friday, April 26, 1957: Colors

After the Boom or Bust board game at Marsha's, we played badminton at my house. Tara's bargain summer clothes got us talking about colors. I said, "I feel better seeing bright, clear colors. The dull brown and gold of our new kitchen radio irritates me."

Marsha said, "I'd paint it blue."

We all giggled, especially after Tara added, "I like black and blue."

I said, "I love pink, red, white, aqua, and blue." Later, I wrote this unrhymed sort of poem:

Pink

Pink is the combination of purity and fire, white and red.
Pink may be the pure softness of a baby's skin.
Pink may be the fiery brilliance of a summer sunset.
It may be a fragrant garden of
Peonies, carnations, roses, tulips, magnolias.
Pink is the color of so many lovely things,
A young girl's first lipstick or nail polish,
Dior's latest chiffon gown,
Baby's cotton playsuit,
Bunny rabbit's eyes.
Pale pink, deep pink, rosy pink, medium pink,
I love them all, whether pure or fiery.

Saturday, April 27, 1957: Onions

I got white Jamaica shorts (more flattering than Bermuda shorts), a pink shirt, and white flats in size 6½AA at Manny's downtown.

On the phone, Doreen said, "I loved this break from school. I'd rather practice ping-pong than go back."

I laughed and agreed. "I loved today's gorgeous weather! It hit ninety! After hours of chores, I rewarded myself by reading *Double Date*, a marvelous romantic teen novel, and planting onions in the yard."

She said, "I don't like digging in the dirt."

I chuckled. "I agree, but seeing things grow is fun! I'm happy Daylight Savings Time is here!"

Monday, April 29, 1957: *Cinderella*

In home ec, I said, "We're back in jail (school), but these cheese toastwiches we made taste yummy."

Tara nodded and said, "I love your haircut." I thanked her while hoping that she wasn't just being polite. I studied early for the English exam to watch the TV ballet, *Cinderella*.

My parents agreed when I said, "It dragged and the wicked stepsisters seemed wrong for the roles." I'm disappointed. I've loved ballet since seeing *The Nutcracker* in NYC at age four.

Wednesday, May 1, 1957: Temples and Jews

After Welshie's fun tennis lesson, I asked Doreen, "Will Artie be at our Ohav Shalom party?"

She replied, "His family belongs to Temple Israel."

I commented, "It's Conservative, like ours, but richer. At the small Orthodox synagogue we used to attend downtown, I never saw kids."

Doreen said, "My father said that the Reformed synagogue, Temple Beth Emmet, is like a church with nothing in Hebrew."

I smiled. "At least they understand the prayers." At dinner, I asked, "Why does Albany have so many Jewish people for its size?"

Dad's answer made sense. "Most European immigrants came to NYC. Moving only 150 miles to Albany for NY State and other jobs was easy for Jews, as well as Catholic Irish, Italians, and Poles."

Thursday, May 2, 1957: Tests and Home Run
I felt good that my spelling test had no errors. Tara said, "We got the only As on the English test. My 84 percent was second highest after your 94 percent."

I replied, "I'm worried about flunking the science test. I guessed at the thirty-point question." I smiled when kids congratulated me on making the first softball home run of the season.

Saturday, May 4, 1957: Jitterbugging
I was disappointed Artie didn't attend our synagogue's rock-and-roll party. I had a wonderful time, jitterbugging all evening with Myles, Frankie, and others to a real (*sic*) good high school band.

Sunday, May 5, 1957: Sisters
In Gloversville for Ella's eighth birthday, I smiled when she said, "I love these girls' cosmetics. Thank you!"

While playing in the backyard, I told her and Lydia, "I wish you were my sisters."

We laughed when Lydia said, "Let's pretend you are! We're adopting you!" At Sacandaga, did a carload of boys even notice our cheerleading jumps nearby? Did they think we looked stupid? At the restaurant, Dad yelled at the waitress when dinner was late. Because we girls were swooning over a blond, muscular doll around eighteen years old, we laughed when Lydia said, "I don't mind the delay."

I whispered to my cousins, "With our own table, we can act as if we don't know my dad." We giggled while overhearing our bossy mothers. Those sisters-in-law are too similar to really like each other.

Monday, May 6, 1957: Fruit and Flirting
Even after sleeping eight hours, I was pooped, maybe from growing an inch since January. In home ec, the stewed prunes

and apricots we cooked made our oatmeal taste better. I was surprised to hear, "Fruits can be appetizers and laxatives."

Tara whispered, "I didn't know that we need at least two fruits daily for vitamins and minerals."

I murmured, "I don't eat much fruit. I'd rather have ice cream for dessert." We got As, even after making faces behind our teacher's back. Because Ari substituted, I was the best Hebrew student. After class, I couldn't resist flirting and laughing at his jokes. He talks less to other girls and seems to enjoy kidding, even though he's twice my age. Doreen laughed when I said, "If the cantor resembled Ari, I'd learn Hebrew."

Wednesday, May 8, 1957: Lucky
On a boiling hot day, 100 percent on my science test amazed me. I told Mom, "While announcing tomorrow's assembly, I'll read these notecards if I go blank." I dislike being on stage, unlike Tommy Sands, who was good tonight in Kraft TV Theatre's *Flesh and Blood.*

Friday, May 10, 1957: Storm
We heard crashing thunder and saw the lights go off and on during the electrical storm. I'm glad the first rain in a month will kill the Adirondack Mountain forest fires.

Sunday, May 12, 1957: Mother's Day and Dreamboat
I'm relieved that Dad's been silent about my report card's B in music and B plus in gym. Everything else was A or A minus. Mom said, "Angela, I like this perfumed drawer sachet and card you made. Herm, thanks for the scented body powder." To be nice, I talked about school and boys (nothing secret) instead of avoiding Mom's questions. How many times have sore throats kept me home since Is-Sho-Da? In between gargling salt water and eating hot soup, I rested while drawing pictures, listening to the radio and our Harry Belafonte *Calypso* album, and reading romantic novels. I'll never show anyone this secret poem I wrote:

Artie

I know a wonderful boy named Artie
And when it comes to marks, he's a smarty,
So handsome, dark, and tall.
We girls all swoon and fall.
And when it comes to dancing,
He's tops, as well as in romancing.
I love this 125 pounds of boy
And with this dreamboat I try to be coy.

Angela's drawing of a typical teen

Tuesday, May 14, 1957: Invitation and Novels

I was glad to say yes when Ken asked, "Will you be my date for the school prom?" He's nice, smart, and a good dancer. I felt excited about pitching well in gym. After rain drenched me walking home, an electric blanket warmed me while I finished *Class Ring* from the library. Teen novels teach me what to say to boys. I enjoy imagining romantic things in books happening to me.

Wednesday, May 15, 1957: *American Bandstand*

Dick Clark's *American Bandstand* from Philadelphia cheered me while sick at home and gargling every hour. I wish Albany teens could dance on a TV show to the latest hits. While I sewed an apron for Grandma, I smiled hearing Tumba chirp, "May I have this dance?"

Thursday, May 16, 1957: Legs and Tonsils

During study hall with an awful, boring substitute teacher, we girls sneaked over to look out the window at the cute legs of boys exercising in gym shorts. I felt afraid to miss more school while Miss Stewart scared us for forty minutes about final exams. Dr. C relieved my worries. "Though your enlarged tonsils make you prone to sore throats, they aren't bad enough for a hospital tonsillectomy."

Kids say, "The only good part is ice cream afterward."

Saturday, May 18, 1957: Parties

We fourteen girls had loads of fun at a birthday party. The three prizes I won included the Del Vikings' hit record *Come Go with Me!* At an evening Bar Mitzvah reception, my new blue piqué prom dress worked well for dancing. It has a scoop neck and flares from an Empire waist. My petticoat makes the skirt stand out. I like the bolero jacket with sleeves. I felt sorry for a girl who looked cheap, necking in public with Mitch downstairs while the other boys smoked and drank. I missed Artie.

Monday, May 20, 1957: Chill and Smart Men

Where's spring? Today's high was only forty-five, a record cold for the date! Watching *Twenty One*, I cheered when brainy Hank

Bloomgarden defeated Junior Snodgrass. I could hardly keep from laughing about a salesman in our living room describing a huge, ugly recliner. Dad was too smart to fall for this:

Mr. Weiss, this chair will be like the throne you deserve
as king of this lovely castle.

Wednesday, May 22, 1957: Polio and Mohican Boys
I'm glad vaccinations now prevent crippling polio. The third shot at Vincentian Institute didn't hurt. The three-story, beige stone building looks like a prison, but I saw no nuns hitting kids for misbehaving. I mumbled to Tara, "I wish Artie was here."

Seeing her Mohican School crush, Tara whispered, "I wish I had the nerve to ask Ben to our prom. He hardly knows I exist."

I murmured, "I'm sure he thinks that you're pretty. It's scary to ask, but with Myles sick, will you be worse off, if Ben says no?"

She chuckled. "I'll be humiliated. He'll know that I like him without returning the feeling."

Thursday, May 23, 1957: Morningstar and C Minus
Mom said, "You're too young for *Marjorie Morningstar*," so I returned this novel about an older Jewish girl to the same place while secretly finishing it. *Reader's Digest* condensers removed the sexy parts I wanted to read. I'm disappointed that it's no wilder than a teen romance. I'm afraid to tell Dad about my worst grade ever: 70 percent in Tuesday's surprise science test. I get As only if I memorize everything in advance and picture the pages during tests.

Friday, May 24, 1957: Prom
Ken, about my height with brown hair and brown eyes, looked good in his suit and gave me a pretty corsage! I love flowers! We walked to the prom with Doreen and Carl. The balloon decorations looked lovely. Sitting at tables, we drank punch from a huge bowl. It was fun when the boys wrote their names on darling dance cards to reserve dances with us girls. I danced almost every time with Ken or a cute blond classmate to rock-and-roll and slow songs by a live trio. The Boulevard Cafeteria French fries

and chocolate milk tasted good. Ken's older brother's cute friend called me a "sweetie pie." What a grand evening!

Sunday, May 26, 1957: Grandma

Yesterday, Mom bought me a red skirt with a matching print blouse and belt downtown. Licking a vanilla ice cream cone, I lost my appetite when I heard:

> Grandma disappeared last month. Uncle Abner and Uncle Peter found her house empty, except for furniture. I remembered that Saratoga Springs mineral water lessens Grandma's headaches. The mystery novels I read at your age helped me find Grandma in a Jewish boarding house on Phila Street.

Today at a park, Grandma smiled more than usual at my cousins and me. She liked my Mother's Day apron and gave me a pretty heart-shaped disk. When Grandma offered icky homemade juice, I politely declined. While she had special food in the shared kitchen, the rest of us ate at Mother Goldsmith's Restaurant. On the walls were signed cartoon drawings of famous customers.

Dad said, "They're caricatures."

At our kids' table, Lydia said, "Let's secretly name our nice waitress Long Nails." How does she lift trays and serve meals with two-inch red nails? While eating delish breaded veal cutlet with French fries, we laughed at our parents.

Driving home, Mom said, "I'm glad my mother has companionship. With friends dead, she was alone, except for my brothers' Sunday duty visits. I should have called more."

I said, "If she spoke English, she'd make friends. Why hasn't she learned?"

"In 1900, she and Pa arrived from Europe with nothing. Ma worked from early morning until late evening, helping Pa escape poverty and raising five kids. Visiting small Adirondack towns and farms, Pa peddled junk and clothes on foot and later on a horse before saving enough to open a store. Ma grew food and scrimped to save for a house. Women back then had no washing machines and other conveniences. By the time Pa died, she was in her sixties, late to learn a language." I felt sympathetic.

Tuesday, May 28, 1957: Changes and Artie

"Today's fifty-degree high is disappointing after eighty yesterday," Tara said before arriving at Doreen's for leftover birthday cake from her sister's party.

I laughed. "We're lucky it hasn't snowed. The nurse measured me at almost five foot three."

Tara replied, "I seem to have stopped at five foot one, which is fine."

"Without clothes before breakfast, I weighed 101½, the most ever. I'm glad I'm not fat. I hope Artie still likes me. I miss him. It seems like years since we've danced."

Wednesday, May 29, 1957: Irene

I had fun playing handball with pretty Irene, who's good at gym and smart in school. She's my size. I like her sense of humor.

I said, "Your baby brother is adorable. With blond hair and blue eyes, he looks like you!"

She answered, "He resembles my nice stepdad. I take after my dad who died in World War II. After being an only child, I love my brother."

"I'd feel the same way. I'm happy we'll bunk together at Girl Scout camp!"

Thursday, May 30, 1957: Memorial Day Rescue

At Sacandaga's Northampton Beach, my cousins and I played baseball with Lydia's new bat, sat on the pier watching a cute boy, and hiked to find more boys. When a mean fisherman dumped a live fish in a garbage pail, Lydia said, "Let's save it." We felt good adding water to keep the fish alive until we left.

We said, "Ugh!" watching Oren Levine clean a fish he caught before cooking and eating it.

Friday, May 31, 1957: Thanks, Marsha

Marsha was a big help! She saw Artie at yesterday's Little League game. If she hadn't called him about today's game, he might not have attended. He and I had fun playing badminton in my backyard! I liked watching his beautiful five-foot-five, 130-pound

Angela Weiss

physique chase the shuttlecock. Seeing Artie was worth hearing three classmates tease the daylights out of me about him!

Sunday, June 2, 1957: No, Artie
Artie invited me to a Temple Israel United Synagogue Youth (USY) dinner party today at a girl's house. When Artie didn't offer to find out about chaperones, I said, "Thank you, but I can go only to chaperoned parties. My family already has plans." I didn't mind not going because the late invitation hurt my feelings. Did another girl cancel? I can't help loving him. After miniature golf and dinner at Howard Johnson's with the Levines, badminton with Dad in our backyard was fun, but less thrilling.

Wednesday, June 5, 1957: Chasing
After Shavuot synagogue services, Marsha and I didn't see Artie at the Little League game. Sneaking by his house, we glimpsed him out back. I hope he didn't see us. He mustn't think I'm chasing him, even though I am.

Friday, June 7, 1957: Class Day and Twins
Wearing my red outfit, red flats, and peds, I laughed at the class will. Does my "inheriting" a graduating eighth-grader's awful handwriting mean that no one can read mine? After kids performed songs, we had fun dancing. At the Little League game, I was disappointed that Artie was absent, but glad that Marsha talked to the cute twins she likes. How can she tell them apart?

Saturday, June 8, 1957: Jewish Star
The synagogue was jammed. Tara whispered, "The juvenile delinquent with long, greasy hair combed in a DA (duck's ass) is a clean-cut Bar Mitzvah star." Like a rabbi, Frankie conducted the whole service. Everything was wonderful, including his speech.

I murmured, "Frankie looks handsome in his new suit. The rabbi and his wife look sweet with tears in their eyes. I'm sorry she's still on crutches from her accident." At the evening reception, I wore my blue dress and ate a delicious buffet dinner. At 1 a.m., flirting with Israeli Ari at the Boulevard was fun.

126

<u>Sunday, June 9, 1957: Unlucky</u>

I'm excited after meeting glamorous Cousin Beth and her adorable nineteen-month-old. Our album has Beth's photos. Mom explained, "After Uncle Abner's 1930s divorce, Beth's mom avoided our family. Beth became a Long Island nurse. After her doctor husband recently died of a heart attack at age thirty-three, she's wealthy and back in Albany." At twenty-four, Beth has gorgeous red hair, an hourglass figure, a charming giggle, and beautiful clothes. Looking like her would be wonderful if I could skip being a widow. I want to babysit June, who has blond curls.

Beth

Tuesday, June 11, 1957: Spit

Yesterday, a mean boy spat on the dress of our old music teacher. Principal Burnsy took him away, probably to give him heck and tell his parents. I felt on the spot when Burnsy asked me, "What happened?"

I shrugged and shook my head, "I wasn't looking." No one tells on a classmate. Today, I was glad that the smart aleck sat quietly with his head down and looked too terrified to spit again.

Wednesday, June 12, 1957: Dates, Popsicles, and Goal

Tara and I dreamed up dates during movies in our final home ec class. On the hot walk home, carrying the cap and apron I sewed, I said, "Tara, thanks for treating me to this cool orange Popsicle! What do you want to be when you grow up?"

"My sister's learning to help people as a psychiatric social worker. I'd like to follow in her footsteps."

"That sounds interesting!"

Saturday, June 15, 1957: Thatcher

It was suffocating out again. After I bought picnic food on New Scotland Avenue, a friend's parents drove her, Irene, Doreen, and me to Thatcher Park, fifteen miles southwest of Albany in the Helderberg Mountains. As we drove through the park, leafy trees shaded everything. We enjoyed swimming in the giant pool and getting tanned. Seeing thirty kids I knew was loads of fun. Why did people compliment my old plaid swimsuit? At home, Mom questioned me about today. Drifting off to sleep, I missed Artie and wondered if the Helderbergs are part of the Catskills.

Tuesday, June 18, 1957: Hank and Heat

Last night after studying, I did cheerleading jumps watching Hank Bloomgarden stay champion on *Twenty One*, before turning in early at 9:30. Today's okay math exam, after difficult cit ed and English finals, was a relief, even though my sunburn murdered me in the humid heat. Tonight, Tara called. "My father read in the paper that the heat of ninety-seven degrees broke an 1892 record for this date and killed a high school salutatorian after his tennis tournament."

Feeling sad, I replied, "That's awful."

"A caddy our age collapsed while playing golf at Wolferts Roost Country Club."

"I thought that these things happened only to old people, like our parents."

Wednesday, June 19, 1957: Downpours and Artie

After roasting during a hard science exam, I made it home before rain poured for about three minutes before the sun came out. Brief downpours followed by sun went on all day. Driving home from Hebrew School graduation, Dad was a good egg to go out of the way past Artie's house. I felt better near his house. My parents approve because Artie's a "nice Jewish boy."

Thursday, June 20, 1957: Grades and Dad

After a scary dream about flunking with 55 percent, I got a perfect score on health! Mom attended her office picnic. Dad and I ate at Waldorf Cafeteria. After paying the cashier, he said, "These turkey dinners are a bargain."

I talked about award day. "As school treasurer, I sat on stage with the teachers. Two graduating eighth-graders won ten awards! On exams, I'm happy about 98 percent in math and a perfect score in science." I can't remember being with just Dad. Because he avoids nosy questions, our Central Avenue walk was fun, including trying on shoes at Michelson's.

Dad said, "Thanks for finding my red Ivy League shirt for only two dollars."

I replied, "Thanks for buying me Levi's!"

Friday, June 21, 1957: Sisters

I enjoyed marking camp clothes and playing hopscotch and Monopoly with Robin Levine, a younger-sister substitute. She's quiet, but I like her. Today was my sister Rowena's birthday. Mom looked sad while wrapping her sister's fortieth birthday presents. I added a homemade card and felt glad to be a younger sister like Aunt Sara.

Saturday, June 22, 1957: Fun

Doreen and I laughed at the comedy *Joe Butterfly*, set in Japan like *The Teahouse of the August Moon*. I ironed and wore my pink blouse with white Jamaica shorts to the Young Judaea dance. After bossing four of us around as we decorated, Ari's pretty brunette sister got mad when we wouldn't play baby games like musical chairs. To be a good Israeli dance and Hebrew teacher, she needs Ari's sense of humor. They're the only Israelis I've met. After dancing and joking downstairs, eleven of us kids walked on Central Avenue and had chocolate milk at Waldorf Cafeteria. Marsha's father, a good sport, drove us home in his station wagon. While we toured the city dropping kids off, we sang, screamed, and waved to boys in cars. What fun!

Tuesday, June 25, 1957: Freedom and Camp

Yay! I'm finally free of pressure! My English final was 97 percent and cit ed, 99 percent. I'm happy that every overall grade was A or A minus, except B plus in gym. I worked hard, but feel lucky. After I marked and packed camp clothes, Doreen's Mom walked Doreen and me to the Girl Scout office for our physicals. I weighed 102, just right, and don't have athlete's foot, which keeps kids from camp.

Wednesday, June 26, 1957: Tumba

Our goldfish died. Afraid, I asked, "How long do parakeets live?"

Dad said, "Longer than goldfish." I was relieved that Tumba may live up to fifteen years. I felt better stroking his soft turquoise feathers and feeding him. His beak nipped me, as usual, when I tried to pet his wings. After he exercised, his long monologue mixed words we taught him with babble we can't understand. When I transferred him to a finger to avoid a dropping, I laughed when he imitated the phone ring.

Thursday, June 27, 1957: *Tammy* and a Hood

Tears came to my eyes as Doreen and I watched *Tammy and the Bachelor*, a marvelous Debbie Reynolds movie. I agreed when Doreen said, "Debbie is so sweet." After cherry ice cream sodas at Stewart's Ice Cream Parlor, we walked home. A car stopped and one of the twins Marsha likes said that Mario, whom I haven't met, likes me.

After they drove off, I asked Doreen, "Why pick me? Don't hoods like fast girls?" She shrugged. We giggled. She's leaving on vacation. I smiled and said, "You lucky thing! You'll get to swim every day!" We hugged good-bye.

Friday, June 28, 1957: Chasing Boys
Licking Stewart's ice cream cones this afternoon, Marsha and I walked past the houses of Artie and the twins. Even though we didn't see the boys, walking a few miles was more fun than school! At home, I flopped down to read a library novel.

Saturday, June 29, 1957: Blabbermouth
Driving downtown, Mom said, "Angela, you aren't listening." I was picturing the big muscles and sexy walk of the air conditioner installer, who had just left our house. He's a double for actor Audie Murphy. Mom pumped me with a million questions about school and boys while I was trapped in the car. She always complains, "Angela, you never tell me anything." She repeats everything to her friends.

To prevent her from getting too mad to buy me a bathing suit, I admitted, "I still like Artie." We looked in six stores for a white bathing suit to contrast with my tan. I was fine getting the second-best suit in stretchy Lastex (white with aqua and gold stripes) for only five dollars.

While I played cards with my parents, the Caplans, and the Levines, Mom blabbed, "Angela likes Artie." Upset, I went to my room to write this.

Sunday, June 30, 1957: Sacandaga
The parents and I rode on the Thruway to visit Breezy Point, my cousins' marvelous knotty pine rental cottage. We enjoyed the warm breeze and Adirondack view. The dense evergreens climbing up the sides of the surrounding mountains looked like soldiers wrapped in green hooded coats. We girls flirted with a cute redhead who caught two silvery fish. They smelled okay, but

looked too slimy to touch. After we played Monopoly, rowed a boat, and fished, we set afloat a bottle with this message inside:

Lydia, Ella, and Angela were at Sacandaga 6/30/57.

Napping in the car on the way home, I dreamed that Mom announced:

I didn't date in school. I blab because I am envious and like to brag about your boyfriends.

How can I trust her?

Monday, July 1, 1957: Embarrassment and Cellar

At Mom's office, I met nice women in the steno pool. Reading the marvelous novel *Fifteen* while waiting, I felt embarrassed that Mom's hair looks like a man's. I wish she looked feminine, like Aunt Sara. When Dad and I got my pretty green suitcase from the cellar, he said, "Prior house owners kept these original 1920s light fixtures after modernizing." As I looked at the dusty chandeliers hanging from the ceiling, I watched for mice or bugs, which scare me. I'm afraid to go down there alone.

Tuesday, July 2, 1957: Don't Read

After doing many chores, I rewarded myself by finishing *Fifteen* and *High Hurdles,* both fabulous. Mom blew her lid. "Why aren't you out playing with other kids?" Why isn't she glad that I read? If I said that my friends aren't around, Mom would reply, "Play with kids on this block."

My parents would start a fuss with other parents if I said, "Bully Jimmy hit my head."

Thursday, July 4, 1957: Independence Day

At Thatcher Park, we had to share a table with other families. I had a long talk with a nice girl with shoulder-length, tan hair from Artie's school. About the same size, we both use Clearasil for acne and know the same kids. She's lucky to see Artie every day. He even went to her party!

Friday, July 5, 1957: Camp Little Notch

Last night, it rained. Keyed up about camp, I didn't sleep well! When I kissed Dad good-bye and thanked him for saving money for camp, his eyes got watery. Mom never cries. She drove me north to Glens Falls and the village of Fort Ann. We bumped along a rutted, narrow dirt road with thick woods all around us. We could hardly see the sky. Getting lost there would be scary. I could never find my way out. Camp is on a clear blue lake surrounded by the Adirondacks. Is that distant tip white with snow? The blanket of mountainside evergreens looks thick. I'm writing this in the john. My diary key is around my neck, but the book is hidden at home. I hope that my parents don't read it.

Monday, July 8, 1957: Icy and Tippy Test
I'm happy to bunk with Irene and Doreen in a cabin with one open side. Without electricity, we use flashlights at night. At 8 a.m., my beginners' swim group has the iciest water. Dr. C said, "Keep your face out of water to avoid tonsillitis." After making myself jump off the dock while holding my nose, I'm glad to learn to swim a little, though I must skip the breathing for the crawl. Each advanced swimmer has to swim to shore with a canoe after a counselor tips it over in the middle of the lake. I'd drown falling out of a canoe. I'm glad we beginners use row boats.

10 July 1980

Mom + Dad,

I found this bark on a birch tree on our hike. We went in these dark soapy caves with deep underground streams. It was very dangerous looking (Don't worry.) But we all made it.

Front page of Angela's letter home on birch bark

Wednesday, July 10, 1957: Bark

My birch bark letter home ended this way:

It's hard to write on bark. We just had a refreshing, cold swim. Our hike took two hours to get there and ninety minutes back. We ate a good lunch there: mashed hot dogs, oranges, and cookies. I skipped relish and mayonnaise, but bought two candy bars. Our counselor, Elsie, is the best! I'm out of bark. Love and XXX (Kisses), Angela

Thursday, July 11, 1957: Pink-Flowered Stationery 9:45 a.m.

Dear Mom and Dad,

We're a bunch of lunatics. Irene goes around saying, "Toothpaste, comb, stamps," to remember them at the TP (trading post). Froggy cracked us up by going around half-dressed with her boyfriend's picture inside her pillow, kissing it and croaking frog-talk. When a girl took her precious pillow away, Froggy batted her with a broom. Doreen got to read only a minute at night by flashlight. We dumped Barbara out of her sleeping bag to get her up in the morning. Gotta go to TP.

Love and XXX, Angela

P.S. We cook dinner, eat, and sing songs around a fun campfire, but I don't like marshmallows.

Saturday, July 13, 1957: Lanyard and Scouts

My jackknife is hanging from the lanyard I braided of flat plastic cords of black and red. I'm only average at making things, but I love arts and crafts. The Boy Scouts visited from their nearby camp before dark! They must have felt self-conscious, standing around in full view of everyone. We were too shy to start conversations. We giggled, especially when the boys' counselors flirted with our counselors, college girls who make everything fun. Looking at the cute males was great! I wish we could have danced.

Wednesday, July 24, 1957: Home

Today was a typical summer day at home. I hung wet laundry from the washing machine on the outdoor clothesline. After more chores, I was free! I relaxed, reading a novel while lying on Grandma's tan wicker couch on the screened-in back porch. Peace ended when the parents arrived from work. Dad blew up after Mom nagged about fixing broken things. He won't let Mom pay someone. We probably don't have the money. Camp was a fun escape. I forgot the parents, but won't hurt their feelings by saying that I didn't miss them.

Wednesday, July 31, 1957: Myrna
Since last Saturday, I've been with our relatives at Breezy Point. Poor Aunt Myrna is cooking and cleaning rather than vacationing. She thanked me for making my bed and doing dishes after every meal, much less than I do at home. While Lydia, Ella, and I had our usual fun while swimming and looking for and flirting with cute guys at the beach, my aunt baked a surprise chocolate cake for Lydia's eleventh birthday dinner tonight.

Monday, August 5, 1957: Cocktail
I'm home after a wonderful week with my cousins, including making fun of our parents. Yesterday, when my parents arrived, we kids were washing dishes. Acting silly and giggling, we served Dad a cocktail of dishwater, tea bags, and other junk. We didn't think he'd actually drink it. After he took one sip, we tried not to laugh when he got really mad at us.

Wednesday, August 21, 1957: Sewing Slub Silk
While taking the bus downtown with Doreen for the daily teen Singer sewing course, I've been too lazy to diarize. We've learned to use a pattern, cut fabric, and sew a dress. My shirtwaist dress with a straight skirt and button-down collar is blue-green slub silk, which looks and feels pretty. I like making clothes, but store clothes look better.

Angela, wearing the dress she made

Saturday, August 31, 1957: Labor Day Weekend

At our hotel on Long Beach, Long Island, I got my period for the first time last night. I'm lucky it didn't mess up my clothes at the beach or restaurant. My parents acted happy, as if it's a big deal. Mom said:

> In her old-fashioned European way, my mother never told me in advance. When my first period started, I said, "I'm bleeding to death!" She superstitiously slapped my face and gave me old rags to use. I was confused and upset until Abner, who was twenty-one, gave me a pamphlet. My aunt, who was visiting, also helped.

Since staying with Grandma in 1949, I've known she can be cold. I'm lucky that Mom told me what to expect. I can't wait to tell my friends.

Tuesday, September 3, 1957: Women

My period's almost done. Afraid of bloody clothes next time, I wrote it on my calendar and will keep a Kotex in my purse. Tara, Doreen, and I agreed: even though we're women at age twelve, no one treats us as grown-ups. We must do what people say. My period's good because it's like a birthday. I'm closer to being free.

Private Diary: Eighth Grade

Wednesday, September 4, 1957: Love School

To start eighth grade, I wore black-and-white, streamlined Ivy League saddle shoes (a half-price bargain at four dollars!); white bobby sox; a gray, long-sleeved crewneck; a gray skirt I made; and my pink striped Ivy League shirt. After a wonderful summer, I'm surprised to enjoy school. Teachers are treating us as leaders. Joys! Mrs. Bern is my homeroom, as well as English (my favorite subject), teacher. I miss Artie!

Saturday, September 7, 1957: Eyes and Autographs

Marsha and I went to Lewis' Bar Mitzvah where I talked with Frankie and Myles. I liked gazing at their light blue eyes. Frankie is interesting and Myles is masculine. I felt good about what the Levines wrote in my lost autograph book, which just turned up:

Dear Angela,
You are one of the nicest girls I know. The best of luck always!
Love, Evelyn

To Angela,
Take the local and change for the express; don't get off until you reach success.
Yours, Lover Boy Karl

Dear Angela,
On this page of blue, I'll tell you what I think of you: 2 sweet 2 be 4 gotten.
Love, Robin.

Sunday, September 8, 1957: Canasta

Aunt Sara, glamorous in a black-and-white dress, was lively, as always. I loved hearing about her exciting life! Smiling, she said, "I still enjoy my one-woman shows, but I want to write a psychology book to help families get along. As the youngest of five kids, I had a hard time and disliked family fights."

Mom sounded envious. "Sara, you were Ma's and Pa's pet. You had music lessons and never had to work in the store, like the boys and me."

Tumba chattered, including "I love you," while we played canasta, a fun card game Aunt Sara taught us. Tumba flew to her the most.

In my room, I confided, "Aunt Sara, I can't wait to see Artie for the first time in months."

She answered, "I understand. I seldom see Mort because of travel."

Monday, September 9, 1957: Rob

Myles and Rob made walking to school fun. After school, I felt like running off when only overweight Rob appeared. Conversation was a strain. He didn't make me laugh. I acted polite to avoid hurting his feelings. Why can't my favorite boys like me and the others ignore me?

Thursday, September 12, 1957: Soon and Confidential
I rolled my eyes when Dad said, "I'll get the broken TV fixed soon." I'm fine without TV. I can concentrate on homework and read more.

After Tumba flew around and said, "Sara," I wrote her a note, knowing that my crushes will stay private:

Walking home alone (Tara missed school), I ran into Myles. At his house, we chatted. His deep voice, blue eyes, and lean body are exciting. When I look up at him, I feel more feminine than with other boys. Artie's still first.

Saturday, September 14, 1957: Heartbroken
For Udeh's Bar Mitzvah, I put a white scarf under the collar of my silk shirtwaist dress. Artie didn't even speak to me! I could tell that he saw me. I looked his way at times, but going up to talk is too forward. To hide my broken heart, I put on a good act, flirting with Myles, Frankie, and Mitch. As Rob walked me home, I wished it was Artie.

Sunday, September 15, 1957: Heels and Disappointment
All the girls are getting their first pairs of heels. Mom said, "We don't have money for heels when your dress shoes still fit. Your next pair can be heels." I love heels, but wearing flats won't kill me. I'm glad that Mom lets me buy bargain clothes. After carrying a torch for Artie for seven months, I'm shocked and hurt that he didn't even say hello.

Wednesday, September 18, 1957: Weight Lifters and Artie
After I wished Tara a happy thirteenth birthday and heard about her presents, she said, "Every year we need more books for homework."

I laughed. "We'll have to become weight lifters or have strong boyfriends in high school." The two peas in a pod, Myles and Rob, arrived to carry our loads. I like Rob carrying my books only with Myles or Tara there. While laughing on the outside with friends, I'm discouraged and confused inside about Artie. Does he have a new girlfriend?

Tara

Monday, September 23, 1957: Bus Stop and Artie

Tara and I, in silly moods on the other side of Madison Avenue, saw Rob and Myles looking for us across the street. Hiding behind a tree, we called out and had a jolly time, kidding around with them until the bus came. I met Mom at her office. She bought me a warm white velvet hat, scarf, and gloves! I thanked my friend at Mohican School for phoning me to say that Artie didn't answer her question, "Do you like Angela?" I'm still wondering what happened.

Friday, September 27, 1957: Mountain and Handshake

At the High Holiday synagogue service, the cantor chanted and the rabbi read the usual monotonous Hebrew prayers. The English translations on the left in the prayer book don't make the service drag on less. During a break, Doreen laughed when I described my dream:

> Walking home from school, I saw Rob buried under a mountain of books as big as a Volkswagen Beetle. When he didn't speak, I walked on, but felt guilty for not rescuing him.

In the synagogue yard, we flirted with all the boys. When everyone shook hands and said, "Happy New Year," Rob's handshake made me feel how much he likes me.

His sweet younger sister whispered, "Rob has really liked you ever since you went with Edwin." That was before I met Artie. How would Artie's handshake feel? Even Doreen and Tara don't know how bad I still feel.

Monday, September 30, 1957: Rob

My load of books weighed down poor Rob on the way home. Why don't boys mind carrying heavy books?

He looked upset when he said, "I have to get ugly braces."

I replied, "I can't wait to get mine off. I'm lucky to have them because my parents don't have much money. I hope my teeth look better."

Rob surprised me by saying, "I have my future planned. Myles wants to be an architect. I'll work with him as a carpenter erecting the buildings he designs."

Sunday, October 6, 1957: No Raise
Dad said, "My boss is a cheapskate. He said no again when I asked for a raise."
　We laughed when Tumba chirped, "Oh, no!"
Friends like Marsha get bigger allowances and more expensive clothes, but I don't need more. Her mother works and her electrician father does well. Doreen's father works in a relative's business and her mother stays home.

Friday, October 11, 1957: Misery
I put on a cheerful face every day, but underneath I feel awful about Artie snubbing me. What could he be mad about? I've cut back on diarizing to avoid repeating Artie stuff. I need something exciting to happen with boys.

Saturday, October 12, 1957: Columbus Day
I got a gorgeous dressy sale coat, dark tweed with blue, white, and orange flecks; push-up sleeves; and a full back with a bow. I wore it over the dress I made to the Center dance, a flop with only about twenty-five kids. I walked by, but the one cute boy never asked me to dance. Maybe my dress doesn't look good. I'm glad to be five foot four, as tall as Mom and Dad, and 104 pounds after dinner with clothes and without shoes.

Tuesday, October 15, 1957: Threat and Tests
We're worried that the Russians are ahead of us after a rocket fired Sputnik, a satellite around the earth. Our teachers are pushing us to do better. "The Soviet Union is a threat to democracy. We must prevail over the godless Communists." I already work as hard as I can. I'm happy with 97 percent in English and perfect scores in cit ed and spelling on the first tests.

Sunday, October 20, 1957: Secretary and Saratoga
About thirty kids, a lot, attended Young Judaea! We planned our hayride! Wearing wool Bermuda shorts with a white pullover, I had fun dancing with two cute boys. Rob said, "Congratulations on winning Recording Secretary."

I replied, "Thank you. Are you glad to be elected President?" He nodded and invited me to the hayride. I enjoyed seeing my cousins in Saratoga Springs on a visit to Grandma.

Tuesday, October 22, 1957: Substitute
Our cit ed substitute teacher was tall, dark, young Mr. K. All the girls were going crazy, screaming and laughing because he's cute and nice. But he's taken. At lunch, he held hands with a glamorous, blond fifth-grade teacher. Because we have to look at our teachers every day, I wish we had other good-looking men.

Wednesday, October 23, 1957: Hayride
Double dating is complicated. While listening to Mr. K's friendly voice, Tara wrote about the hayride:
> I put off Lewis, hoping Myles will invite me, so we can go with you and Rob.

I wrote:
> I put off Rob because it won't be fun without you and Myles.

After dinner, Frankie and a handsome pal came by to reserve hayride spots. Mom gave Frankie a hayride publicity sign to put on the synagogue bulletin board.

Sunday, October 27, 1957: Conversations
Despite cramps from her period, Doreen made her pajama party last night fun. We discussed the hayride and boys. I declined a hayride invitation from a boy who's worse than Rob. After telling Rob, "I can go with you," I wished that I'd waited.

Brainy Neal called to say, "Can you come to the hayride with me?"

I sadly said, "Thank you. I wish I could, but I've accepted another invitation."

Myles called to ask, "Who should I take to the hayride?"

I answered, "Tara, so you can double with Rob and me."

When I called Tara about her family's move, she replied, "It was easy staying in the same building. I love my new room with gray built-in cabinets. But I'm still sick. I'm putting off Lewis about the hayride, hoping Myles will ask me."

I replied, "I told Myles that I hope to double with you and him."

Monday, October 28, 1957: Hayride Plans
Myles and Rob walked me home from school. Tara waved from her new room. On my porch, while the boys kidded around, I wondered why Myles asked my hayride advice and ignored it to ask a different girl.

Tuesday, October 29, 1957: Running
Kids at school kept saying, "Congratulations on being nominated for school president!" In an excited daze, I thanked them.

Pam, a smart go-getter, said, "If you don't have a campange (how do you spell it?) manager, I volunteer."

I enthusiastically replied, "Thank you!"

Looking serious, she said, "I'll talk to as many kids as possible to get them to vote for you."

I smiled and answered, "That's perfect! I'll write my speech." Does anyone enjoy giving speeches? Ugh! It makes me nervous.

Wednesday, October 30, 1957: Dates
Udeh called for hayride reservations for him, Aryeh, Artie, and their dates. My heart sank. I didn't ask whom Artie invited. I was afraid that Udeh would tell Artie that I still like him. Calls from Neal and Rob didn't cheer me up. If we girls want to go out, we're stuck accepting and acting nice to any boy who asks. I wish it wasn't forward and unfeminine for girls to choose boys for dates.

Thursday, October 31, 1957: Halloween
For Halloween, I wore a hair ribbon, drew freckles on my face with an eyebrow pencil, and dressed as a little girl in a short skirt. At our school dance, I was popular: I got asked to dance almost every dance, maybe because of my costume. My main partner was Ken. On the way home, Rob and Myles complimented my costume.

Friday, November 1, 1957: Flirting

The best way to get through boring synagogue services is flirting with boys sitting on the other side of the aisle. I stared and then looked down or away before Myles and Frankie caught my eye. When I felt one of them looking at me, I'd try to catch him in the act before he looked away. I ignored Rob to avoid encouraging him. I joked and laughed with other kids downstairs. Flirting is my second favorite thing after dancing. Reading novels is third.

Saturday, November 2, 1957: Jitterbug and White Tower

At the Center, would I have been asked to dance more than twice if I'd worn my new slacks? I hid feeling hurt that Artie ignored me. Neal had a date. I pretended to have fun jitterbugging with girls. Few boys know this dance. The turns and toe-heel, toe-heel, rock step footwork are harder than slow dances where boys lead the box step. A bunch of us snacked at White Tower, a cool diner! The tower and outside walls are gleaming white. Everything inside looks attractive! It's brightly lit and white, except for shiny chrome trim and red seats and Formica counters. We sat in leatherette booths. I sipped chocolate milk with a straw while we played favorite jukebox tunes: *Wake Up Little Susie, Little Darlin', Peggy Sue, You Send Me,* and *Come Go with Me.* I made the best of tonight. Moping won't get Artie back.

Sunday, November 3, 1957: Ray and Neal

While I nervously memorized tomorrow's campaign (dictionary spelling) speech about how hard I will work if elected, Ray and Neal arrived to reserve hayride spots. I'm glad Neal will take Doreen, who likes him more than I do. I smiled at strong-looking Ray, around five foot six. He'd make a good book carrier. Ha! Ha!

Monday, November 4, 1957: Speech and Grades

In the auditorium, my index cards got me through the speech when I went blank. I hope that my friends meant what they said: "Your speech was good." I'm nervous about our election on adult Election Day. I'm pleased with my all-A report card, except gym (B). On character marks, like attendance, punctuality, and dependability, I got twenty-eight excellents. Gym effort was satisfactory.

Tuesday, November 5, 1957: Guys Galore

My heart raced as I stared at tons of handsome boys in CBA (Christian Brothers Academy) military uniforms at the annual football game against AHS (Albany High School)! I wore AHS garnet and gray: a checked blouse and gray wool slacks and crewneck. I saw loads of kids I know, including Artie, who made my heart thump. I smiled back when handsome Mario, the hood, grinned and said, "Hello!" Having fun with Patroon classmates, I forgot about today's school election.

Wednesday, November 6, 1957: Shock

It's unreal! I'm president of the school! I'm in shock, but happy. My parents said, "Congratulations." They take good things for granted and say more only when criticizing. Mom, who wasn't a school leader, seemed envious. No matter what I do, she's not happy.

Friday, November 8, 1957: Telegram

Aunt Sara, who makes a fuss when good stuff happens and never criticizes, sent my first telegram:

Congratulations on being president of your school!

Feeling grown-up and important, I giggled hearing, "Spended (*sic*)!" from Tumba.

Saturday, November 9, 1957: Best Time

Wearing gray slacks and crewneck, I had the best time of my life on my first hayride. Sitting in the wagon on hay with blankets over us was romantic and fun. Rob had his arm around me and held my hand. The farmer up front drove the decrepit, stinky brown and beige horses. We ignored the odor while joking and singing at the top of our lungs. After a snack shack stop, the horses were comical. When one started to move and the other five didn't, the moving horse stopped. The farmer yelled, "Gidyap!" and cracked the whip on the ground. Another horse or two moved, but not all. The farmer got madder as we giggled uncontrollably until all horses started at once. At the synagogue, hot cocoa warmed us thirteen couples. Five boys danced with me, including Myles and Frankie. Doreen had fun with Neal. I'm interested in Ray. I had a super-marvelous, wonderful, lovely time! I'm lucky that Artie didn't show up with a date.

Sunday, November 10, 1957: Playing the Field

At Young Judaea, Ray was the best of six boys who kept me dancing to every song. I nodded yes after hearing his low voice say, "Let's keep dancing after I return from the restroom. Can you please wait?"

When Rob immediately started dancing with me, I explained, "I promised to dance with Ray."

Looking angry, Rob said, "Ray had you all afternoon."

I replied, "No one keeps tabs on me."

After being too mad to ride home with us, Rob called to ask, "Do you like me?"

I don't, but answered, "I play the field. I don't want to get tied down."

He said, "I understand. Nothing will change."

On the phone, I told Doreen, "Thanks for suggesting that I dance with other boys to get rid of Rob! Ray was fun! He even jitterbugs! I hope the four of us can double!"

Saturday, November 23, 1957: *Silhouettes*

My parents let me attend Ray's afternoon party because his parents chaperoned upstairs. Doreen and Neal were there. Ray and I laughed about both wearing gray slacks, black shoes, and red socks. My red blouse and gray scarf matched his striped T-shirt. It was exciting to fox-trot, jitterbug, and cha cha with a good dancer. We danced the stroll in a line to the great hit song, *Silhouettes*. We laughed because the group that sings it is The Rays. Doreen confided, "Neal said that Naomi turned Ray down."

I chuckled. "I should thank her."

Sunday, November 24, 1957: Actress for a Day

At Young Judaea, everyone laughed at this silly skit Doreen and I wrote. We put it on for the talent show, even though it shows no talent:

Teens in the Ladies' Room at a Dance in Israel

RACHEL (Angela)

You're here too, Naomi?
(Naomi walks from a stall to the mirrored dressing table.)

NAOMI

After not dancing for twenty minutes, I escaped here. I wish Haym would ask me. He's lazy. If the place was burning down, he wouldn't get off his big, fat uh...seat.

DEBORAH (Doreen)

Your petticoat shows, and your lipstick is smeared. Maybe that's why he hasn't asked.

RACHEL

Your nose can use powder, and your hair needs combing.

NAOMI

Now they tell me.
(Naomi corrects these problems.)

DEBORAH

You danced with the tall, thin dreamy blond with the crew cut! Dig the cool white sports jacket, black pants, and black shirt! He looks good enough to be in a magazine.

RACHEL

Yeah! I was sure sad when the last record ended. Dan's a swell dancer who attends Haifa High.

NAOMI

You lucky thing! You danced three times with him!

RACHEL
But I also danced with that overweight drip with the squeaky voice.

DEBORAH
I suffered through his bad breath for two dances. His bulging eyes were glued to my chest.

NAOMI
Did you come here to escape from him?

RACHEL
We needed rest. Dancing the hora killed us!

DEBORAH
It's as fast as the American jitterbug. I loved jitterbugging with my date, Amnon, the only boy who can do it.

NAOMI
Did you see Schlomo Schlemeal on TV last night? He sang his new record, *Rock, Chopped Liver, Rock*. He's the Israeli Elvis.

DEBORAH
I like Schlim Schlimozzle even more. I bought his hit, *Gefilte Fish Rock*.

RACHEL
After the dance, we're going to Moshe's Potato Latke Joint. Naomi, do you want to join us?

NAOMI
No, thanks. I've got to go.
                    (Naomi exits.)

DEBORAH
If Naomi had a date tonight, we could all have fun together.

RACHEL
Yeah. Let's go. We don't want to miss a chance of dancing with Dan!

DEBORAH
Let's bop out of this joint!

Saturday, November 30, 1957: "Let's Go to the Hop"
Danny and the Juniors' hit song, *At the Hop,* went through my head before the Young Judaea hop. What a cool word for a dance! Wearing my gray skirt, black flats, and new aqua twinset, size 34, I danced with seven boys, mainly Ray. I was thrilled to see Aunt Sara sing and play her accordion for an audience for the first time. Her best songs were *Everybody Loves Saturday Night,* in French, Spanish, Hebrew, and English, and *Tumbalalaika* in Yiddish. While we danced, Ray said, "The kids think your aunt is marvelous!" After my parents, Sara, Neal, Doreen, Ray, and I cleaned the synagogue hall, we piled into our car. I had to sit on Ray's lap. We forgot the cupcake, wrapped in a napkin in his pocket, until he pulled out the empty napkin. When I felt Ray's pocket squish and pictured the cupcake mashed inside, I laughed until my stomach ached. Ray's arm was around me while we had chocolate milk and French fries at the Boulevard Cafeteria. When I kissed Doreen on the cheek, Ray said, "How about letting me in on this?" Ray and Aunt Sara made it a stupendously fabulous evening. I'm lucky and proud to be her niece. I love Ray! Rob gave me a dirty look when I was with Ray. I had told Rob that my mother wouldn't let me go with him.

Monday, December 2, 1957: Invitation
I wasn't in the mood to explain things to Rob, but he seemed calm after I said, "Saturday, my parents invited Ray." Ray and I skipped a movie yesterday because he and Neal had seen Elvis' *Jailhouse Rock* and Doreen and I had seen Pat Boone in *April Love.*

Friday, December 6, 1957: Good Day
I'm pleased with my all-A report card, except for gym and math: B plus. I was happy to accept Ray's phone invitation to the synagogue Hanukkah affair, but too chicken to call him by his secret nickname: Raykins. Good news: I need a 32A because my 30AA bras are too small.

Saturday, December 7, 1957: Undefeated
As one of our school's twelve players, I jumped up and down with excitement and played most of the time at the Livingston Junior High volleyball tournament for Albany girls in seventh through twelfth grades. The team ahead at the end of a timed period won. Thanks to Welshie's excellent training, we were the only undefeated team with scores of 25-7, 35-25, 20-16, and 55-5. We played twice against older girls, who looked more at boys in the bleachers than at the volleyball. Will we be as crazy next year? A new coral (a popular shade I love) lipstick was my reward.

Sunday, December 8, 1957: Hanukkah Invites
At our Young Judaea meeting, Ray held my hand and danced close. I like him more and more. I'm sorry for Doreen, heartbroken after annoying Neal invited Marsha to the Hanukkah affair. Rob sounded nervous on the phone when he said, "Can you come with me to the Hanukkah affair?"

I was relieved to answer, "Thank you, but I've already accepted another invitation."

Rob asked, "From Ray?"

I replied yes, before politely getting off the phone.

Wednesday, December 11, 1957: Captain and Ten
I'm happy to be elected captain of one of two volleyball teams. Rob and Myles still walk Tara and me to their turnoff every morning. Aunt Sara sent a lot of money, ten dollars, for Hanukkah and my birthday. I can buy a nice anniversary present for my parents.

Angela Weiss

Friday, December 13, 1957: Unlucky
Why do bad things happen on Friday the thirteenth? We had three tests. I'm relieved about math (100 percent) and English (96 percent), but don't know about science. After synagogue services, a girl talked about her father's sudden heart attack death this morning! I felt awful and sad for her.

Saturday, December 14, 1957: Swell
Downtown, I bought Hanukkah presents. Mom bought me mittens, an ear warmer, a 32A bra, a Tune-Tote for records, and stationery. At the Center, I danced with Ray mainly and others. Rob took me to the Boulevard. Doreen sat with six boys, including Ray, Neal, and Frankie. Marsha went with a handsome Italian boy. Her nice father drove ten kids home in the back of his truck. I enjoyed sitting on the lap of Marcus, my first date in sixth grade. Tonight was swell!

Sunday, December 15, 1957: Rehearsal
Ray, Neal, Myles, Doreen, and I rehearsed for the candle-lighting ceremony. With a found hair clip, Doreen and I curled Ray's and Myles' hair. They were good sports and seemed to enjoy the attention. We had fun singing, talking, and running up and down the stairs. When cute Ray called later, we were in silly moods and had fun. Neal's call was a pain:

> My best friend Ray is mad because I'm dating Marsha instead of Doreen. Ray listens to you. Can you help me patch things up with him?

I got off the phone without agreeing to help. He acted like a jerk, dropping my friend for no good reason.

Wednesday, December 18, 1957: In Love
Ray sent me a Hanukkah card and called for our usual talk of over a half hour. We know each other's classmates and discuss what's going on in our schools. I love Raykins. We're excited about holiday social activities. He's sweet, like a Teddy bear.

Friday, December 20, 1957: Christmas

I was relieved about a perfect score on my science test. With a record-setting warm temperature of around sixty outside, we laughed a lot in class. Even the teachers were in wonderful moods, maybe because they like vacations. The Christmas party included carol singing. Even though I felt left out, I ignored these feelings and enjoyed dancing with four boys. Winning a silk hankie in the grab bag helped. I told my parents, "Our school has many Jewish students and a Jewish teacher. Why is Hanukkah ignored?"

Dad said, "Dan O'Connell, dictator of Albany, allows only Christmas programs." I felt better after my parents gave me an interesting 1958 almanac and big USA map for Hanukkah.

Saturday, December 21, 1957: Missile Toe

I love the crisp, silky feel and whispery sound of my new red taffeta dress with a low-cut back! A size 5 junior, it fits perfectly. It has a boat neckline, good for any kind of necklace, and multi-color, striped sash to tie a thousand ways. At the Hanukkah affair, a wonderful triple-layer petticoat of fifty yards of white nylon ruffles made the full skirt stand way out. My parents, Ray, and I hung Japanese lanterns, put blue checkered tablecloths on card tables, and set out refreshments. I danced with five boys, mainly Ray and Neal, who was at our table with Marsha. Boys, wanting to kiss, held missile toe (spelled right?) over girls' heads. I couldn't kiss Ray with my parents there. He smiled at my Woolworth necklace, engraved: Angela and Ray. His I. D. bracelet was too big on me and my ring was too small for him. After a Boulevard snack, we walked while holding hands. The fifty-degree evening felt like spring. Today set another high-temperature record for the date. Ray confided, "I like science and math and hope to be an atomic scientist."

Raising my eyebrows in surprise, I replied, "Wow! Most boys say doctor, engineer, or lawyer." I felt feminine and protected when Ray opened doors, pulled out chairs, took my coat, got my order, gave me napkins and salt, and kept me warm in the car. He's adorable and I love him! He even speaks Yiddish!

Monday, December 23, 1957: Gentleman
Shopping on Central Avenue, I enjoyed Ray's opening all doors and walking on the outside. He bought gifts for his parents, sister, and brother. I bought perfume for Mom and the nice lady at the dry cleaners. I liked Rob even less when he gave me a dirty look and didn't return my polite hello after he saw Ray holding my hand. On my porch, Ray had his arm around me and warmed my hand. Later, I imagined really kissing Raykins while listening to great Hanukkah gifts: Jimmie Rogers' songs *Honeycomb* and *Kisses Sweeter than Wine*. Ummm!

Tuesday, December 24, 1957: Hates Your Guts
In an anonymous call, a boy said, "Rob said to tell you he hates your guts." What nerve! Rob's not a gentleman. The third time Ray called, we talked a long time. I didn't reveal the nasty call to anyone. To stop feeling upset, I imagined slow dancing at a party with Ray:

The hostess turns out the lights and says, "Champagne."

Everyone stops dancing and kisses until the lights go on.

I wonder why our champagne dances have the same name as the square music Lawrence Welk plays on TV.

Wednesday, December 25, 1957: Turkey Farm
From Thanksgiving to Christmas every year, Dad must work twelve hours, Monday through Saturday, at the Surplus Store. Today, he finally got a day off. After an hour on the Thruway, we met my cousins for Christmas dinner at the Turkey Farm near Gloversville. Everyone sat at long tables, family style. We ate all the food we wanted from big platters of delicious turkey, dressing, and vegetables. The food smelled wonderful. Dad liked it and didn't yell. I loved being with Lydia and Ella, who gave me a pretty red wool crewneck, size 34. At their house, Aunt Myrna served yummy green apple pie.

Friday, December 27, 1957: Unready to Settle Down
Aunt Sara came to visit! In my room, I confided, "I love Ray. He's fun, intelligent, a good dancer, and a gentleman."

She said, "I'm happy that he's a good boyfriend. I remember your wanting to see Artie more."

I replied, "I wonder if you've seen Mort."

Aunt Sara answered, "Besides travel, a famous soprano, Martha Schlamme, is keeping us apart." She looked sad when saying, "He leads too exciting a life to settle down with one woman." I gave my aunt a hug.

Saturday, December 28, 1957: Angel and Heaven!

Doreen, in a white robe, seemed like an elegant angel during her Bat Mitzvah. Mrs. Bern, our wonderful teacher, smiled and waved when she saw me with Ray. Wearing a navy silk dress, Mrs. Bern looked more like Aunt Sara. With short brown hair and glasses, Mrs. Bern looks like a librarian at school. I can't wear my red taffeta everywhere, so Mom's dressmaker removed the sleeves from my ugly striped nylon dress. It looks a little better and costs less than a new dress. Wearing it to Doreen's evening party, I was mainly with Ray for dancing and kissing games. His arm was around me all evening and his soft lips sent me to heaven. I love, love, love him.

Sunday, December 29, 1957: Ungentlemanly

Rob stopped by to ask, "Did a boy call you?"

I answered, "On Christmas eve."

Rob asked, "What did he say?"

I replied, "Rob hates your guts."

Rob said, "It isn't true. I never told him to say that."

"What did you tell him?" Ungentlemanly Rob didn't reply or apologize. I got my mind off it by enjoying Hanukkah gifts: a lovely blue sailor blouse and white leather key ring with gold tooling from my parents.

Monday, December 30, 1957: Voices and Period

Ken invited me to the school dance! I remembered his soprano solos of my favorite carol, *O Holy Night*, in school Christmas programs. I'm glad boys' voices have changed, even though they can't hit high notes. I enjoyed Ray's deep, sexy voice during two phone calls. Four months after my first period, the second arrived.

Tuesday, December 31, 1957: Two Dates

Doreen's party was wonderful. Ray, who plays ping-pong well, didn't mind my winning. Neal beat me by two points. Playing doubles, we laughed while shooting the ball on the walls and ceiling! Doreen and I giggled while giving Ray and Neal the purity test. They did okay, answering no to most questions about whether they ever:

Had a date past 1 a.m.?

Danced cheek to cheek with a girl?

Kissed a girl?

Kissed a girl on the first date?

Kissed a girl on the neck?

French kissed a girl?

Nibbled on a girl's ear?

Necked continuously for an hour?

Removed a girl's bra?

Put a hand under a girl's skirt?

After sodas, we champagne danced. Ray's nice kiss was medium long. Wearing my striped nylon with Ken, I danced with him and three others until midnight. We ran around grinding noisemakers, breaking balloons, and screaming, "Happy New Year!" The souvenir noisemakers and big red bow on my bulletin board remind me of many fun times in 1957!

1958

Thursday, January 2, 1958: Pink

On the way home, Tara and Doreen agreed when I said, "Seeing everyone was great, but homework and tests make school feel like jail, even though our classroom's now painted pink."

Tara said, "Rob still likes you." I made a face, remembering the bad phone call. I wasn't pleased when he appeared and called later. After Ray called twice, I went to bed happy.

Friday, January 3, 1958: Rowena

My parents liked the anniversary card I made. Before they went out to dinner, Dad joked about the snow in Northville, where they lived for five years. Mom said, "After our wedding, we needed work. We ran a tiny branch of my father's clothing store."

Dad added, "Albany is better than that hick town of 5,000 prejudiced people. Only one other person was Jewish."

I said, "I didn't like being the only Jewish kid at Mayfield." To avoid spoiling their anniversary, I didn't mention Rowena's sad death, which Mom once described:

After marrying in 1937, I was nine months pregnant in June 1940. Even though we sprayed, the outside of our Northville house was black with spiders. Some got inside, even through screens. I was afraid that a huge spider above the bedroom window would get in our bed. When I climbed on a chair to kill it, my big stomach made me lose balance and fall to the floor. I felt pain and turning inside. The Northville doctor said, "I hear heartbeats. You'll be fine if you rest." I should have rushed to the Gloversville hospital. A few days later, I felt no life. The Gloversville doctor heard no heartbeats. After the induced hospital birth, they discovered that the cord had turned around Rowena's neck, gradually strangling her. She was a big, beautiful baby with round cheeks and dark hair.

Saturday, January 4, 1958: Kicked Out
At Woolworth's, I bought a dollar neck chain with a medal engraved: Ray and Angela 1958. At the Center dance, I wore my Orlon-and-wool black slacks and tan birthday crewneck from Uncle Peter. Ray treated me and danced with me. At the White Tower, we shared Boston cream pie. A bunch of us got silly and almost died laughing. I can't blame them for kicking us out for throwing salt around and playing volleyball with gloves and hats. Ray had his arm around me going home while Marsha's father drove. The whole evening was fun!

Sunday, January 5, 1958: Can't
Because I'm trying out for cheerleading, I wanted Ray to go out for basketball. He said, "I can't."

I asked, "Why?"

Eventually, he said, "I can't take gym because of a heart murmur." I felt awful. Unathletic boys have it hard. Young Judaea was less fun than usual.

Tuesday, January 7, 1958: Thirteen
I'm officially a teenager, but I've felt like one since starting seventh grade. I'm glad to be five foot four and not fat. Eating my favorite steak and cake, I tried to forget that thirteen is unlucky. I'm not superstitious. The parents gave me an orchid blouse, size 32, and a slightly flared wool tweed jumper with an Empire waist, size 10 preteen! Rob sent a birthday card. Julia from school and darling Ray made birthday calls. I love him more than any other boy.

Saturday, January 11, 1958: Perfect
While the parents and Aunt Lila gabbed, Ron and I talked in my room, confiding as always. Like all Dad's relatives, he's smart with a good sense of humor. Excited about a pretty blonde, he's taller and less chubby now. Ron's studying for his Bar Mitzvah. I said, "I can't wait to dance with your friends."

At my party, I couldn't help laughing when Doreen said, "Frankie accidentally spilled the perfume he was supposed to give you." Always in trouble, he's no goody-goody rabbi's son.

Before and after eating, we danced, including champagne dances with kisses. I danced with all the boys, but mainly Raykins. I love Ray! Everything was perfect, including my presents: a gorgeous robe in light blue quilted rayon (Doreen, Tara, Marsha); pretty charm bracelet (Ray); tan Morocco leather wallet (Myles); clutch bag (Neal); skin sachet (Lewis); blouses from three cousins; Pat Boone's *April Love* record; and a blue music box for powder.

Afterwards, Ron said, "I fell for Doreen and liked Ray a lot. Everyone seemed to enjoy bingo and the word game. The cake was delicious."

I replied, "Thanks to your mother, the table decorations were elegant. I appreciate your wonderful gift: the Waterman cartridge pen!"

Monday, January 13, 1958: Sneezes and Escape
My bad cold with loud sneezes and nose-blowing, maybe from champagne dance kissing, made me zip school. The slang zip is cooler than skip. I felt too sick to take Ray's call. Mom opened her birthday gifts before Dad took her to dinner. She's nagging more. "Do this. Do that." For weeks, Dad listens before losing his temper and shouting at us. I hate being yelled at and can't wait to grow up. Does the strange watercolor I painted show my escape from home? A two-lane country road between golden wheat fields passes a deserted gray building. Unless it's the CIA, a government building wouldn't be in the middle of nowhere. Does the pretty blue sky show my being free as a bird?

Sunday, January 19, 1958: Snowballs
At Young Judaea, I wore my jumper and Cousin Justine's pretty birthday blouse. Tara was happy to see Ben! Raykins got me a soda, paid my dues, gave me his picture, had his arm around me during the movie, and danced with me. Lewis cut in during dancing. Later, three of us girls and four boys couldn't stop laughing while making fun of teachers and discussing exams. Tara's father drove Ray and me to her house, where we played in the snow. When my boot got full of snow, Ray shook it out for me. Laughing, Tara said to Ray, "Angela and I threw eight snowballs

before hitting the sign. You hit it the first time." Because Ray is strong and throws well, I'm sad about his heart murmur.

Wednesday, January 22, 1958: Last Exam
After a murderous cit ed exam Friday, I'm pleased about 99 percent on Monday's cinchy English exam. I'm glad that Tara's 99 percent was first on yesterday's fair science exam. Thank goodness that today's math exam was the last! Doreen was happy to hear that a boy she likes said that he likes her. At my house, Tara and I made lists comparing Ben and Ray and ourselves. The fifth time Ray called, I finally got the nerve to use his pet name, Raykins. I enjoyed Ron's thank-you letter.

Saturday, January 25, 1958: Perfect Boyfriend
Ray's mother drove Ray, Doreen, her date, and me to see good movies: *My Man Godfrey* and *Kiss Them for Me*. I wore my aqua twinset and tweed jumper. I like peanut-less chocolate, so Ray got my half of a Reese's Peanut Butter Cup. He was romantic and well-mannered. He held my hand and had his arm around me, making me feel protected and loved.

Sunday, January 26, 1958: Playmates
I wore a white blouse with my jumper to a fun and tasty Bar Mitzvah dinner for a toddler playmate, who often hit me. Mom said, "If you hit him back, he won't bother you." I was afraid, but finally got mad enough to beat him up. Mom was right. He never hit me again. I fell for another former playmate, Barney, who's now five foot eight with black hair and dark eyes. Another only child who wants a brother or sister, he attends AHS.

Wednesday, January 29, 1958: Second
I got my period only a month after the second one. It's good to feel grown-up. I confided in Doreen, "I like Ray best. I really love him. Barney is second, but I'm not sure."

Doreen said, "Barney is handsome. I've always sort of liked him."

I said, "Something must be wrong with me for liking more than one boy at a time and not wanting to go steady, even with Ray."

162

She replied, "We've been dating for over a year, but we're only thirteen, too young to get serious."

I said, "Doreen, you are smart and know how to make me feel better."

On the phone, Ray said, "Barney told Neal that you're cute and nice." I felt warm inside, but couldn't admit liking Barney without hurting Ray's feelings.

I told Ray, "I'm relieved that studying for exams paid off." I left out my exam average of 99.5 percent, including a perfect score in health, in case Ray's was lower. I bought a secret pal Valentine for Barney.

Saturday, February 1, 1958: Heavy
I said to Ray, "I had no idea bowling balls were so heavy."

He replied, "I haven't bowled either." We ran around to find the lightest one to share. I was excited about winning the Buddy Holly record, *That'll Be the Day*, with the highest girls' score. My sixty-five included two strikes and two spares, along with gutter balls. Ray did marvelously with eighty-five. The pinsetters, high school boys, were cute! After cookies and cocoa at the synagogue, I was popular for some reason. Dancing with other cute boys was fun.

When Doreen slept over at my house, I said, "I went for Hy tonight."

She laughed and replied, "I don't blame you. He's so cute." We enjoyed gabbing about boys until late.

Tuesday, February 4, 1958: Guard
At extracurricular basketball, I had fun, as center guard, running around and jumping up and down in front of the shooters to prevent baskets. Playing well made me feel strong. Winning at sports puts me in a good mood.

Sunday, February 9, 1958: Chinese
My fear of falling while walking on ice hidden under new snow came true. After a painful bang, I enjoyed being examined at St. Peter's Hospital by the first Chinese person I've met. The young doctor's accent made me ask, "Did you live in China?"

He smiled and replied, "I'm from Taiwan." The only Asian people I've seen in town are doctors around Albany Hospital. Being X-rayed by a cute young technician was the frosting on the cake. Nothing is broken, thank God.

Tumba cheered me by saying, "Angela," more than usual.

Tuesday, February 11, 1958: Dance Fun

At the Center dance, Mitch, Frankie, and Rob danced so much with me that I didn't miss Ray. Did the blue full skirt I made in home ec make me popular? Mitch took me to the Boulevard on a fun triple date with Rob, Tara, Myles, and Marsha.

Thursday, February 13, 1958: Angelina and Anne

I'm excited about Cousin Justine's new baby, Angelina. I bet she's like her name: little angel! My cold kept me home on our day off school. I finished Anne Frank's famous diary. I want mine to stay private.

Friday, February 14, 1958: Romance

I love romantic things, like flowers. Dad bought Mom roses. He'll take her to the synagogue Valentine dance. Home with my nose red from blowing, I missed getting school Valentines. Three Valentines signed Ray XXX made me happy! Rob sent one, as did Ron. I liked the enclosed pictures of his girlfriend and of Pat Boone, the singer. In bed, I make up wonderful romances, like this:

> July 1958: Looking my best in a shirt, shorts, and sneakers, I'm washing our car. Four boys I like stop to talk. I flirt and offer cool drinks. Sitting on the porch, Hy says, "We've come from Center Day Camp."
>
> Barney adds, "We're planning a formal dance."
>
> I say, "Can I guess your dates?" After they laugh, I continue. "Barney will go with Rose. Ray will ask Naomi. Lil will be Ty's date. I don't know about Hy. I'll get lemonade." Barney, Hy, and Ty follow me into the kitchen. I'm surprised. "Are mighty juniors helping a humble freshman get lemonade?"

They say in unison, "I want to ask you to the formal."
Everyone laughs.

"Because everyone asked at once, I can't accept the earliest offer. I don't want to hurt anyone's feelings. I'm crazy about all of you, so I can't choose by my feelings." Then I cry in frustration. "I want so much to go." They pat me on the back and comfort me. I dry my eyes and say, "I'll go with the boy you pick for me. Does anyone want to bow out?" I am relieved when Ty returns to the porch. Looking at my favorites Barney and Hy, I say with a flirtatious smile, "Maybe I can go with both of you."

Barney says, "Half is better than none." We all laugh. When Hy carries the lemonade to the porch, Ray and Ty politely rise.

I propose a toast, "To the formal dance!"

"To the formal dance!" they repeat. I wink at my future dates, Barney and Hy.

Tuesday, February 18, 1958: Advice and Flattery

No school yesterday was the only good thing about snow two feet high and cold way below zero. Today, my twenty school Valentines made me smile. Three were unsigned. Who secretly likes me? When I ran into Myles, I asked, "Saturday night, can you and Marsha bowl with Ray and me?"

He said, "I'll find out. I still like Tara better than Marsha and another girl."

I said, "I shouldn't stick my big foot into your affairs."

He laughed and said, "I need advice."

I said, "Tara's wonderful. I wish she'd get over someone. You'd be a better boyfriend, if she'd stop treating you as a friend."

When he asked, "What's his name?"

I answered, "Tara's my friend. I can't tell."

He said, "I understand." I seem to be over my crush on him. He's an awfully good kid.

I called Doreen to say, "Imitation is the sincerest form of flattery. I love your quilted, flared skirt. I got a silky black-and-white plaid, size 11. The faint red stripes match my red velvet blouse."

"Let's wear our skirts if our social lives ever revive."

I laughed and agreed. "For two weeks, I haven't seen Ray, but he calls daily."

Sunday, February 23, 1958: *Sayonara* and Beth

We saw the movie *Sayonara*, a love story with a sad ending for Red Buttons and cute Miyoshi Umeki. I've liked her since she was on the Arthur Godfrey radio show. Are people prejudiced against the Japanese girlfriends and wives of American military men because Japan was our World War II enemy? We visited fashionable Beth, whose toddler is darling! I said, "I wish we could see them more."

Mom answered, "Beth's too busy."

Monday, February 24, 1958: Report

Mrs. Bern is my favorite teacher. Her English grammar lessons have helped me. When I mentioned Anne Frank's diary last week, her eyes lit up. "I've been looking for time to read it." Her husband and two sons must keep her busy.

I said, "You can borrow my copy."

She smiled. "Thank you. I have one. A brief book report about it will earn extra credit."

Today, the kids clapped and I got an A for my report:

The Diary of a Young Girl is a heart-warming and heart-breaking story about a German Jewish girl our age. She wrote her 1942-1944 diary while hiding from the Nazis in the Netherlands. She used an autograph book with a red-and-white-checkered cover and lock. I loved reading about her relationship with her boyfriend, also in hiding. I felt her constant fear of being found and killed. The book showed how awful war is. I'd rather live in peace and write a less exciting diary. It's hard to believe that someone our age wrote as well as an adult and created the best book I've ever read. Anne Frank wrote:

I need...something besides a husband and children...I want to go on living even after my death!...Will I ever... write something great?

I think she did. On a scale of one to five stars, this book deserves ten.

Thursday, February 27, 1958: Restless

The game at the Mohican School gym was fun because I knew many kids, including Marcus, Artie, most of the cheerleaders, and four basketball players. Tara was excited about seeing Ben. We won by two points, even though their players are good, including Mario, who made the anonymous call for Rob. If he's already scaring people in a sneaky way, will he end up in the Mafia? Both cheer squads did well, but theirs rudely ran out first, instead of letting us visitors start. Talking to Ray, I felt eager to flirt with others. In the school bus on the way home, we sang and acted nutty!

Friday, February 28, 1958: White Bucks and Freer

I loved cute Pat Boone's song and movie, *April Love,* and his cool white buck shoes. My new pair, size 7AA, is low-cut with only four eyelets and has black ties and soles. I enjoyed buying a slip, a 32A bra, size 32 pajamas, and Serena Modess sanitary napkins. My fourth period brought stomach cramps. Not eating and taking Midol, which contains aspirin and stuff, helped. Wearing my new plaid skirt to synagogue services, I had fun with Frankie, Myles, Rob, and two girls. I felt freer with Ray absent.

Saturday, March 1, 1958: Predictable and Guilty

Am I normal to want to date other boys when I'm lucky to have a mature, polite, smart, romantic, fun boyfriend, who's a good dancer? Why do Ray's predictable calls leave me feeling trapped? Petting Tumba, I asked him, "Does your cage bother you?"

I laughed when his monologue included, "No" and "Angela." I feel guilty because Ray's done nothing wrong. I wish he'd read my mind and find someone new.

Sunday, March 2, 1958: Moving On
At Young Judaea, I felt mean paying less attention to Ray and hoping he gets the idea. Saying anything will hurt his feelings more. Waiting for Dad's ride, I enjoyed being the only girl with Myles, Frankie, and others. At the Purim holiday dinner, Marsha, Myles, Doreen, her date, and I had a good time playing records and kidding around.

Wednesday, March 5, 1958: Myles and Lukewarm
Lately, Myles sticks up for me. He may still love Tara, who likes only Ben. I've always had a weakness for Myles. I felt perked up when he went out of his way to walk Tara and me to and from Iroquois School for the basketball game. Thanks to our easy win and yesterday's victory in a close game, our school will play in the championship game! When Ray called, I was lukewarm and got off the phone quickly after saying, "Is it okay if we don't talk every day? I'm studying for tests this week." I want Ray to save face and I do have to study. I felt the same with Edwin.

Saturday, March 8, 1958: Mr. Peanut
I took the bus to State and Pearl downtown. As usual, I had fun talking to kids I know who were shopping on North Pearl Street south of the Palace Theatre. Mr. Peanut, in front of the Planters' store, made me laugh. Dressed as a giant peanut with black arms and legs and top hat, he handed out free peanuts. I love fashion shows, including today's Whitney's Department Store parade of summer clothes. I enjoyed looking at all eight floors at the two department stores and at pretty clothes in my size in smaller stores. I feel better without Ray's calls. Is everyone repetitious eventually? Would Artie have bored me? Feeling in a rut, I want someone new, like Barney.

Sunday, March 9, 1958: Carnival
The Purim carnival was mobbed with kids running around turning groggers to make noise against wicked Haman. My grogger had a picture of Queen Esther, who saved the Jews in Persia. I helped with the booths and was surprised to be popular with boys. Did personality, looks, or my red Bermudas, blouse, and

knee sox make them flirt? The synagogue raised money selling dollar Purim-grams, telegrams hand-delivered to people there. Frankie's Purim-gram said:

Angela, I like your art picture.

Mitch sent me a gag gram:

I like you. From your secret pal, Myles

When Myles talked Mom into letting me attend the dance tonight, did it mean he likes me? Wearing a skirt and sweater, I danced mostly with him! Mmmmm!

Monday, March 10, 1958: Hark and D-E-A-Rest

At Dad's birthday dinner, he laughed and liked my proclamation birthday card:

Hark! Hear Ye!

The Royal Order of Weisses, who reside at 549 Merritt Street, otherwise referred to as Weissdom, want it known that they wish a happy, happy forty-seventh birthday to one of their most faithful clan members, Herm Jonah of Weissdom, on this tenth day of the third month of the year 1958 common era.

Signed: Angela Weiss, Daughter

Fern Weiss, Wife

I answered Aunt Sara's warm letter using her gift: pink music notepaper! I love it because the music notes on the front spell out D-E-A-Rest. I felt okay talking to Ray because it's been a while.

Tuesday, March 18, 1958: Dreams

My wonderful daydreams include this ongoing one:

An eighteen-year-old, starting the second year of pre-med, and I, thirteen, are counselors at the Center camp. We go for each other and kiss. The other girl counselor is jealous when he uses teaching me to swim better as an excuse to hold me and touch my legs and arms in the water.

My colored paper dream wheel includes twenty-one cute boys' names on pie slices. Last night's spin stopped at tall, lean Myles, who's been on my mind. I dreamed:

Grown-up architect Myles and I lived in NYC. I was an interior decorator. He said, "In Albany, I had a secret crush on you." I smiled and admitted my crush on him. We got engaged and kissed and ALL. He's the kind of boy you want to kiss and ALL.

Unlike Albany where everyone knows you and gossips, you're free to do things in NYC without people disapproving. I want to live in a big city without snow and cold winters.

Friday, March 21, 1958: Second

At a Bat Mitzvah, I had fun, dressed in my red velvet blouse and plaid skirt. It was fine that Ray and Neal ignored me. Myles asked, "Are you going to the joint Bat Mitzvah party?"

Hypnotized by his blue eyes, I said yes.

He mumbled, "Good. I won't go unless you do." When he smiles at me and sticks up for me, I can't tell whether he likes me romantically or platonically. I'm okay being second to Tara. Not tied down, I can enjoy different boys.

Tuesday, March 25, 1958: Ray and Rewards

At dinner, Mom asked, "Is Ray still your boyfriend?" I kind of shrugged. If I say no, Mom's big mouth may cause word to get back to Ray and hurt his feelings.

Changing the subject, I said to Mom, "Have you thought of growing longer hair? It looked pretty when I was young."

"Working full-time, I don't have the extra time."

I replied, "Thanks for the black-red-and-white-striped T-shirt." To hold up my stockings, Mom got me a panty girdle, which is more like a chastity belt than my garter belts. I also appreciated a strapless 32A bra.

Dad said, "It's a reward for your report card with As in everything, except B plus in art."

As usual, I mainly listened, gobbled down my food, and asked, "May I be excused?" Escaping to my pretty green room was relaxing. After homework, I wrote Aunt Sara:

I'm surprised not to miss or think about Ray. He calls every few days to talk a little. I don't want to hurt his feelings, so I am nice, but not encouraging. He doesn't mention the change but seems to know our romance is over. I love flirting without guilt.

Before falling asleep, I finished the hilarious book, *We Shook the Family Tree.*

Saturday, March 29, 1958: Wild

I wore my best red taffeta to Marsha's evening Bat Mitzvah celebration, the wildest party I've attended. Many kids necked and petted. I didn't and couldn't believe my eyes. Mitch kissed a girl for a long time while his hands were feeling her up. Does she mind a fast reputation from doing things in public with someone who isn't her boyfriend? I'd rather be a respected girlfriend a boy takes to dances. After dancing mainly with Myles, I ended up dancing and joking with Frankie. He got me in a silly mood by saying, "I'll write my tall, blond Ohio friends about you. When I left in 1956, I was the only short guy." His descriptions were exciting; it was like shopping for boys.

I told Frankie, "The more, the better!"

He laughed. "Most girls are happy with one boyfriend, but you want twenty-five." I giggled while picturing myself flirting with a pack of cute boys. The evening was a gasser!

Sunday, March 30, 1958: Matzoh

The parents and I drove to South Pearl Street for Passover food. When we passed the Surplus Store where Dad works, he said, "The tightwad who won't give me a raise owns this store." At the grocery, we ran into Myles, who gabbed enthusiastically about Marsha's party. We bought gefilte fish, Manischewitz Seder wine, and matzoh, which tastes better than most bread, except Jewish rye. I love to eat the heel when it's still warm from the bakery oven.

Saturday, April 5, 1958: Passionately

After Myles called, I made up this story while lying in bed:
Myles took me to a formal dance at Sacandaga. In a little shack at the beach, we changed clothes for a midnight swim. I asked, "Can you please unzip my dress?" He stood behind me and unzipped it. I kept it from falling down by holding it against my chest in the front.

171

With his hands on my shoulders, he said, "Your back is bare. No bra?"

Turning my head back, I enjoyed a whiff of his after-shave lotion before replying, "My dress has a built-in bra." He smiled and I smiled back before closing the curtain and putting on my best white swimsuit. Opening the curtain, I admired his lean body in a tight, black knit swimsuit. After we swam to and from a raft, he carried me around in shallow water and kissed me. When we got cold, we returned to the shack. Behind the curtain, I took off my wet suit and put on white shorts. On top, I put on a bra without hooking the back. I was a 34B, instead of a 32A. Holding my loose blouse against the bra in the front, I opened the curtain. Myles looked good in only tight Levi's. I said, "Can you please hook my bra in the back?"

"My pleasure." He smiled and hooked it.

I said, "Maybe I shouldn't wear a bra. Can you unhook me, please?" I heard his deep laugh and felt him unhook it. I closed the curtain to put on a low-cut sheer blouse. As we walked through the woods, he kept looking at my blouse front in the moonlight. When he hugged me, I stood on tiptoe with my arms around his neck. After kissing for a while, we walked until I said, "Oww!" When I bent down to remove a stone in my sandal, he looked down the front of my blouse and saw everything. I was happy to have more to show off. When I stood up, he kissed me passionately.

Sunday, April 13, 1958: Fear and Circus

Yesterday's movie, *A Farewell to Arms* with cute Rock Hudson, was sad! I cried a lot, partly because of my period, which makes me emotional. Seeing Jennifer Jones suffer in childbirth, I felt afraid to have a baby and die if things go wrong. I escaped by finishing two wonderful Betty Cavanna romantic teen novels: *Love, Laurie* and *Lasso Your Heart*. Today, our Gloversville relatives, my parents, and I loved the circus, especially the animal acts and acrobats!

Saturday, April 19, 1958: Spring Clothes

Sleeping over at Doreen's, I saw her pretty new clothes. When she asked about mine, I said, "My sleeveless, green-tan-and-gold harlequin print dress, in size 7, has a full skirt and green sash, like Audrey Hepburn's dresses. I'd love to be like her playful characters. Her face and slim figure are perfect, like a ballet dancer."

Doreen agreed. "What else did you buy?"

"The cord middy top and skirt are the latest chemise style with a bloused back and dropped waist with a hip cuff."

"I like chemises! What will you wear to Ron's Bar Mitzvah?"

"As a graduation present, Mom paid a fortune, $25 at David's, for a heavenly, white nylon semiformal with blue trim in size 7. I feel like a princess in it!"

"I can't wait to see everything!"

Friday, April 25, 1958: Chemise and Emotions

I wore my pink-gray-and-white-striped chemise for our graduation photo of both eighth-grade classes. I'm happy about growing up, but sad to leave wonderful Mrs. Bern and Mrs. Lewis at Patroon. I can't imagine a better gym teacher than Welshie. Was my chemise the reason I was popular at the school dance? I need to know why I'm popular sometimes, so I can do it every time.

Saturday, April 26, 1958: Marjorie

Last year, our abridged *Marjorie Morningstar* book without sex scenes kept me from learning more about sex. Marsha, Doreen, and I saw the romantic movie with Natalie Wood perfect as Marjorie. Gene Kelly dances well, but why would a girl of eighteen want a boyfriend as old as parents?

Sunday, April 27, 1958: Panel and Click

Albany hosted Mom's Jewish women's convention. Frankie and I represented Young Judaea in the Hadassah panel discussion. My chemise felt fashionable, as we discussed how teens feel and what they want. We went out with Myles, Doreen, Ray, and others. Doreen deserves someone special, like Ray. I'll be happy if they click.

Wednesday, April 30, 1958: Will Will Like Me?

Last week on the bus that took us to a play, Tara and I talked to the new boy in our class, tall Will from Syracuse. Today, we overheard a boy ask Will, "Do you like Angela?"

Tara and I looked at each other and smiled after Will replied, "I'm not telling anyone who I like."

Thursday, May 1, 1958: Tallest, Strongest, Fastest

At assembly, a teacher introduced me: "Here's our school president to announce today's program."

Tara later said, "I heard Will ask, 'Who's the president?' When a boy answered, 'Angela Weiss,' Will smiled."
I wrote to Aunt Sara:

> I hope Will likes me better because I'm president, instead of being scared off. From the school yard during gym, Will waved up at me as we girls watched from a classroom window. He has the cutest smile, runs the fastest, and is the strongest boy. I love athletic boys!

Friday, May 2, 1958: Sincerely

In homeroom, Will told Doreen:

> I went to a party last night. My whole family is tall, including my cool stepfather. My dad died in World War II.

During study period, Doreen and I joked and showed off for Will sitting behind her. When his eyes met mine and we both smiled, I felt excited. In cit ed, I laughed when Will caught my eye. He showed off by pushing a boy off his chair. In math, Will grinned and asked, "Have you done your homework?" I nodded. I look at and smile at him all the time. While the other kids finished an art project, which I finished early, I gave Frankie a haircut. Will watched and later knocked down Frankie during tag. Was Will envious? He signed my autograph book around page margins:

> Dear Angela, when you go to the country, walk around the hedges and rember (*sic*) it was I who wrote around the edges. Sincerely yours and all my best wishes, Will

174

Saturday, May 3, 1958: Neal and Will

When Doreen slept over, she said, "I love your first pair of heels!"

I answered, "I can't wait to wear them! I like the one-and-a-half-inch height, square throat, pointed toes, and narrow size 7AA/AAAA!" Talking about favorite boys was fun.

She said, "I'll get Frankie to ask you to the hayride."

I answered, "I'll talk to Neal." She looked at his picture. I looked at Will's autograph, imagining the prom with him.

Monday, May 5, 1958: Invites

Doreen succeeded! I accepted Frankie's hayride invite. I called Neal and said, "Hayrides are loads of fun! Frankie and I can double with you and your date."

Neal replied, "I'll think about it." I told Doreen.

She smiled. "Thanks for doing everything possible! He's a tough nut to crack." Will smiled a couple of times and borrowed my textbook. He smokes, like most boys. If it stunts his growth, it won't matter since he's already six foot one at fourteen.

Tuesday, May 6, 1958: No Chasing

Will, sitting next to me in math, said, "I get up at half past five for my paper route and go back to sleep from seven to eight." Interested in everything about him, I feel lucky that he talks to me. Doreen shared his telephone number. I wish girls could call boys.

Thursday, May 8, 1958: Male Insecurity

At school, I hid my happiness about report card straight As for the first time this year. I feel honored that the teachers nominated me for the best citizen award! I wrote a note to Aunt Sara:

> When I grow up, will men still be threatened by and avoid women with brains? It's disappointing. I refuse to miss out on dates because boys aren't confident. When I won't tell my grades at school, people assume they're low.

I've called Will's number to hear his voice and hung up. When our eyes meet, I can't tell whether he knows or what he thinks.

Front row, left to right: Marsha, Marie, Tara, Barbara
Second row, third from left: Doreen, Pam; eighth from left: Angela, Irene
Third row, fourth from right: Ken; third from right: Carl
Back row, fifth from left: Mitch; eighth from left: Will; fourth from right: Frankie

176

Saturday, May 10, 1958: Ray and Doreen

I'm disappointed about rain cancelling the hayride, but glad we danced instead. Wearing my blue dress, I danced and talked with Frankie. Doreen and Ray came with us to the Boulevard for chocolate milk. After Ray's mother drove us home, Doreen and I were on the phone for an hour. I'm glad that Ray and Doreen seemed to hit it off! Ray seems like a better person than Neal.

Sunday, May 11, 1958: Mother's Day

The Mother's Day card I made looks better than the apron I sewed, but Mom liked both. We dressed up to visit Grandma in Saratoga Springs. God bless her! She looked happy to see our families. Wearing my chemise and heels, I felt grown-up. At Mother Goldsmith's, we had the excellent Long Nails. Lydia, Ella, and I acted silly and laughed at our parents, who couldn't hear us at a different table. Our favorite veal cutlet with French fries was delicious. Lydia, who's taller than I, liked hearing about tall Will and said, "Send him to my school. Most of the boys come up to my chest."

Tuesday, May 13, 1958: Teacher Recognition Day

We girls mobbed around Smitty, shouted compliments about her gorgeous silk print dress, and had a ball. But she wouldn't let Will sit next to me in math. Darn! After four years of putting up with us, Welshie deserves recognition. Of the fun sports she's taught, my favorites are volleyball and basketball. I can also play softball, climb ladders, and tumble a little on mats. I'd like to see her husband. I try to picture whether he's bigger. Is he tougher? Is she bossier? Maybe he says, "Go to the beauty parlor. Your gray hair sticks out all over, like curly silver wires." At least my ugly short hair needs little setting. I cut the back and bangs shaggier.

Thursday, May 15, 1958: Will

We kids are signing class photos. Will talked to me in math and art where he asked for a signed copy of my picture. He signed his:

Best Wishes and Best Luck Always, Will R

When Will shows off, he makes sure I'm watching, which I always am. I called his number and hung up. Despite our flirtation, I'm afraid he won't invite me to the prom. It's on my mind because I'm reading *Senior Prom*, a good paperback romance I got by mail.

Friday, May 16, 1958: Syracuse
My period came; it's not the best timing. On the Greyhound bus to the Syracuse Young Judaea convention, Lewis, Frankie, and I talked to a pleasant eighteen-year-old boy. I stayed with a friendly family with a teen girl and boy. At the synagogue, I met a doll!

Sunday, May 18, 1958: Closing
An Albany girl I know was on the Greyhound bus home. When she asked about the convention, I replied:

Saturday, I had fun at the synagogue, our meeting, and the luncheon. Hardly any boys attended the dance, but I had a good time in my semiformal dress, competing in the dance contest and watching a girl crowned queen. Sunday, we elected regional officers and kidded around during the closing banquet. I enjoyed it, even though nothing happened with boys and we didn't sightsee in Syracuse.

Maybe there's nothing to see.

We both laughed.

Monday, May 19, 1958: Track
We had fun at the track meet watching our boys win. I felt excited when Will, our star, came over to chat. I mentioned being in his hometown yesterday. At home, I giggled when Tumba repeated for the first time, "Tumba's the greatest."

Tuesday, May 20, 1958: Perfect
In math, Will passed me notes. After I called him conceited, he wrote:

I am not conceited. I am perfect. I'm only kidding. Why do you think I am conceited?

I answered:

Do you really want to know and why?

Before he could answer, class ended. After dialing his number, I hung up when his mother answered.

Thursday, May 22, 1958: Scoring and Hard to Get

In softball, I was happy to hit three singles and come in for two runs. Our bigger balls are easier to hit than boys' baseballs. At Doreen's after school, I said, "I'm discouraged about Will. Nothing's happening. I don't know what to do."

She replied, "How about playing hard to get?"

I nodded. "As a last resort, I'll try ignoring him."

Thursday, May 29, 1958: President

I wrote Aunt Sara about class day:

I felt pretty in my white semiformal. As president, I gave a speech of thanks for a new school flag. I won the citizenship award certificate, plaque, and pin. Three girls and I got first prizes in the four main subjects: English, math, cit ed, and science/art. I laughed when the class prophecy predicted that I'd be the first female American President. I appreciated the compliment, but I'd rather be an interior decorator. Sitting behind me, Will talked and shared his song sheet. We joked about the class will being named after him and laughed at kids' inheritances:

A boy's wolf whistle went to a shy, bookish girl.

An unathletic boy received Irene's cheerleading jumps.

Ken left his singing voice to a girl who sings off-key.

A girl who never dances inherited Mitch's dancing skills.

The tallest girl left four inches of height to a short boy.

Frankie's duck-tail haircut, back since his Bar Mitzvah, went to a boy with a crew cut.

A girl with unstylish hair inherited my hair-cutting ability.

A girl who hates gym received Will's strength and speed.

Watching me dance almost every dance with Frankie, Mitch, and Ken, Will seemed to want to ask me. Maybe he doesn't know how. I was dying to be in his arms. At the Center dance, I was popular, dancing with Frankie, Myles, Mitch, cute Hy, and others. The awards, fun activities, and two dances made today the most exciting day of my life!

Saturday, May 31, 1958: Antiques and Flirtation
Aunt Rhoda, Uncle Harvey, Ron, Uncle Bert, and Aunt Lila arrived yesterday for Memorial Day! For some reason, my aunts love antiques. They liked the furniture in the mansion of Philip Schuyler, the Revolutionary War general. I skipped the tour I had in fourth grade. Wearing a white blouse, black Jamaica shorts, and white flats, I enjoyed being noticed by a teenager with a turned-up nose, brown crew cut, and clear blue eyes. As I stood in the doorway watching his slim, medium-height physique walk away, he romantically turned back for a last look. I kept missing Will.

Monday, June 2, 1958: Albany Newspaper
I'm excited because The Times Union printed my class day photo above this:

> Van De Loo-Miller Post No. 1022, American Legion presented a flag to Patroon School. Angela Weiss, president of the school, accepted the flag for her schoolmates. Making the presentation are William Gannon, left, and Philip Swartz, post commander.

Mrs. Bern said, "Van De Loo is an old Dutch name meaning From the Woods."

Tuesday, June 3, 1958: Let Down
Last night on the phone, I silently prayed that Will would read my mind and invite me to the prom. His sexy voice said, "Hello, who's this?" before he sighed and hung up. Today, he said, "Good morning," and loaned me paper during math. Tired of waiting about the prom, I invited Myles. I'm glad that Doreen invited Ray. Too chicken to invite Ben, Tara invited Neal. No boys in our class invited us.

Saturday, June 7, 1958: Prom
I felt special! The Times Union printed my name as one of five kids on our prom planning committee. When I got home around noon from sleeping over at Doreen's after the prom, I wrote to Aunt Sara. I love sharing everything with her:

Myles smelled good and looked handsome in his blue suit. After he complimented my semiformal, we walked to the prom with Tara, Neal, Doreen, and Ray. When my friends got corsages, I wished for one. After our grand entrance, the teachers beamed on us and seemed to love Myles. Looking into his blue eyes, I was in the best mood. His dancing was marvelous, including the jitterbug and cha cha. Myles was very attentive, a swell escort. Everything was perfect: the girls wore beautiful dresses and got free corsages; the Four Half Notes played well; and Irene and Ken were queen and king. After delish prom punch and cookies, we ate French fries and ice cream at Joe's Deli. At Marsha's, we danced and played party games. Sitting on chairs roped to the back of Marsha's father's truck, we rode around town, waving to people, singing, joking, and laughing, as we got dropped off at home. Myles held my hand, had his arm around me, and kept me warm. The prom was one of the best times of my life! Not all eighth graders have proms, so we're lucky.

Sunday, June 8, 1958: Kissing
Doreen called to say, "You were smart to hold off Myles when he tried to neck in the truck. I just heard he's after a fast girl."

I responded, "I'd feel used because kissing means nothing to Myles. He'll do everything possible with any girl, leaving her with a fast reputation. If I neck, it will be only with a regular boyfriend in private when we love each other. I'm so glad you had a great time with Ray!"

Friday, June 13, 1958: Upset
Despite studying, I didn't do well on the health final. After a difficult English exam, my mouth fell open when Mom announced, "I must get false teeth after getting most of my teeth pulled in the hospital." I'm in shock. This is scary. I must brush my teeth better. Will Friday the thirteenth ever be good?

<u>Wednesday, June 18, 1958: Recovering</u>
Dear Lydia and Ella,
Thank you so much for the letter and graduation gift! The two pairs of shorty pajamas are cute! I'm wearing the pink ones now. After our tough cit ed final Monday, I felt sick. The school nurse said, "You've caught German measles, which are milder than regular measles." Missing the art and math exams may lower my final grades. Bad luck! I painted a watercolor of us at the beach where I'd love to be.
Love, Angela

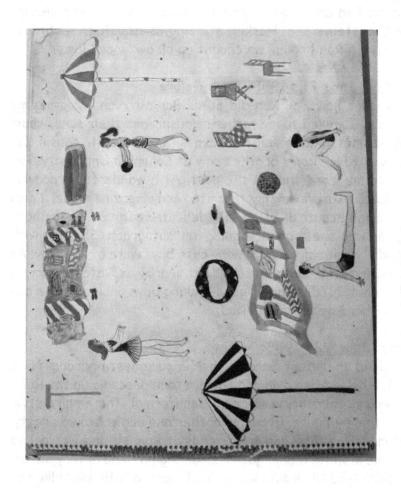

Angela's colorful watercolor

Friday, June 20, 1958: Family
Dad's upset about missing Ron's Bar Mitzvah. His mean boss won't let him off Saturday, the busiest day at the store. In NYC, Mom and I saw Ron's presents and enjoyed Aunt Lila's tasty chicken dinner. Aunt Rhoda played the piano while soprano Lila sang old tunes, such as *Over the Rainbow, Bei Mir Bist Du Schoen,* and *Stardust.* Ron and I got bored listening to the adults discuss Rabbi Lookstein's son, Haskel, starting as assistant rabbi last Saturday. In Ron's room, we caught up on our social lives.

Saturday, June 21, 1958: Boys Galore
I'm proud of how well Ron did in his Bar Mitzvah. Wearing my blue dress, I talked to my father's cousins and their sons, whom I've never met, like Farrell. His mom is Dad's favorite cousin. I'm crazy about Hal, Ron's brother now at Columbia University. Hal talked to me more than in the past. At a wonderful Broadway play, *Blue Denim,* we saw my favorite teen magazine model, Carol Lynley. She's beautiful, blond with delicate features. At the back door, she was sweet about signing her autograph. She left with a friendly, dark-haired boy. Many cute boys were at the play. At a restaurant, two handsome dolls sat nearby as I ate a delicious steak dinner. NYC is full of good-looking boys, including the bus station where we picked up Dad.

Sunday, June 22, 1958: Happy
I'm thrilled that Aunt Sara will live in our guest bedroom for a year! We helped her plan and pack before dressing up for Ron's Franconia Hotel party. I wore my semiformal. The Empire style is good for my figure. Even my mother and aunts looked pretty. I met many relatives and fun friends of Ron. He and Hal looked handsome in white dinner jackets. Ron's girlfriend is very sweet. Rich, blue-eyed Gil, Ron's best friend, danced with and talked to me. My parents say, "Being rich isn't important."

Dad's sisters, who go for fancier things, say, "It's better than being poor." A photographer made a movie of Ron's candle-lighting ceremony, including me. Dinner was delicious. It was a marvelous affair!

Angela and Ron

Monday, June 23, 1958: Gil and Ben

Interested in my weekend, Tara asked, "Ajax (my nickname), what's Gil like?"

I answered, "He's thirteen, blond, five foot eight, polite, intelligent, and outgoing. I wish he lived here." To help Tara with Ben, I called to invite him to Marsha's painting party. I can't wait for it!

Tuesday, June 24, 1958: Toothless and Birthday

Losing your teeth is horrible! I was upset seeing Mom in the hospital awaiting false teeth. Dad and I sang *Happy Birthday* to Aunt Sara, who liked the card I made.

She said, "I was born in 1917, five years after your mom."

Surprised to learn Mom's exact age, I replied, "I was born five years after Rowena. I wish she were alive. I hate being an only child. I get annoyed, but must smile politely when people say that I am spoiled and probably get whatever I want."

She said, "People can be tactless. You're the opposite of spoiled."

I replied, "Thank you. I'm happy you're here to write your book."

She said, "I hope that my music book publisher, E. P. Dutton, accepts my family relationship book."

She smiled after I said, "Thanks for dedicating *Musical Tales* to me in 1946. I love the stories and beautiful colored pictures!"

Wednesday, June 25, 1958: School's Over

Aunt Sara congratulated me after I did a cheerleading jump and said:

Yay! I've earned my NY State Regents' Certificate! All eighth graders pass the same finals for it. To avoid being called a brain and scaring boys away, I didn't tell anyone that my report card has A, A plus, or A minus in all eight subjects. I'm relieved and happy!

Thursday, June 26, 1958: Painting Party

Aunt Sara laughed when I reported:

At Marsha's, over twenty kids used green paint on one another and the party shack her father built. The Albany afternoon newspaper sent a photographer, who took crazy shots of us acting silly. We danced, played kissing games, joked, and picnicked on hot dogs, salad, watermelon, and soda. After I sat near Myles, he invited me to the Tower of Talent and tried hard to neck in public. He walked me home and held my hand. It was a terrific day!

Friday, June 27, 1958: Suits
Doreen and I had fun buying swimsuits. Doreen said, "Your turquoise-and-white-striped knit suit is a bargain! My parents would smile if I could find a seventeen-dollar suit on sale for five dollars!"

"I hope that Mom's okay with eleven dollars for this grown-up, white Lastex suit." Home from the hospital and looking better with dentures, Mom approved my suits.

Saturday, June 28, 1958: Fame and Eternity
The Knickerbocker News must be hard up for news. A cute photo of us painting the party shack is on the front page with our names listed! I said, "Doreen, your photo is excellent! Wearing Dad's baggy old shirt, I don't look good." The article, three columns and twenty paragraphs long, shows how nice Marsha's father was to build a "rumpus house." Aunt Sara, the parents, and I saw a superb movie: *From Here to Eternity* with Burt Lancaster and Frank Sinatra at the Madison Theatre!

Monday, June 30, 1958: Talent
Tara enjoyed hearing about the ball I had with Myles, Mitch, and Marsha at Hawkins Stadium for the Station WPTR Tower of Talent:
> We had good seats and were in the best moods. Myles had his arm around me and complimented my green dress. We were thrilled to hear famous people sing their hits: Dakota Staton, Rose Marie June, The Jive Bombers, Jack Scott, Fabulous Fabian, Dicky Doo and the Don'ts, and the Kallin Twins. The Everly Brothers were stupendous

performing *Wake Up Little Susie.* Connie Francis sang *Who's Sorry Now!* The Lane Brothers' *Boppin' in a Sack* about dancing in a chemise dress was funny. "You once did the bop and wiggled a lot, but in that smock you ain't got no rock." I sat on Myles's lap in the taxi to Calsolero's. While we had pizza and soda, Mitch was a riot, waddling around with his pant legs rolled up and his hairy, muscular calves showing!

Wednesday, July 2, 1958: Newman
At Tara's, Doreen hugged us good-bye before leaving for a long family vacation at a lake near East Greenbush. Doreen said, "I hope to meet a cute boyfriend."

I said, "Have fun! We'll miss you!"
At the drive-in theatre, *The Long Hot Summer* was good! Dad smiled patiently while Mom, Aunt Sara, and I raved about handsome Paul Newman's blue eyes!

Thursday, July 3, 1958: Izzy
After Kirk Douglas' movie, *The Vikings,* Aunt Sara told me, "Years ago, I dated Kirk, who was Izzy Demsky from Amsterdam, NY. I lost track of him until seeing him, bigger than life on a NYC movie screen. I was so shocked that I blurted out loud, 'Izzy!' People in the theatre turned to stare at me."

After laughing, I asked, "Was he as handsome when you dated?"

She said, "No, but he was charming."

I added, "I like his chin dimple and blue eyes."

Monday, July 7, 1958: The City
Dear Lydia and Ella,
How are you? I hope you're having a great summer! I'm so excited to be in Manhattan after an easy bus ride. Aunt Sara and I taxied to her cool studio apartment on West 73rd Street to close it. The kitchenette is tiny. Ludwig van Beethoven, the ebony baby grand piano, takes up half of the big room. I love the matching curved couches. Our aunt sleeps on the banana-colored couch with black piping. I get the black one with yellow piping. When I

admired her huge painting, she replied, "Mexican artist Orozco painted *Zapatistas* to honor the memory of Mexican Revolution leader Emiliano Zapata."

I said, "The white frame with gray streaks is beautiful."

She replied, "Thanks! Its convex shape makes the inexpensive print look special. 'It's better to die on your feet than to live on your knees,' was Zapata's motto."

I answered, "I understand feeling that way." I miss you two and hope to see you soon!
Love, Angela

Tuesday, July 8, 1958: NYC
After I packed boxes all morning, Aunt Sara said, "Angela, you've done a lot. Lila is on the phone, inviting you to visit." Ron came and took me by bus to his East 70th Street apartment. We had a good talk about our crushes and sent a birthday card to Gil at his summer home. It was fun to buy a light blue skirt, size 22 waist, with Aunt Lila.

Thursday, July 10, 1958: Dreamboat and Puerto Rican
Aunt Sara, Ron, and I saw the Statue of Liberty on our boat ride around Manhattan Island. Back at Aunt Sara's musicians' building, a real doll was standing not far from a motorcycle. Around eighteen with blondish, curly hair, he wore a tight, striped gondolier T-shirt and black slacks. Walking around the motorcycle, Aunt Sara said to me, "Isn't it cute?" I nodded, smiled, and saw the doll beaming at us with his knockout smile.

Upstairs, Aunt Sara agreed when I said, "Any girl would go for him." Leaving for dinner, we ran into him again! In the coffee shop where we had cheeseburgers, a cute Puerto Rican waiter looked at me whenever he walked by. After we smiled at each other, I felt grown-up that a man who looks at least eighteen paid attention to me.

Aunt Sara said, "Many restaurant workers are Puerto Rican."

I commented, "I never see Puerto Ricans in Albany."

She said, "Thanks to your efforts, most of the packing is done. I'm concerned about Ludwig, who's too big to take to Albany and too special to sell." When we returned, the dreamboat was getting on his motorcycle! My aunt, a conversation whiz, spoke to him while I shyly stood back and smiled at him.

He said, "I take voice lessons in the building." My face felt hot when he smiled at me. Older, handsome guys make me tongue-tied. Aunt Sara is so much fun.

Friday, July 11, 1958: FDR
Aunt Sara took me to the most moving play I've ever seen in my life: *Sunrise at Campobello*, the Broadway show at Cort Theatre. Watching Ralph Bellamy in the lead, I learned about FDR's early life, his strong mother and wife, and his paralysis. Aunt Sara said, "I loved FDR. As President, he saved our country during the Depression."

Saturday, July 12, 1958: Coney Island
Aunt Sara said, "I'm relieved! My friend will babysit Ludwig."

I replied, "I'm glad that you don't have to sell your piano!"

She said, "Angela, you've been a big help. I'll put the unsold things in storage. Have fun at Coney Island!" Uncle Bert, Ron, and I enjoyed the beach and Skee-Ball in the arcade. Loads of people walked on the boardwalk and swam in the ocean!

Sunday, July 13, 1958: Hail and Tumba
Mom called. "Yesterday at 1 p.m. and 4 p.m., hail bigger than marbles hit Albany briefly." I'm glad we missed getting bopped on the head.

Back in Albany tonight, Tumba seemed to say, "I love you," more than usual after flying around and landing on our shoulders.

Monday, July 14, 1958: Anonymous
I told Aunt Sara, "The trip made me feel grown-up. If I had kissed a boy on a boat ride here, Albany gossips would tell everyone."

She said, "Except in my neighborhood stores, I was anonymous in NYC."

I replied, "Maybe I'll move there after I graduate. NYC has so much to do." I wrote seven letters about my exciting trip. At the Center after dancing with Lewis, Frankie, and another boy, I felt less let down to be home.

Friday, July 18, 1958: Bargain and Painting
I listened to hit songs on my $36.35 (one-third off) GE transistor radio in black, gold, and red. Painting a watercolor of a beauty contest let me design fourteen swimsuits.

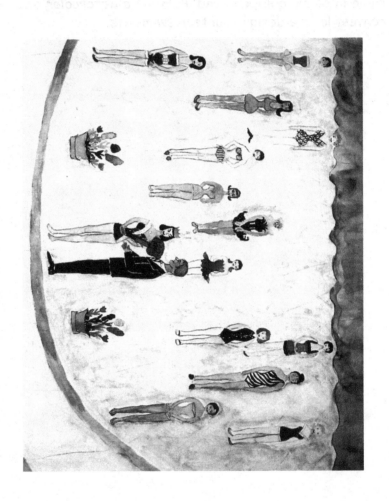

Angela's colorful designs

Sunday, July 20, 1958: Catskills

I sent Aunt Sara a postcard:

Young's Gap is a fabulous resort. The green lawns, white buildings, and large pool remind me of country club pictures. After a delicious dinner in the big dining room with our families, we teenagers met in the basement. Imitating you, I bravely talked to a tall, dark doll, a junior from Queens. In the nightclub, we danced once and sat together. Donald, who wants to be a writer, is marvelous: intelligent, handsome, and funny.

Monday, July 21, 1958: Donald

In my white suit, I swam with Donald, who has a good physique and dresses well. Basketball with his friend and their fathers, ping-pong, and volleyball with other teens were fun. In the nightclub at a long table, we teens drank cocktails. My Singapore sling without liquor was tasty. The top-notch NYC singers and comedians, whose names I've forgotten, seemed good enough for the Ed Sullivan TV show! Dad said, "What a bargain: the same meals, entertainment, and activities at only fifty-two dollars a week per person, half the price of newer rooms!"

Tuesday, July 22, 1958: Variety

Picturing Aunt Sara, I ignored feeling nervous with older NYC sophisticates and made myself talk to new boys, including a tall, blond college boy who's seventeen! I sent Sara a card:

I love it here! Near the teen room, a girl and I talked to a cute Brooklyn guy. We all jitterbugged and played ping-pong and checkers to a draw. In the main building, none of us got three identical pictures for nickel slot machine prizes. I really like fourteen-year-old Donald, who is witty and likes the *New Yorker*.

I had fun until feeling let down when Mr. Brooklyn looked away, said less, and seemed bored. He was with an older girl tonight. While it rained, I enjoyed ping-pong with Donald and read my novel when he wanted to read *Bleak House* by Dickens.

Wednesday, July 23, 1958: Jackpot

I hung around Mr. Brooklyn, who talks to me only if no one older and better is around. While Donald picked up his older brother, I wrote Doreen a card:

> We all love it here! I'm playing ping-pong and shuffleboard and swimming in the pool. When we teens gathered on the front porch, I talked with a cute boy, who sits nearby in the dining room, and three boys from another hotel. I danced twice with one, who's fifteen. I got annoyed when NYC boys called Albany a hick town! The singers and comedians were good. Flirting with six boys today felt like hitting the jackpot, including my favorite, Donald!

Thursday, July 24, 1958: Castle

I wrote Tara:

> Like ducklings behind their mother, we teens followed our leader down a country road to a high, fancy iron gate. Inside, we hiked up the winding driveway, shaded by evergreens, and through a meadow to stone Craig-E-Clare at the edge of a mountaintop. The view of higher mountains and a river below was stunning. Rich Mr. Dundas built Dundas Castle for his wife, who went crazy before it was finished. Sadly, he died in 1921, without ever living there. Though kids joked, "It's haunted," I don't believe in ghosts.

Back at the pool, I took dips and got up my courage to say hello to new boys. None seemed interested in me. Donald and I played ping-pong before and danced after the funny game night show. All the boys here are living dolls. Except for Mr. Brooklyn, who greets me, the older ones ignore me. Only younger boys are interested, like Rich, fourteen and pretty cute.

Friday, July 25, 1958: Sports and Books

Avoiding swimming because of my period, I enjoyed volleyball with teens, basketball with Rich, tennis with his father while Rich changed, golf as a tournament spectator, and shuffleboard with new boys, none spectacular. Cute Donald and I danced and watched the dance contest. He asked, "What's the best book you've read?"

I answered, "I love novels, but Anne Frank's diary is my favorite book."

He said, "I keep a journal. Do you?"

He laughed after I looked into his eyes, smiled, and replied, "Maybe."

Saturday, July 26, 1958: Music
My volleyball team got beanies for winning! I won once at shuffleboard and shot baskets. At the pool, I took candid pictures of boys and talked to new boys. I wore my best evening dress to the lawn sing-along for teens. Rich and Donald took my address and escorted me into the nightclub. Being the only girl with five boys was exciting. One boy had us in stitches. Donald and I watched the nightclub entertainment and danced. After he bought me a malted milk, we spent our last night together talking until late. He said, "I'll be glad to listen to Beethoven symphonies again when I get home."

Curious, I asked, "Which is your favorite?"

"I like the *Fifth* the most, followed by the *Ninth*. Of course, the *Eroica* is superb!" He's such an interesting talker that I paid attention to his detailed description of the music.

"You'd make a good teacher!"

After a charming laugh, he said, "I might have to work as an English professor if my novels don't sell."

He smiled when I responded, "For variety, you can teach music appreciation. My favorite aunt, who has written classical music books, used to teach music." When he showed interest, I mentioned Aunt Sara's Haiti trip and one-woman shows.

Sunday, July 27, 1958: Sweet Sorrow
Donald and his dad visited our room to say good-bye to my family. I was disappointed never to kiss Donald. What would it take for him to kiss? I hope he writes as promised. His address is 97-37 63rd Road, Rego Park 74, NY, and his phone is TW6-2563. The teen leaders kissed me good-bye. We teen girls cried or were choked up. As we drove home through the nearby village

of Liberty, Dad said, "That was some vacation, especially the nightclub entertainment!"

I said, "I had fun with teens every day. May we please come back?" I'm sad to leave heaven and relieved that I wasn't a wallflower with younger boys.

Monday, July 28, 1958: Crying
Missing Donald and emotional from my period, I cried secretly in the bathroom. At the Center, dancing with Frankie and kidding with him and others cheered me up. Frankie and a pal took me to the Albany Waldorf Cafeteria (opposite of the fancy NYC Waldorf) for a snack and walked me home.

Tuesday, July 29, 1958: No Letter
Aunt Sara and I are in the same boat, hoping for letters from Mort and Donald. We felt better after a good movie: *Indiscreet* with Ingrid Bergman. On the bus home, three cute boys stared at me. When they left and one waved at me, I enjoyed waving back.

Saturday, August 2, 1958: On Top Of The World
I got a sweet letter from Donald! Does "Very truly yours" mean that he's my boyfriend? Looking at my Young's Gap snapshots of Donald, Aunt Sara smiled and agreed that he's a doll!

Sunday, August 3, 1958: *The Brain*
Driving the half hour to Thatcher Park, Mom said:
> The NY State Director of Psychological Services complimented me. "We're lucky to have a Secretary who earned a Merit Award." My two new bosses love *The Brain,* my two-act play explaining my master filing chart with the same name.

Why did she call it *The Brain?* I'm afraid she got it from my diary. At the synagogue picnic, Myles and I were together all day, dunking, swimming, holding hands, and laughing with others. I liked his arm around me. On the way home, Mom continued:
> Working for three directors, who supervise professionals in state mental hospitals and schools, is never boring.

Reading the files, I wish I were an occupational therapist
or psychologist.
Figuring out people is fun. What's occupational therapy?

Monday, August 4, 1958: Damn Mom
At the Babe Ruth League baseball diamond, Will was playing. I'm
finally over him. Damn Mom made me stay home from tonight's
dance without any reason. Even Aunt Sara couldn't change her
mind.

Thursday, August 7, 1958: Sheath and Heels
Mom said, "Grandma's hundred dollars a month for Sara's rent
helped pay for your Singer teen sewing course."

During class, I thanked Doreen after she said, "I like your
flower-printed polished cotton sheath in orange and brown. The
brown gathered overskirt adds another look." We saw a good
movie: *Light in the Forest* with pretty Carol Lynley from *Blue
Denim*.

Afterwards, I mentioned my new shoes. "I love the three-
quarter-inch black heels with bows above the pointed toes.
They're size 7AA with super narrow AAAA heels to keep them on."

Saturday, August 9, 1958: Champagne Kissing Dances
Ten of us, including Cousin Ron, had fun at my party, including
hot dogs, a scavenger hunt, dancing, Spin the Bottle, and other
kissing games! I danced with various boys, including Myles for
the champagne kissing dances. Ron said, "Everyone had a good
time!" He has crushes on Doreen, Tara, and Marsha.

Sunday, August 17, 1958: Thrills
In NYC, Donald took me to and from Radio City Music Hall in
cabs! I loved the Rockettes, dancing and kicking high in glamorous
costumes. *The Reluctant Debutante*, a movie with John Saxon,
Sandra Dee, Rex Harrison, and Kay Kendall, was a riot. After
juicy hamburgers at a fancy place, we talked on the couch at
Aunt Lila's. He asked, "Do you enjoy classical music?"

I replied, "When Mom and I clean the house Saturdays, we listen to the Metropolitan Opera on the radio. I like singing, including operas."

Smiling, he kept all four vacation photos and said, "I'll try to visit you." I wondered how a kiss would feel. I wore my best white dress at Aunt Rhoda's and Uncle Harvey's twenty-fifth anniversary party with a delicious catered dinner. I fell for Uncle Harvey's fourteen-year-old blond cousin from Vineland, New Jersey! Joe wore a cool red sports jacket and is six foot with cute freckles and hazel eyes. He has perfect manners and is a sophomore.

Describing his interests, he said, "I collect rare foreign stamps and play basketball, baseball, and football. I can't wait to get my license and drive our 1958 Cadillac." I was in heaven dancing the jitterbug, fox-trot, and cha cha to live music with this excellent dancer! He and Ron cut in often and fought to pull out my chair. As the only girl, I felt like a princess! Today was perfect!

Wednesday, August 27, 1958: Love and Kissing
It seems like a month since the party. Joe's letter, signed "Love," made me happy. I answered, "With Love." Donald's recent "Very truly yours" seemed less romantic. I picked new reading eyeglass frames and finished my dress in sewing class. Aunt Sara asked whether I had fun at a friend's party. Grinning, I reported:
> We danced and played every kissing game we know! I kissed five boys, including fast, funny Mitch and smooth Wolf. My kisses were pecks because they aren't boyfriends and we aren't in love. Myles, whom I kissed the most, walked me home. Rob walked Tara. I understand why she still prefers Ben.

Saturday, August 30, 1958: Letters
I had forgotten about a Catskill couple's taking my address for their son. His nice letter said that he is fifteen and five foot ten, weighs 165, and loves being a rock-and-roll DJ (disc jockey). He's been at camp, where he edits the newspaper. Donald sent

a terrific short story! After reading it, Aunt Sara said, "He's a talented writer. I see why you consider him special."

Monday, September 1, 1958: Family Reunion
Tonight, I wrote to Lydia and Ella:

Yesterday, we drove to Mohegan Lake, a summer cottage resort north of NYC. We saw Grandpa's brother, over ninety, and the families of six of his kids. Some of his grandkids are around our ages. I enjoyed boy watching at the pool and a jam session with cute musicians on the accordion and drums. I laughed and whispered to Aunt Sara, "The drummer sounds like Dad tapping silverware on the dinner table."

She replied, "Your dad's trio played at weddings and Bar Mitzvahs until transporting drums on the NYC subway became too difficult." Back at our hotel after a concert, Aunt Sara and I talked to a lifeguard and a counselor, both nineteen and adorable. Today, we talked to the lifeguard and swam with a tall, dark, handsome Manhattan junior and a cute Bronx freshman. At our cousins' colony, the same good-looking musicians jammed.

On the drive home, Mom mentioned our second cousin, Rita. "Living near Vilna in Eastern Europe, Rita, at age twelve, saw the Nazis shoot her parents and two brothers in their home during World War II. After Rita escaped, kind non-Jews hid her until 1945. In the US, Mom's cousin took her in and helped her finish college and become an artist." Hearing what she'd been through made me cry. I didn't get all the cousins straight, but the weekend was terrific. It would have been even more fun with you two there!

Tuesday, September 2, 1958: Kisses and Nerves
Marsha's party included kissing games. I broke off Myles' long kisses. He walked me home and kissed me goodnight. Of the boys there, he was the best. I can't love a boy who will neck with any girl. After feeling trapped with Edwin and Ray, I'm avoiding going with one boy. At home, while putting away my new red print wool

dress, size 7, and black wool Bermudas, I felt excited about starting ninth grade and nervous about finding my homeroom. Hackett Junior High is twice as far away.

Wednesday, September 3, 1958: First Day

I walked a mile to school past Albany Hospital grounds on the right and two- and one-family houses on the left. At dinner, when asked about my teachers, I said:

> Mrs. C for science is young and pretty. We're sorry our first male teacher, young Mr. P for cit ed, is married. He's six foot five and makes us laugh. Nice, grandmotherly Miss W teaches English, Latin, and homeroom, which has the smartest kids from Albany elementary schools.

I loved seeing Paul from fourth grade! Artie's in my classes! If funny Hank, manly Luke, and other smart kids top my grades, I can stop hiding mine to have dates.

Paul

Saturday, September 6, 1958: Money and Hits

While I babysat for Myles' sweet, blue-eyed sister, he arrived home early, talked, and walked me home after his parents returned. Dad will put the fifty cents an hour I made into my college account. What a cool surprise! My DJ pen pal sent these great hit records: *For Your Precious Love, Good Golly Miss Molly, La Bamba, Purple People Eater*, and *All I Want to Do Is Dream*.

Tuesday, September 9, 1958: Steve

Steve, one of many smart boys in my homeroom, has been talking to me, including making me laugh. He has light brown curly hair and craggy features. He seems strong and is about five foot eight. When I asked what he wants to be, he said, "I love animals and want to be a veterinarian."

I replied, "Just like Marsha. She has a cat."

He answered, "We've always had dogs, my favorites."

I joked, "Can I be your pet?"

He laughed. "Here's your leash!"

Friday, September 12, 1958: Fourteen Crushes

Aunt Sara laughed when I said:

I have crushes on three pen pals, Myles, Luke, and Hank (who ate lunch with me), and eight other homeroom boys. Doreen, Tara, Marsha, and I had fun walking home with four of them.

Though my period arrived, I was in a good mood, thanking my DJ pen pal for another box of pop records, including favorites like *Witch Doctor, Chantilly Lace, Twilight Time,* and *Jailhouse Rock*! I enjoyed Joe's letter about his school clubs and sports this year.

Saturday, September 13, 1958: Architect

How did Rob and then Myles find Tara and me on our walk? When Myles called later for a flimsy reason, I was happy because he seldom phones. Excited about starting AHS, Myles said, "I like geometry, which will help me as an architect."

Monday, September 15, 1958: M&M Candy

Sara, on a writing break, chuckled while listening to my description:

Escaping from hours of boring Jewish New Year synagogue services, our teen herd stopped for free sodas at Mitch's parents' grocery during a long walk. I felt happy, holding Myles' hand with his arm around me in my red chemise and later in Bermuda shorts at Washington Park. Fifteen of us played tennis! Wearing my quilted plaid skirt with black tights at a fun dance party, I laughed after secretly nicknaming Myles and Mitch after the candy: M&M. I let Myles kiss me once while dancing and couldn't resist Mitch's dance dips, twirls, and turns! M&M walked Doreen and me home.

Wednesday, September 17, 1958: To Lydia

I answered Lydia's letter:

I'm glad you're enjoying junior high! Enclosed is a magic potion to make your male classmates grow taller than you. Latin helps with English words and lets me get to know smart boys, including Luke with an ideal physique. School would be fun if I could forget homework and tests and spend all my time flirting. Brown-eyed, cute Craig made me laugh all day, including at lunch where he loaned me his notes. He's about five foot seven with freckles and a turned-up nose. While Steve talked to me at the bus stop, tall Myles stopped to talk on the way to visit past teachers. After Steve walked me almost home and left, Myles reappeared. After talking on the porch, we did homework inside. Our chaperone, Aunt Sara, made me happy by saying, "You're grown-up enough to drop 'Aunt.'" Love to you and Ella

Thursday, September 18, 1958: On the Spot

Steve, Frankie, and I enjoyed visiting Mrs. Bern and Mrs. Lewis at Patroon. After teasing me about boyfriends, Frankie annoyed me by saying, "Angela likes you best, Steve." I stopped talking to Frankie.

Friday, September 19, 1958: Kisses
When Sara asked about Mitch's party, I replied:

> Tara and smooth Wolf, Doreen and Mitch, and Myles and I talked, played kissing games, and danced. Except for Mitch's two kisses, I was with Myles, who kissed me goodnight. Am I more popular this year because my hair is longer?

Sara considers longer hair my best look.

Saturday, September 20, 1958: Mushy
M&M walked me to a party with Marsha, Doreen, and their dates. When we phoned radio station WPTR, I voted for *Nel Blu Dipinto Di Blu* for the Top Forty hit tunes. Its Italian words kept going through my head. In Latin, *volare* means to fly. Mitch's dancing, especially spins and dips, seemed to give me wings. He asked, "Do you like Myles as a boyfriend?"

Looking up at his glossy black pompadour, I replied, "Yes. But he's mushy, trying to kiss, when I'd rather dance or laugh."

Mitch said, "Don't I act mushy?"

I answered, "You act nice."

He said, "Oohh!"

He didn't reply when I asked, "Do you like someone as a girlfriend?" During Spin the Bottle and Apples, Peaches, Pears, and Plums, each pair left the living room to kiss in a dark bedroom. I got good kissers M&M a lot. Instead of pecking, I put all I had into each kiss to see what would happen. Even after a minute, nothing special occurred.

Monday, September 22, 1958: Five Boys
When Sara asked if I'd had a good day, I said:

> Yes! After an A plus on a Latin test, I got all thirty answers right in cit ed. Craig, Steve, and others made me laugh so much at lunch that I could hardly chew the bologna with mustard sandwich I'd made. I liked walking home with Steve and Luke, who has a sexy body and smooth personality. He shaves already, dresses well, wears glasses, and is almost six feet tall with dark coloring. For

the first time, Donald signed a letter, "Yours, Donald."

Is this more romantic than his usual "Very truly yours"? Sara responded that it's hard to say for sure.

Doreen called about the upcoming XEA (Greek Chi Epsilon Alpha) sorority pledge tea and also said, "I heard that Mitch likes you."

I replied, "I think that he's just flirting."

Tuesday, September 23, 1958: Mitch's Shoes
On our walk home in almost eighty-degree weather, I accepted Steve's invitation to Frankie's party. At evening synagogue services, we got tired of standing for the cantor's long chant of the Kol Nidre song, which started the Day of Atonement. I was fine with Myles being with Marsha. Mitch probably repeated my "mushy" remark. During a walk, Mitch, who knows Doreen likes him, said, "I don't like anyone as a girlfriend."

He smiled when I confessed, "Saturday, while blindfolded during Apples, Peaches, Pears, and Plums, I looked down, recognized your shoes, and chose you to kiss." Today's favorites are M&M, Steve, and Luke. Life's exciting!

Wednesday, September 24, 1958: Driving
Wearing my orange print dress, I fasted for Yom Kippur. At the synagogue, I couldn't remember any sins. Hours of prayers bored us kids. M&M and I walked and talked. Mitch, only fourteen, showed me how his father taught him to drive, but didn't start the car. I was happy that Mitch asked me to the movies! When a girl said, "Rob still likes you," I tried not to frown to avoid anything hurtful getting back to him.

Thursday, September 25, 1958: Steve
I enjoyed Steve's company in classes, at lunch, in study hall where we wrote notes, and on the walk home. I was happy that it was about eighty degrees and that he carried my coat!

Friday, September 26, 1958: Lola
Mitch, another couple, and I enjoyed *Damn Yankees*. Blond, gorgeous Tab Hunter was the lead actor. I loved Gwen Verdon's

red hair and the way she sang *Whatever Lola Wants, Lola Gets.* I liked Mitch's arm around me. In his kitchen, Mitch and his friend, clowning around, were a riot. When they mimicked and made fun of people, I was glad not to be the butt of their jokes. Mitch's three kisses were just right!

Saturday, September 27, 1958: Unmushy
For a party, I dressed sharp: pink shirt, charcoal Bermudas, pink knee sox, and black, bubble-toe saddle shoes. Mitch pecked me a few times, sat me on his lap, and asked, "How old do you have to be to go steady?"

I replied, "I don't believe in it."

He said, "You will." On the way home in the car while I was on his lap, he asked, "Am I acting too mushy?"

I said, "Just right."

He asked, "Who are your dates for the next two parties?"

I answered, "Rob and Steve."

He said, "Don't get too chummy. I'll call you." I like Mitch's attention without possessiveness.

Sunday, September 28, 1958: First Tea
When Sara asked about the DeWitt Clinton Hotel XEA sorority tea, I said:

> The pretty light blue room with navy carpet had a long side table covered with a white tablecloth, plates of sweets, and tea stuff. I think I did okay in my red wool dress, standing around and talking to different sorority members. Holding our cups and saucers, we drank bitter-tasting tea and ate little cakes and cookies! I'm glad I didn't have to take Dad, who would have gobbled up all the sweets. Mom's interrogating questions would have gotten me dropped from XEA.

Monday, September 29, 1958: *Sukkot* and Dancing
Sara said, "After writing alone in the house every day, I get vicarious enjoyment from hearing about your activities."

I asked, "Does vicarious mean secondhand? It sounds as if it has a Latin root."

Sara responded, "Secondhand or indirect is a good synonym."

"I'll look in my Latin dictionary. During a walk with M&M on a Sukkot synagogue service break, Mitch's coat kept me warm. In the Sukkot harvest hut, we ate raisins at the table as someone waved a lemon and palm leaf. Dried corn cobs in husks hung on the unpainted plywood walls. Marsha and Myles were among four couples at a party. Mitch and I had fun, eating pizza, talking, and dancing a lot! I loved his twirling turns and low dips with kisses." Sara laughs when I use my M&M nickname.

Tuesday, September 30, 1958: Tears

I confided in Sara:

Dancing with me at his party, Mitch said, "Someone said that you like me. I like you." When we rubbed noses, he almost kissed me. I felt good when he said, "Hey, Beautiful." Walking me home, Mitch and a pal made fun of my full apricot topper jacket. "It looks like a maternity dress." Mitch held my hand, but stared and laughed at me for three blocks. I got annoyed, so he said, "I'm sorry," and kissed my hand. When he dragged me along, I tripped and fell, cutting my wool slacks. Seeing my knee bleeding, he said, "I apologize." When they ridiculed my topper again, I couldn't help crying, but felt embarrassed. After my tears stopped, they were quiet.

At my house, I said, "Sorry for crying and all."

They said, "It's all right."

Mitch probably thinks I don't like him, but I do and hope he calls. I loved my topper. Now, I'll feel funny wearing it. My only good slacks are too ruined to fix and too expensive to replace.

Sara was sympathetic.

Wednesday, October 1, 1958: Yankees

Putting yesterday out of my mind, I answered Ron's letter:

Are you glad that Dad, Steve, and I are Yankee fans, like you? Braves fan Mitch must be happy about Milwaukee beating the Yankees in the first World Series game. I find baseball unexciting, except for cute players. Mickey

Mantle's my favorite! Steve was with me at school, walked me home, and talked on the porch for an hour. With attention from several boys, I'm never bored. I loved getting a letter from Donald and was happy that Luke called about homework and talked awhile. I called Myles for help with algebra. Sara and I laughed at Tumba saying to his mirror, "Tumba's the greatest." What's new in NYC? Love, Angela

Saturday, October 4, 1958: Why Not Both?
I've worried that Mitch has dropped me. Wearing my chemise, I greeted him and Steve at the synagogue party. Mitch asked, "Do you still like me?" After I nodded, he asked, "What about Steve?" I didn't answer. Frankie looked mad because I won't give up Mitch for Steve. I was happy being with Mitch and Steve and dancing with Myles.

Sunday, October 5, 1958: *A Certain Smile*
I told Sara about my lovely romantic novel. "In *A Certain Smile*, a French girl has a love affair with an older married man."

Sara smiled. "Did it include, 'My wife doesn't understand me,' a favorite line of cheating married men?"

I laughed. "Older unmarried boyfriends interest me. I love the romantic Johnny Mathis song *A Certain Smile*." My family admires handsome Johnny, Nat King Cole, Louis Armstrong, and Ella Fitzgerald. We get upset when people act prejudiced against Negroes.

Tuesday, October 7, 1958: Who's Boss?
After fun with M&M made synagogue services bearable on the last day of Sukkot, today is another Jewish holiday: *Simkhat Tora!* Frankie tried to find out whether I prefer Steve to Mitch. Walking home, Tara, three boys, and I acted real gone. (Sara likes this slang for crazy and carried away.) Mitch showed me an engraved medal: Mitch and Angela. "Shall I change it to loves?"

I smiled. "If you feel that way."

He said, "I think you're pretty," which was probably flattery. He put me on the spot: tact forced me to say that he's handsome.

He held my hand and put his arm around me. "At Frankie's party, don't get too friendly with Steve. Don't kiss him too long or sit too close."

I felt glad that Mitch likes me, but free to do as I please. It's exciting to play the field and get to know different boys. I said to Mitch, "Please tune my transistor to the hit songs."

He replied, "No! Who's boss?"

I answered, "You."

He responded, "Good." I like an outgoing boy who takes charge and isn't shy about speaking up about things. Saying good-bye, Mitch again mentioned Steve, without annoying me. I just smiled.

Wednesday, October 8, 1958: Tie and Love

On our porch, Steve, Frankie, and I cheered while hearing the Yanks tie the Braves in the World Series on my transistor! Tomorrow's the final game. On the phone, after inviting me to the ULP (Greek Upsilon Lambda Phi) fraternity party, Mitch asked, "Did you date other boys when you went with Myles?"

Taken aback, I stopped myself before blurting out: I never went with Myles. I wished I had known that Myles thought that we were going together. To avoid hurting Myles' feelings when Mitch repeats my answer, I finally said, "Why not?" Remembering that "Discretion is the better part of valor," I resisted the temptation to add, "Wasn't he making out with other girls?"

Mitch warned, "Don't get too friendly with Steve." I think he said, "Good-bye, dear." Am I falling in love for the fourth time? He discusses things better than other boys do. Mitch is fun and the best dancer!

Thursday, October 9, 1958: Attention

When Sara asked how I was doing, I replied:

Smiling with his eyes crinkled, handsome Paul looked into my eyes and said, "I remember when you were my fourth-grade girlfriend." He told me about his trip to his birthplace, Sicily. He's better than ever.

After Steve was with me all day and walked me home, Mitch arrived and said, "I like you first, second, third, fourth, fifth, one hundredth, and more. I saw you with

Steve. Didn't he carry your books?" After we discussed the Yankees winning the Series (Yay!), Mitch left. Frankie called for a long talk.

When Sara asked what Frankie wanted, I replied, "When he tries to find out my feelings about Steve and Mitch, I say only things I'd say in public. All this attention from two nice boys is wonderful. Mitch is slick, but I like his confidence."

Friday, October 10, 1958: Competition

After spending the school day with me, Steve walked me home carrying my books in lovely Indian summer weather of almost eighty! Frankie and Doreen were there when Mitch, on his bike, joined us. Mitch and Steve exchanged dirty looks. On our back porch, Mitch told Steve, "Angela likes you and not me." Though I've already accepted Mitch's invitation, Mitch asked Steve, "Why haven't you asked Angela to the dance?"

Steve said, "I'll get around to it." I'm always surprised about how boys compete.

Saturday, October 11, 1958: Tied

Tara laughed when I mentioned that Steve had pieced together my torn note to her. Fortunately, it contained nothing revealing. At Frankie's fun party, Steve kissed me five separate times really well! Frankie cracked me up, trying to kiss with his arm around me on the other side. I laughed at his algebra jokes. How many math words contain girls' underwear? I danced with and pecked Frankie and two others during kissing games. On the phone, Doreen giggled when I said, "Steve tried for a goodnight kiss as I opened the front door, causing him to miss. Mitch was first until I kissed Steve. They're tied."

I agreed when Doreen commented, "We're lucky to be invited to the second XEA sorority rush. I hope that no friends get dropped."

Sunday, October 12, 1958: Nomination

Sara and my parents raised their eyebrows when I said, "After being voted secretary of my homeroom and of the fifteen ninth-grade homerooms, I got nominated for president of Hackett, including grades seven and eight. I don't want to run." I told Sara, "I dislike giving speeches and probably would lose. Unlike being president last year, being secretary shouldn't hurt my social life."

Sara commented, "I understand. It's sad that women must hold themselves back to avoid threatening the fragile male ego." I've learned about ego from hearing Sara talk about the psychology book she's writing.

Monday, October 13, 1958: Playdium
Because Steve called for a bowling date first, I couldn't accept Mitch's movie invitation. Steve and Frankie took Doreen and me to the Playdium. Using the lightest ball and distracted by the cute pinsetter, I bowled sixty-five. My second score was the best of our group: ninety-four. Talking to Luke, Lon, and Hank from my homeroom as we bowled convinced me to decline the presidential nomination for a better chance to date these attractive, smart guys.

Tuesday, October 14, 1958: Declination
I told Miss W, "I appreciate the honor of being nominated for school president. I've decided to decline. I'm already ninth-grade secretary. I want to keep my grades up."

She replied, "Angela, in my thirty years here, no one has declined to run. You'd make a good president. If your parents agree, I'll let the principal know."

Nodding, I said, "Thank you," and felt relieved.

Thursday, October 16, 1958: Downtown
M&M, Rob, and I shopped. Mitch bought cool black boots. After we ate hot dogs at the Walgreen's counter, Mitch said, "I'll call after my camping trip." Alone, I found a blue print shirtwaist dress, size 8. I felt happy to run into and talk to Beth.

Later, I told Mom, "I wish we'd been invited to Beth's wedding."

Mom said, "As a widow, she probably kept it small."

I said, "I'd love to see Beth more."

Mom replied, "Married to a doctor and now an attorney, she socializes with country club professionals, not sales and clerical workers like us." Beth is twenty-six, a little older than Tara's sister.

Sunday, October 19, 1958: Veep and Pork

While Sara and I improved Tumba's manners by repeating "No, thanks," after his chirps of "No," I said:

I hope that being elected Young Judaea vice president doesn't keep boys from dating me. Mitch took me for a submarine sandwich. The pork in his sandwich was unappealing. Only half my friends keep kosher. I don't miss shrimp or other foods I haven't tried. At Washington Park, I was the only girl with M&M, Frankie, and seven other boys. After Tara and Wolf arrived, M&M, Rob, and I laughed even more on our front porch. I sat on Mitch's lap as he held my hand with his arm around me. His good-bye kiss had no taste of pork, which made me smile.

Monday, October 20, 1958: Mix-Up

Teachers' meetings ended school at noon! Mitch called to say, "I'll meet you at the library." Frankie, Tara, and I joked and laughed all the way to the library. Mitch wasn't there. Later, he called to ask, "Why weren't you there?" We laughed after learning we had gone to different libraries.

Wednesday, October 22, 1958: Pining and Competing

Sara and I laughed when Tumba said, "Mort," in between gibberish.

Sara joked, "Maybe Tumba and I can record an album to compete with Martha Schlamme's album with Mort."

I laughed and said, "I'm sympathetic after months of pining for Artie."

When Sara asked if anything amusing had occurred today, I said:

After Steve walked me home, M&M joined us for laughs. On the back porch after Mitch gave me a peck, Steve asked me to sit on his lap. When I did, Mitch put his arm around me. After Myles left, Steve and Mitch competed to outdo each other. No one owns me, so flirting with both was fun.

Thursday, October 23, 1958: Reply
I answered Lydia's letter:

At school, I weighed 107½ pounds. I was five foot four, the same as last year. Hearing your frustration about shorter boys, I'm happy at this height. Willpower is helping me stop nail biting for the first time. You're lucky not to get much homework. Every day, I rush to finish homework to have time for chores and talks with boys, friends, and Sara. I feel lucky that she lives here! It's great, but no surprise that you are getting all As! Because I need the best grades for college scholarships, I'm relieved to be one of six Hackett kids with an A in each subject on the first report card. The character ratings were all excellent. I hope I can keep it up. Love, Angela

Saturday, October 25, 1958: Heavenly
I answered Ron's newsy letter:

I'm glad that you and Gil had a fun double date! I've been having a ball! Dancing with six boys at the Center was one of the best times ever. Mitch complimented my new dress and was a heavenly partner. We ate pizza at Calsolero's. Playing the field, I enjoy romantic Mitch. Although Steve is a better student, I'm sad that he's starting to repeat himself, like Edwin and Ray. At synagogue services yesterday, I kidded with Frankie, Rob, and Myles! Frankie and I, in silly moods, had arms around shoulders. It's a dream come true to enjoy more than one boy I like. Have you told Gil that his deadline for moving to Albany is Hanukkah 1958? Ha! Ha! Love, Angela

Monday, October 27, 1958: Greek and Party
At the sorority meeting, we freshmen got red XEA pledge ribbons to wear. We're learning the Greek alphabet. I want to be a full member next spring. When Doreen asked about Earl's party yesterday, I said:

Hackett kids, mostly from Mohican School, were there. Wearing my favorite red taffeta, I danced with Artie. During kissing games, his brief kiss was good, but the earth didn't shake.

Doreen laughed and asked what else happened. I said:

After kissing in a game, husband Tad and I laughed about our 1950 wedding. I'm glad he's in my class.

Friday, October 31, 1958: Sal

I answered Lydia's letter:

I hope you had fun on Halloween. My costume at school was Levi's. Without needing to speak as a candidate for president, I had fun at the political rally. With all the attractive Italian boys at your school, you might be interested in my new Italian crush, Sal, honor roll veep of his homeroom. He's about five foot eight with dark hair, brown eyes, gorgeous teeth, and a winning smile. He walked me to my homeroom and talked to me after school. I said, "I look awful with lipstick on my cheeks from the political rally."

I was happy that he replied, "You look pretty good. How about coming to the big football game with me next week?"

"I'd love to!"

Later, Frankie said, "Sal once said that you have a cute figure." At school, I'm always glad to run into my first Italian boyfriend, Paul, more charming than ever! I can't wait to see you on Thanksgiving! Love to you and Ella!

Saturday, November 1, 1958: Movies and Party

On an average double date with classmates, I saw these movies: *The Defiant Ones* about a Negro and a white prisoner chained together and *Careless Years* about a teen couple. Doreen loved her fourteenth birthday surprise party. She deserved all the attention. She's one in a million as a friend! It was terrific jitterbugging with M&M and dancing with two boys, who fought to dance with me. During kissing games, M&M, Frankie, and others kissed me.

Monday, November 3, 1958: Cut-Ins, Sal, and Order

After sorority, I brought Sara up to date:

Young Judaea yesterday was fun with pecks from Mitch and cut-ins while dancing with M&M and others. Two overweight boys, who are okay as pals, walked Tara and me home. Today, handsome Sal waved between classes; got my address and number from Frankie, who walked me home; and called before sorority. Myles got a sorority sister to order me to kiss him, which was fun!

Tuesday, November 4, 1958: Game

The AHS vs. CBA game with Sal was thrilling, though AHS lost. M&M didn't say hello when Sal's arm was around me. My sorority order was to get a nickel from four cute CBA boys! Sitting on one's lap, I flirted by asking, "Will you marry me?" When Mitch called to apologize, I said, "Sal bought my ticket."

He answered, "I shouldn't have ignored you when I didn't invite you." I admire a boy who apologizes. I'm glad we made up. I like Mitch and think about dreamboat Sal constantly!

Thursday, November 6, 1958: Steve, Mitch, and Sal

Recent boredom caused me to politely decline Steve's dance invite. I was happy to accept Mitch's invitation to the dance. I'm in a good mood after talking to Sal at school and during his call. When he said that he wants to be an engineer, I said, "I don't know what an engineer does."

He responded, "Neither do I, but it sounds good."

I laughed and said, "I always see you with your cousin."

I chuckled when Sal said, "I don't know why, but he wants to be a cop."

"What should he do instead?"

I giggled, hearing, "Something safer so we can drink beer in our rocking chairs at age ninety."

Friday, November 7, 1958: Socializing

Walking me to classes, darling Sal, whom I've known a week, said, "I might call this weekend." I felt excited.

Luke asked, "Have you been invited to the ABG (Alpha Beta Gamma) fraternity dance?"

Hoping Luke would ask me, I said no.

He said, "You will." He wouldn't name the boy. After Frankie walked me home, I took a walk with Myles.

Sunday, November 9, 1958: Canasta

My parents, Sara, and I laughed during canasta, our favorite card game. Using two full decks, we each laid out as many canastas of seven cards as possible.

Right after Mom picked up a huge discard pack to use for several canastas, Tumba made us laugh by saying, "Oh, no!" We laughed again when he repeated it after Mom won.

Monday, November 10, 1958: Good for a Girl

At the Center, M&M and Frankie danced with me. When Doreen slept over, I said, "Guess what that guy said when we played ping-pong."

She replied, "You're good for a girl."

Laughing, I asked, "How did you know?"

Doreen answered, "He irritated me with that backhanded compliment when I played with him." We giggled awhile before she said, "Sal is really cute."

I replied, "Why do boys wait until the last minute? Yesterday, Sal called about visiting that day and going to a CBA dance tonight. I had to say, 'Thank you for asking. I wish I could say yes. As a pledge, I can't miss sorority without being dropped for good. Today, after homework, I have family plans.'"

"I prefer respectful to conceited boys. Last-minute invites suggest that we have nothing better to do than await their calls."

Nodding and chuckling, I answered, "Your opinions always make sense. You'll make a wonderful teacher!" Doreen is very sweet!

Wednesday, November 12, 1958: Sal and Mitch

I'm happy because Sal walked me to class and spoke to me outside school. He's so good-looking, especially when smiling, that I don't mind conversation lagging. When Mitch called and said, "I still like you," I felt glad.

Thursday, November 13, 1958: A Plus
On the yellow cover of my *Teaching as a Career* paper, I like the magazine photo of sixth-grade kids at classroom desks. Inside, I included:
> Teachers are at least twenty and no older than eighty
> years old.

Mr. P wrote:
> I don't believe there are many eighty-year-olds teaching.
> Seventy is the maximum in our state.

He liked my magazine cartoon of one kid saying to another, "Considering Mr. Heath is a teacher, he's pretty human." After spending many hours typing fourteen pages, the longest thing I've written, on Mom's portable typewriter, I was thrilled to read:
> Your paper has a fast-moving, breezy style. I enjoy reading
> this kind of paper. You have answered the question "What
> I need to be a teacher" excellently. I can find no technical
> mistakes in your paper. To sum up, you have done an
> excellent job.

Choosing a familiar occupation made it easier.

Saturday, November 15, 1958: Frankie
When Frankie walked me home yesterday, he said, "Sal is after a blonde he met at a CBA dance."

I replied, "I'm not surprised. He's stopped coming around. We had little in common, so it's okay."

Frankie said, "Let's go to the Center dance tomorrow."

I smiled and said sure. Wearing my red dress and new underwear (32A bra, girdle in size small, and red tights), I danced with him and Mitch tonight.

Frankie mentioned, "I'm thinking about being a lawyer."

I said, "You talk well. You'll be good at it." When he glanced at me to see if I was teasing, I couldn't help giggling. The ideal boy combines Frankie's brains, blue eyes, and interesting conversation with Mitch's dancing and romantic, fun, direct personality.

Tuesday, November 18, 1958: Married

Sara mentioned, "At Parents' Night with your mom and dad, a teacher flirted with me."

I asked, "Mr. P?"

She replied, "I declined the movie invite of Mr. B, a light-skinned Negro wearing a wedding ring."

I said, "His poor wife. I'm glad you discouraged that wolf." Men go for Sara, but the synagogue has only one single man: an unmasculine Holocaust survivor, who may prefer men. His tattooed arm saddens me.

Saturday, November 22, 1958: Boredom

At the beauty parlor, I got a permanent. My hair looks better wavier. Downtown, I bought a slip, French purse, and Hanukkah presents for friends. Not much is happening socially, except for Mitch's calls.

I asked Sara, "Why do things always seem more exciting in the beginning with boys?"

Sara asked, "Could eventual boredom mean he isn't the right boy for you?"

I answered, "Probably."

She said, "Someone who keeps you interested will come along."

I said, "I love talking to you. You know everything about boys."

She laughed and said, "Then how come Mort has lost interest in me?"

Sunday, November 23, 1958: Unappreciated

Ugh! Instead of thanks for all the chores I do, I got criticism at the family meeting, as usual. Mom said, "On November 17th, I went to your room with two plates with food stuck on after you washed them. You said, 'I'll clean them after I finish algebra homework.' On Tuesday, I reminded you again to rewash them. I'm working full time with too much to do. Do your chores right the first time." Then Mom complained, "Herm, the sink has leaked for three months. Let's call a plumber."

Dad answered, "Fern, we can't afford one. I'll take care of it."

Mom asked, "When?" Dad blew up, yelling at everyone. I escaped to my room. I hate these meetings. I want to dia-write (*sic*) only about good things, like boys.

Monday, November 24, 1958: Broken
The ugly meeting caused bad dreams. I don't know whether friends' mothers nag and fathers yell because we'd rather talk about fun things. Dad's from NYC where apartment building "supers" fix everything. Our dishwasher hasn't worked for years, but dishwashing beats ironing, dusting, vacuuming, laundry, and weeding. I don't miss TV.

Thursday, November 27, 1958: Embarrassed and Thankful
Mom drove us to Gloversville for Thanksgiving. I'm embarrassed that Dad's the only father I know who drives worse than his wife. My cousins and I had fun with Sara, whom we all adore! I thanked Aunt Myrna, an excellent cook, and said, "I loved the turkey, dressing, and green apple pie!" I'm thankful: my braces are finally off! I don't mind wearing a night retainer. Smiling with my teeth showing helps with boys.

Friday, November 28, 1958: A Boy Tried
In a terrif (*sic*) movie musical, *Mardi Gras*, singers Pat Boone and Tommy Sands played military cadets who sold raffle tickets for money to visit New Orleans. Christine Carere was good as the homecoming queen. Tara and I laughed after I said, "I can't believe that, during the movie, a cute boy I don't know sat next to me and tried to make out! What nerve! Of course, I moved far away."

Tuesday, December 2, 1958: Hospitalized
I'm sad because our white-haired, sweet homeroom, English, and Latin teacher is in Albany Hospital. Although Miss W has wrinkles and old-fashioned dresses, she makes Latin fun. We can't find out what's wrong. It must be bad: she'll be gone for three months! We kids made and signed a big card of colored paper. Walking to the hospital to deliver the card, Craig cracked fewer jokes because we're worried that Miss W might not come

back. He said, "When I grow up, I want to be a lawyer who helps people, rather than makes money." We were stopped at the doorway of Miss W's room. When the nurse gave Miss W our card and we waved, Miss W smiled and waved from her bed. Seeing cute boys at the hospital cheered me a little.

Craig

Saturday, December 6, 1958: Hank and Artie

My straight-A report card surprised me. Many classmates seem smarter. Hank has finished tons of history, science, and philosophy books. Up late reading every night, he wants to be an astrophysicist. He said, "It relates to astronomy." I flirt with him and wish he'd ask me out. Wearing my new peach Banlon cardigan in size 32 and gray-and-white-plaid pleated skirt at the Center dance, I enjoyed dancing twice with Artie. I can't help liking him. In the gym, I had a ball flirting and shooting baskets with a cute athletic guy. He took my name. I love muscular bodies in skimpy basketball uniforms.

Friday, December 12, 1958: Hanukkah

When I gave Mom the muffler I knitted in her favorite color, purple, she said, "I don't want your presents. All I want is a good daughter," as if I'm bad. I said nothing, but felt let down after spending so much time making it to please her. With mean Mom disliking me, I'm thankful to be loved by Sara. She and I combined our money to buy Dad a blue-and-gray tie. Doreen and I exchanged presents. I love her gift: a gray rabbit fur collar in the latest Peter Pan style! I can't wait to feel the soft, silky fur warming my neck. Sitting with Mitch at synagogue services was fun. Since he calls only every few days, I'm not bored. We joke around and have enough things to say. I enjoyed the new dance step we tried Sunday at Young Judaea.

Saturday, December 13, 1958: Norwegian

At Julia's party, I felt lucky being with funny Craig, one of the best dancers I've met and the best of five kissers during kissing games. I laughed a lot with other intelligent classmates, like well-read Eva, whose personality is wonderful. During a rare serious moment, I mentioned our current English class book. "Do you like *Giants in the Earth?*"

Eva replied, "We must be reading *Giants* to learn about the American immigrant experience. My first choice of a novel written in Norwegian by someone born in Norway is *Kristin Lavransdatter* by a woman who won the Nobel Prize."

"Eva, thanks for the *Kristin* tip! I'm always looking for good novels."

Thursday, December 18, 1958: Card and Dances

We made a big Christmas card for Miss W. I hope the hospital lets relatives and friends visit her. During our homeroom party, I was glad to dance with Craig and Artie! I loved that girls got to ask boys to dance! I picked two boys I want to date. At the school dance, my partners were Craig and a new boy. December is fun with parties and presents. I thanked Aunt Rhoda and Uncle Harvey for five dollars!

Monday, December 22, 1958: Thanks

Dear Lydia and Ella,

Thank you very much for the pretty wool pullover in pink, one of my favorite colors! I wore it with a pleated skirt to the Center dance. I danced mainly with Frankie and Mitch, who took me to the Boulevard for chocolate milk and French fries. I love romantic missile toe (*sic*), even though it's a Christmas thing. At Young Judaea, boys waved the twigs with berries over our heads for kisses. Mitch's two kisses were the best. Myles and Rob also missile toed (*sic*) me. I'm so glad to be off school! Doreen and I saw *Tale of Two Cities*, a good black-and-white movie about the French Revolution. We went for handsome Dirk Bogarde and enjoyed the English accents. Thank you again for the great Hanukkah gift! Have a fun vacation! Love, Angela

Tuesday, December 23, 1958: Terrific Movies

At the end of romantic, sad *An Affair to Remember*, I couldn't stop crying. Handsome, charming Cary Grant is a favorite actor. Deborah Kerr was wonderful. I'd love to slow dance with Mitch to the title song from the movie. In *Left Hand of God,* Humphrey Bogart fell in love with pretty Gene Tierney. I'd like to look like her, including her light-colored eyes!

Saturday, December 27, 1958: Mr. Oneonta

Kids from other cities are visiting for the Young Judaea convention! I thought I had no chance with a good-looking, charming boy from Oneonta, fifty miles away. He dresses nicely and has dirty-blond, curly hair. About five foot six, he was in my discussion group. Sitting opposite, I gave him flirtatious smiles. After he talked to me, I got next to him in an Israeli folk dance. At the evening party, I danced mostly with him. He's the rare boy who can jitterbug! He and I went with Frankie and Doreen to the Boulevard for French fries, chocolate milk, and hamburgers. In the car, I was glad I had to sit on Mr. Oneonta's lap. When we sang, I noticed his good voice. My parents, the chaperones, let four couples dance at our house to my radio. Doreen slept over. We were so excited that we talked all night about the convention and this exciting boy!

Sunday, December 28, 1958: Idiot

After the Young Judaea meeting, the visitors left. I told Sara:
> My favorite boys are good at everything. Mr. Oneonta is fourteen; captain of the basketball, football, and baseball teams; and president of his freshman class and Young Judaea group. He gets top grades, plays three instruments, sings in the choir, and has good manners! I doubt that he'd bore me. Diagonally opposite at lunch, he said, "I'd write if I had your address." Instead of giving it to him, I idiotically said that a girl from his group had it.

Monday, December 29, 1958: Fun

Vacation's flying by too fast with only a week left. After fun with Mitch at the Center dance, I slept over at Doreen's. I said, "I'm enjoying a bunch of teen novels from the library, especially romances and mysteries. Do you agree that real lives are just as interesting?"

She nodded. "I liked reading a biography of Marie Curie, the scientist, from the school library. I don't need a novel's conflict and climax. I enjoy learning about real lives."

"I like biographies. I wish there were more diary books, like Anne Frank's."

<u>Wednesday, December 31, 1958: Mame</u>

My favorite aunt and I saw *Auntie Mame* about a wild woman who never worries about what people think. Sara thanked me after I said, "You're better than Mame! I'm luckier than her nephew. You make my life easier and happier. The parents listen to you." For their anniversary, I used a mix to bake a yellow cake.

Before their New Year's Eve dance, Dad asked Mom, "Remember dancing to Ella Fitzgerald at the Savoy in Harlem when we were courting?" They enjoy dancing as much as I.

Mitch called to say, "Happy New Year!"

Our recent repetitions paid off: Tumba chirped, "Happy New Year."

We laughed and started repeating, "Tumba's a good boy," and singing *Happy Birthday*.

1959

Thursday, January 1, 1959: Resolutions

Sara's New Year's resolution: finish the book in 1960. My parents want me to spend more time with them, instead of friends. I'd enjoy them if they praised my grades and all my housework and stopped criticizing and ganging up on me. They seem jealous of Sara, who gives compliments, keeps secrets, and treats me like an adult. Teachers like me and give good grades, but Mom acts as if she dislikes me.

Sunday, January 4, 1959: Lydia

Fun Lydia came to Young Judaea with me! At around five foot eight, she enjoyed dancing with taller Myles. I danced with him and Mitch. Lydia confided, "I like a boy in my class, but he hasn't asked me out."

I smiled. "Welcome to the club! Nothing happens when I flirt with several smart classmates. What else can a girl do?"

Monday, January 5, 1959: Alaska

I told Sara, "In cit ed, we learned that Alaska is now the forty-ninth state. Mrs. C said, 'Alaska now has daylight for only a few hours and is colder than Albany.' I won't be moving there when I grow up."

Wednesday, January 7, 1959: White

I'm fourteen today! I love my white gifts: extension phone, cardigan, and Perry Como vest. I got plaid wool pleated skirts in size 12 preteen: pink with orange and tan with green. I don't mind saving Grandma's ten dollars and Aunt Rhoda's and Uncle Harvey's five dollars for college. Mitch called to sing *Happy Birthday*. I stay interested because he avoids jealous comments and doesn't call too much. I chuckled when Tumba sort of sang, "Happy birthday to you."

Sunday, January 11, 1959: Bowling

Cousin Stu from Gloversville is six foot one, sixteen, and cute. Oren Levine, Stu, his date, and I bowled. Stu bowled 150! I wish I could invite a cousin to the XEA formal dance. I was happy to bowl ninety-two. Oren, who bowled 120, is also Stu's cousin, but unrelated to me.

Monday, January 12, 1959: XEA Date

While I bowled eighty-two, cute Mu Sigma fraternity guys bowled in the next lane. Getting up my nerve, I approached Artie, smiled, and said, "The XEA dance is coming up. I'd like to go with you." I'm thrilled that he smiled and accepted!! I've liked him almost two whole years.

Saturday, January 24, 1959: After Exams

Dear Diary, I've neglected you during exams. I'm relieved to get 97 percent to 99 percent on the four main tests. Cutting loose at the Center dance, I was lucky to dance with Artie! For ladies' choice, I chose a tall, thin, blue-eyed boy from homeroom. After Frankie and a pal danced with me, they took me to a fun party. I have my period.

Thursday, January 29, 1959: Bargain Days

After Tara described her gorgeous bargains, she was interested in my finds:

> I got a size 36 sweater, a Coty compact, boots, and a red poplin coat with white Orlon pile lining in size 10. I was lucky to find soft black leather Sandler oxfords in size 7AA/AAAA. For the XEA dance, Mom found a yellow net formal for five dollars. We cut it to ballerina length, so it looks in style. The prettier dresses were expensive.

Friday, January 30, 1959: Choir

I confided in Sara, "I never criticize the parents' off-key singing, because it's peaceful when they're gone for choir." They sent copies of their choir photo in The Times Union to all our relatives. It's National Jewish Music Month.

Monday, February 2, 1959: Semifinals

When Eva asked about my weekend, I said:

The Sherwood Swingout Dance Saturday night was marvelous. Because radio DJ Sherwood was master of ceremonies, loads of people paid to attend. It was a synagogue fundraiser. Craig and I reached the semifinals in a jitterbug contest! He bought me sodas. I danced a lot with six boys, including Artie. For ladies' choice, I danced with a cute boy. He took Doreen and me to the Boulevard. How was your weekend?

Chuckling about hers being unexciting, she mentioned finishing Thomas Mann's masterpiece, *The Magic Mountain*.

When I expressed curiosity, she said, "I related to the main character, also an only child with a chronic illness. I learned about European philosophy. I liked the hopeful idea that someone intelligent can use illness to become heathier and wiser. I understand why Mann won the Nobel Prize."

"It sounds interesting. I'll add it to my reading list."

Wednesday, February 4, 1959: Roses and Nerves

I told Sara:

I got these dyed yellow satin flats and yellow stockings for the XEA formal. I was happy when Artie asked, "What color dress will you wear?"

I smiled and replied, "Yellow."

He said, "I'm getting you roses. Do you prefer a wrist or regular corsage?

I beamed and answered, "Regular."

He said, "We're going to a house party before the formal." It's cool that Artie knows the sorority leader who's giving the party. Their parents are friends at their ritzier synagogue. I don't mind being poorer, but I'm jittery about going blank without anything to say. It's embarrassing. I'm not nervous with boys I don't care about or who already like me.

Sara asked if I ever plan a few questions to show interest. I replied, "Thank you! I'll try it. I'm excited enough to burst! I can't wait to go with Artie and maybe win him over as a boyfriend."

Saturday, February 7, 1959: XEA Dance

For the first time, a beauty parlor set my hair and did my nails! The polish is gold! I was thrilled seeing handsome Artie in a dark suit and red tie. I loved the corsage of six white roses. At the party, we drank punch and mingled before going to the Hampton Hotel ballroom with lovely balloon decorations. A local trio, The Humoresques, played good music. I danced with terrific Artie, marvelous dancer Rex, and Craig's pal. When I asked whether Artie has a hobby, he replied, "Amateur radio." He explained how he uses code to communicate with people in other places. At Joe's, Artie ordered us roast beef sandwiches and orange sodas. In the car, I was glad crowding made me sit on his lap.

Sunday, February 8, 1959: No Kiss

Sara said, "I've enjoyed hearing you describe the dance. These dance programs and tiny red suede purses with XEA in gold make lovely favors."

I said, "Artie was well-mannered and a perfect escort, but said little. Making conversation was hard, so my planned questions helped. He didn't kiss me goodnight. I go for him, but will be surprised if he asks me out."

Sara said, "Maybe he's too much of a gentleman for a first-date kiss."

When I answered, "He invited me to an unchaperoned party in 1957," we both laughed. I asked, "When you dated Kirk Douglas in the 1930s, did you guess that his nephew, Rex, would dance with your niece?"

She chuckled and said, "Never!"

Saturday, February 14, 1959: Favorite Holiday

I was happy about Valentines from pen pal Joe in NJ, Ron, and Gil. At Earl's fun party, I danced with him, Craig, and others. Kissing game partners included Earl and husband Tad. Wishing for a magic wand to make Earl interesting, cute, and a good dancer, I reluctantly accepted his date invites.

Sunday, February 22, 1959: Ben

Tara eagerly listened about Ben, who's in her homeroom and French class:

> I wish you'd been at the Center. I'm sure that Ben would
> have asked you to dance. After we danced, he said little,
> except, "French is my worst subject. I can't pronounce it.
> I wish I was a genius, like my cousin."
>
> I replied, "I can pronounce Latin, but the grammar is
> hard. Is your brother a sophomore?" He nodded.

Tara said, "The best boys seem to pick cool girls from Mohican or Iroquois School."

> I agreed. "I was overjoyed to dance once with Luke and would
> love to date him, Hank, or Lon from Iroquois. I miss having you
> in my classes."
>
> Tara said, "I miss you, too. Your dance snapshots with Artie
> look good."

Tuesday, February 24, 1959: Bowling and Deaths

Eva asked how I spent our school holiday. I said, "Yesterday would have been even more fun if you had bowled with us. Craig came with friends from a Catholic high school. One is sixteen, blond, a good bowler, and very nice. The better-looking boy with a dark brush cut was quieter. We all liked the Big Bopper, Buddy Holly, and Ritchie Valens. Three weeks after the plane crash, we're still sad that they died so young."

I agreed when Eva said, "I hope their great hits, like *Chantilly Lace, Peggy Sue, That'll Be the Day, La Bamba,* and *Donna,* keep their memories alive."

Friday, March 6, 1959: Parents

I felt cranky until my period arrived today. Following my New Year's resolution, I tried to be with my parents. As usual, Dad sat in the living room reading the newspaper. He's on his feet all day, selling men's clothes six days a week. He was pooped after working twelve hours yesterday. Mom's always occupied. She mended clothes tonight. Tumba was funny, pecking his mirror and saying, "Tumba's a good boy."

Tuesday, March 10, 1959: Birthday

Dad happily ate his cake after dinner and laughed at Sara's forty lines about him, including these:

You are many things to many people.

They enumerate as high as a steeple.

In shul you rate very high.

I would say high as the sky.

The Mr. and Mrs. Club and many others

Regard you as one of their brothers.

Your contributions to the choir

Are zestful as a burning fire.

Your rhythmic variations on drums are inspirations

For all to create interesting lamentations.

Saturday, March 14, 1959: Poughkeepsie

I said to Sara, "For the first time I can remember, nothing bad happened on Friday the thirteenth. It's good that Dad hasn't fixed the washing machine."

Chuckling, Sara asked, "Why?"

I answered, "Hardly any Orientals live in Albany, so I enjoyed meeting a nice Chinese Albany Pharmacy College soph from Poughkeepsie at the Laundromat! As we washed clothes, he talked about his two sisters and landlady, who just died."

"How was the Center?"

"I met another older Poughkeepsie man at the basketball game! He's a senior going to Rider College in NJ next year. He's five foot seven with brown hair and eyes and a nice smile. I had a ball dancing with him. What a spectacular evening, one of my best! I'm excited to look more grown up and have boys up to five years older talk to me!"

Wednesday, March 18, 1959: Most Popular

In our yearbook election, I was amazed and happy to win most popular girl and most versatile girl in my homeroom! I told Sara, "Artie got most popular boy! I'm glad that best personality went to my hilarious favorites: Craig and Eva. Smart homeroom veep Eva got and deserved most likely to succeed! Cute Lon won best-looking and best-dressed boy. Homeroom treasurer Luke got

Angela Weiss

best physique and biggest flirt. The school dance included a real jam session by a terrific band. Dancing with five boys, mainly Craig, was fun!"

Smiling, Sara said, "I'm happy about your two wins!" Dad congratulated me.

Tumba said, "Spended (*sic*)!" Mom said nothing. Because she wasn't popular in school, is she envious?

Eva

Monday, March 23, 1959: Sister

I'm finally an XEA sorority sister! I dislike snobbish behavior and feel sorry for the girls dropped for not being cool, popular, or well-dressed. Our XEA officers are popular at AHS and most sisters are nice.

Tuesday, March 31, 1959: *Wonderland*

On vacation, Doreen and I enjoyed *Rio Bravo*, a good Western with John Wayne and Dean Martin. Cute Ricky Nelson was fun to watch. Doreen said, "Can you help with my yearbook composition? You're good in English."

I replied, "So are you, but I'm happy to help!"

She continued, "Thank you. Can you suggest corrections?"

Smiling, I replied, "Sure!"

She blushed and handed me a lined page from her purse:

Winter Wonderland

The sky contained light gray nimbus clouds, spotted with soft tones of blue. Transparent icicles hung from the dormant maple trees in the still and peaceful park on the severely bitter-cold December day. The bushes, decorated with heavy burdens of snow, were collapsing. Shrill notes were heard in the intensely calm, cool air from the birds that had remained for the winter season. The park benches, partially covered with flakes, were now vacant. Everything was frozen and did not move when the violent wind suddenly came rushing in. Not a person or animal was visible, except for three small, brown squirrels' heads, which were huddled together. Their tiny eyes peered earnestly out from their moderately warm and cozy dwelling in the tall, stately trees. That once-vivid green ground was covered with a pure-white blanket of snow, which glittered like diamonds. Lacy snowflakes whirled in the air and looked as if they were dancing. This picturesque scene appeared like a winter wonderland.

"Doreen, it's beautiful! Such poetic images!"

"I appreciate that! Do you see English errors or anything to improve?"

"It's well-written! I'd love a copy to show my aunt."

"I feel better now. Keep this copy. I have one at home."

"Thank you!"

She laughed. "I'm flattered that you'll show it to a writer." After thanking me, she gave me a hug.

After Sara read it, I called Doreen. "My aunt said, 'It shows observant intelligence and a flair for writing.' I'm lucky to have a gifted friend!"

Friday, April 3, 1959: Romance and Prejudice

Since seeing the fabulous movie *South Pacific* on Wednesday, I've been singing outstanding songs:

Some Enchanted Evening, Younger Than Springtime, This Nearly Was Mine, A Cock-Eyed Optimist, I'm in Love with a Wonderful Guy, Happy Talk, There Is Nothing like a Dame, Bali Hai, Bloody Mary, My Girl Back Home, I'm Gonna Wash That Man Right out of My Hair!

You've Got to Be Carefully Taught made me think about prejudice. Cute Mitzi Gaynor was unsure about marrying handsome Rossano Brazzi because his kids were half Polynesian. Lieutenant Cable hesitated about Bloody Mary's Polynesian daughter. I always agree when Dad says, "Prejudice is wrong."

At Hudson, I hated hearing kids say, "Nigger." I hear it less now, but am upset when kids act bigoted. I love seeing smart, popular Negro kids prove them wrong. Today, *The Sound and the Fury*, starring bald, handsome Yul Brynner and Joanne Woodward, best actress Oscar winner, was good, but nothing beats *South Pacific*.

Saturday, April 4, 1959: Dance

The beauty parlor polished my nails blue and curled my hair too tightly for the Mu Sigma dance. Wearing Mom's cut-down, navy nylon dress with flared skirt and portrait neckline saved money. Because Earl is short, I wore navy satin flats with sheer blue stockings. After the dance, I told Sara, "A cab took us to the

Sheraton Ten Eyck Hotel where each girl got these favors."
I showed her the red rosebuds, leather nail kit, and program.
"We danced the jitterbug, cha cha, and slow fox-trot to a great
band. While drinking punch, we laughed at a comedian. A group
of us ate delish Joe's cheeseburgers, French fries, and fried
onion rings. Exciting activities made it fun. Earl, who goes to the
Reformed synagogue, wants to be a rabbi."

Sara smiled. "Can you see yourself as a rabbi's wife?"

I cracked up. "I'm lucky the parents let me skip services.
The best Jewish boys belong to Earl's synagogue or Conservative
Temple Israel."

Sunday, April 12, 1959: *Gigi* and Grilled
My family saw *Gigi,* a romantic musical comedy. I enjoyed sweet
Leslie Caron, handsome Louis Jourdan, and charming Maurice
Chevalier. A Hungarian Gabor sister also appeared. The songs
were fun, but nothing compares to *South Pacific.* I survived
yesterday's interrogation about boys' religions, grades, and
date activities on my shopping trip with Mom. My New Year's
resolution made me share about the dance with Earl to avoid
talking about boys I like. Mom bought me pink gingham pajamas,
a 32B bra, gold and green nail polishes, and a gorgeous white
pleated skirt and coordinated print blouse in size 10.

Friday, April 17, 1959: DJ Stu
I was pleasantly surprised at Robin Levine's poise during her Bat
Mitzvah. She conducted the whole synagogue service. Wearing
my new white outfit and rust suede ballet slippers, I sat with
Oren and Cousin Stu. At the Levine's house, I loved dancing with
tall Stu to records. While we walked the dog, I felt excited when
he said, "Working as a DJ is fun. Can you come to Gloversville
for a dance? Give me your address so I can write." I had a ball
with Stu. Oren gave me college practice tests. I'm put off by his
terrible acne and high-pitched voice.

Sunday, April 19, 1959: Oscar Winners
Sara and I saw terrif (*sic*) Academy Award pictures. *Separate
Tables* is about guests in a hotel dining room. Rita Hayworth

arrives to get back with ex-husband Burt Lancaster, but he likes the female hotel owner. Shy Deborah Kerr has a crush on ex-Major David Niven with a shady past. He got a best actor Oscar. For *I Want to Live*, Susan Hayward got a best actress Oscar for playing a real woman trying to escape the death penalty. Her difficult childhood and life made us sympathetic. She got executed, though innocent of murder. She was guilty of lesser crimes. Sara said, "I'm against the death penalty. Mistakes occur. Angela, what do you think?"

I said, "I don't know. People like Hitler should be executed for killing millions of people."

Sara said, "Good point." I love talking to Sara. She never laughs at my opinions.

Saturday, April 25, 1959: Capital Punishment
I'm glad about good movies showing because no boys have asked me out. Sara and I saw *Compulsion* with talented Orson Welles as real defense lawyer Clarence Darrow in a famous 1920s trial. Cute Dean Stockwell and Bradford Dillman play rich, smart, crazy students accused of kidnapping and murder. Sara said, "This movie also illustrates what's wrong with capital punishment."

I said, "It showed that no one can commit a perfect crime."

Sara smiled and said, "You're right, Angela." Sara's so supportive that I'm willing to express ideas. My parents never say that I'm right about anything. The gunfight Western, *Warlock*, with good actors Henry Fonda and Anthony Quinn, was okay.

Tuesday, April 28, 1959: War
Home from school, I walked past Sara's open door. A cigarette in the ash tray made the room smoky. Sara sat at the card table typing. Stopping and swiveling her chair around, she said, "After struggling to present psychological ideas, I need a break. How was your day?"

Lounging on the bed, I shared, "We discussed war in cit ed."

"Did you learn that big business influences governments to start wars to profit from making weapons and war supplies?"

My jaw dropped before I replied, "We heard that countries fight for land or religion."

Sara commented, "Manufacturing creates profit. Greedy businessmen try to hide the sacrifice of young soldiers for wealth."

"I would never have known. Thank you!"

Wednesday, April 29, 1959: Can't Blame Them

Sara and I saw an interesting Lana Turner movie, *Imitation of Life*, about two mothers with teen daughters. Feeling sympathetic about the hard time Negroes have, I said, "Who can blame those with light skin for passing as white?" Cute Sandra Dee and handsome Troy Donahue played a young couple in love. The sad ending made Sara and me cry.

Saturday, May 2, 1959: Rebellious

At the Center, I wore my new white lipstick! Frankie was the best of the four partners who kept me dancing to every song. Frankie's rebellious, funny remarks make up for shuffling around the dance floor. At the Boulevard, he treated me to French fries and chocolate milk. We pecked goodnight.

Sunday, May 3, 1959: Drive-In

Despite the speaker box squawking, the drive-in is fun! During bad movies, I sleep in the back seat. We saw *Some Came Running*. Mom loves Frank Sinatra, who played the lead. Shirley MacLaine and Dean Martin were good. I nodded when Dad asked, "Remember Dean's funny ex-partner, Jerry Lewis?" Seeing couples in other cars making out made me glad to stay a virgin until I marry after college. Why get a fast reputation and risk pregnancy?

Monday, May 4, 1959: Obnoxious

We visited Beth, her husband, and their new baby. I'd love to babysit for both adorable girls. Poor Beth could hardly answer each of Mom's questions before being interrupted by another obnoxious one fired at her. After giving gifts and acting loving to Beth as a child, Mom resents that her niece isn't warmer. Mom said, "Beth's divorced mother set Beth against us."

Thursday, May 7, 1959: Ladies' Choice

The best part of XEA sorority is asking boys to events. At lunch, I got up my nerve and smiled while looking into the blue eyes of smart Phil, our good-looking homeroom president. A little taller than I, he has a good physique. When he smiled back, I said, "XEA is having a picnic May 17. I'd enjoy going with you."

When he replied, "Sure, that sounds good," I wondered whether my winning most popular girl made him accept. It didn't hurt that my report card with straight As is a secret. Letters from Ron and Gil felt like rewards.

Saturday, May 9, 1959: Tulip Court

I answered Ron's letter:

Thanks for your great letter! I'm happy that Gil also wrote. Are you having a June birthday party? My parents and Sara came to our school musical about Albany's history. Act One, *Land of the Mohicans*, included classmates singing *The Indian Love Call* and performing Indian dancing. The best part of Act Two, *Old Dutch Albany*, was Negro students singing spirituals. Kirk Douglas' nephew, Rex, was entertaining as master of ceremonies for Act Three, *The Tulip Ball*. I'm glad that a lovely, intelligent, popular Negro girl, who dresses beautifully, got elected queen. We dozen girls, lucky to be elected to her court, received yellow tulips. I wore my formal (yellow net) and eye makeup. I felt good when Phil, my sorority picnic date, waved from the audience. Classmates sang *Smoke Gets in Your Eyes* and *Wunderbar*, which went through my head at Cousin Beth's fancy catered party after her sister-in-law's piano concert. What a *wunderbar* evening! I'm in a great mood after three boys called about the tulip queen court. One was the blue-eyed boy who won best smile and has danced with me at the Center. Husband Tad and fun Craig talked awhile after complimenting my appearance.

Sunday, May 10, 1959: The Hill
While eating out for Mother's Day, I told my family about my first job interview:

> The Albany Hospital head of volunteers asked, "Are you prepared to do routine tasks for the nurses this summer, to free their time to take care of patients?" After I said yes and she asked about my grades and school, she said, "You're accepted as a candy striper volunteer." The red and white uniforms are adorable.

Dad said, "Angela, when you walk to and from the hospital, avoid the short cut across the hill."

Mom said, "Herm, weren't the nurses attacked late at night?"

Dad said, "I don't want Angela taking chances. New Scotland Avenue is safer with more people around."

I nodded, afraid to ask what happened to the nurses.

Wednesday, May 13, 1959: Excellent Dancers
After the science honor exam, I changed to my ugly formal for the Hackett tulip dance. I danced almost every tune with excellent dancers: Artie (six times), Rex (twice), and Craig (the rest)! I'm happy after an exciting time!

Saturday, May 16, 1959: Superlative Movies
The sad ending of *Green Mansions* made Tara and me cry. Audrey Hepburn played a South American jungle girl who wore animal skins and spoke a language birds understood. Anthony Perkins discovered and loved her. I want to read the book. I enjoyed *Mating Game*, a romantic comedy. Debbie Reynolds, a farmer's daughter, meets a tax collector auditing the farm. While shopping, Tara said, "This white Arnel dress looks great on you."

"Thank you! I like the silky pleats. This size 9 fits perfectly." After Mom approved the bargain by phone, I said, "Tara, I was wondering if you've had duties as homeroom vice president."

"Even the president does little. Vice president is my favorite office." We giggled.

Sunday, May 17, 1959: Picnic

I shared with Sara:

Despite my feeling nervous, Phil and I talked steadily as the bus climbed the road to Thatcher Park. We played gin rummy in the bus until the rain stopped and we could hike the narrow Indian Ladder. The most fun was volleyball. I said, "Phil, I'm impressed with this fire you made. These hot dogs taste great." Sara, thanks for suggesting planned questions.

When I asked his career goal, he answered, "Physicist."

When I asked, "What will you do?" he talked about electromagnetic fields, protons, electrons, ions, and more things, which made me afraid to take physics at AHS. Ha! Ha! We had the best ice cream at Toll Gate. I like Phil and I felt let down about no hand-holding or good-bye kiss.

Friday, May 22, 1959: The Mostest!

I hardly remember *Room at the Top*. I was in heaven with Artie and Tad next to me and nine boys I like nearby. Sara enjoyed meeting Kirk Douglas' nephews! Later, I said, "Neither resembles Kirk. Tall, thin Rex with pale, freckled skin resembles Kirk's sister. Francis gets his black hair and eyes and tan skin from their dad."

Saturday, May 23, 1959: Good Girl

I liked the movie *Count Your Blessings*. Pretty Deborah Kerr divorced handsome Rossano Brazzi, whose uncle was Maurice Chevalier. At the Boulevard afterwards, Luke and a pal laughed and asked, "What's the difference between a nice girl and a good girl?"

I shrugged. "I don't know."

Luke answered, "A good girl goes on a date, goes home, and goes to bed. A nice girl goes on a date, goes to bed, and then goes home." Boys using girls for sex bothers me.

Tuesday, May 26, 1959: Combinations

I said to Doreen, "Ping-pong at the Center was fun with those cute boys. You've gotten really good!"

She said, "Thank you! Practicing in our basement helps. What color are your new clothes?"

I answered, "The blue-striped shag cloth Jamaicas, the blue doeskin Jamaicas, and the blue doeskin skirt go with either the shag cloth or white blouse for six outfits. I hope they inspire a rescue from this dating dry spell."

Doreen and I giggled after she joked, "We're lost in the Sahara."

Thursday, May 28, 1959: Hardly Breathing
After school, Craig and Eva kept me laughing during tennis and at my house. Later, I told Sara, "The most wonderful thing in the world happened: Artie came up to me in the cafeteria, smiled, and said, 'I'd like to take you to the youth council picnic.' I beamed and accepted! I'm so excited I can hardly breathe!"

Friday, May 29, 1959: Sara's Life
Sara said, "Progress on my book has been sloooowww all day. Let's see Shirley MacLaine in *Ask Any Girl*." After the amusing movie, Sara said, "Romantic comedies motivate me to find a way to get Mort to call or write."

I replied, "All other men go for you, especially the rabbi when he visited Dad."

She answered, "The rabbi shouldn't flirt, especially with his wife disabled."

"I wonder if he was wild like Frankie."

Saturday, May 30, 1959: Memorial Day
As we drove south to the summer cottages of Mom's uncle's big family, Sara told anecdotes about fun experiences with these NYC cousins. Was Dad's tantrum because Sara was getting all the attention? Mom once said, "Dad's older sisters and parents spoiled him. As the only boy, he got his way by yelling."

Sunday, May 31, 1959: With Artie
I told Sara, "At the picnic, Artie took me hiking on the scary Indian Ladder trail. We passed behind the waterfall without getting wet. Volleyball and games kept us too busy for much talk. I enjoyed his arm around me. We also held hands!"

She asked, "How do you feel about him?"

I replied, "I can't help feeling attracted to Artie, but I'm more comfortable with talkers, like Craig and interesting Luke, who wants to be a psychiatrist."

Friday, June 5, 1959: Prom Date
I politely turned down Earl's prom invitation after enough of his company at that dance. I'd rather stay home. After Paul Newman's fabulous *The Young Philadelphians,* I said to Sara, "Mr. Newman can be my prom date!"

Sara laughed. "His acting and blue eyes are mesmerizing."

Sunday, June 7, 1959: Tad and Paul
When Tad picked me up for our barbeque date, I pitied him when Mom pumped him with questions about his parents, whom we haven't seen since 1950. The party was the best with volleyball, badminton, good food, and talk with fun classmates. Charming Paul said, "Congratulations on winning most popular and most versatile in your homeroom!"

"Thank you, Paul!" My face felt hot with a blush. Sure that he'd won in his homeroom, I flirtatiously said, "I wonder who won your poll."

Smiling, he replied, "We didn't have most popular. I got best athlete and best-dressed. Marcus got most likely to succeed and Neal got smartest."

I smiled and batted my eyelashes. "I would have voted for you for all of them, including biggest flirt. You were our *Quizdown* hero, answering that impossible question." When he laughed and looked down into my eyes, I went into a trance, imagining a prom invite until Tad arrived with my drink. Yesterday, seeing Luke, Hank, and Lon on the bus going downtown and at the swimming pool, I longed for a prom invite. Hearing that Artie likes a pretty green-eyed blonde, I hid my disappointment.

Friday, June 12, 1959: New Job
After an interview, I accepted an unpaid counselor-in-training job. I told Mom and Sara, "Helping kids with arts and crafts at

McKownville Day Camp sounds better than hospital work. Albany Hospital didn't mind because they have a waiting list."

Mom said, "Fresh air is healthier."

I laughed hearing Tumba say, "No, thanks!"

Tuesday, June 16, 1959: DeMolay
I was thrilled to accept Craig's invitation to the DeMolay picnic! I asked, "What's DeMolay?"

He said, "My father belongs to the Masons, a fraternal order. DeMolay is like the junior Masons."

I said, "My mother's brothers may be Masons. What happens in DeMolay?"

Craig said, "We meet and do charity projects."

Later, Mom said, "The Masons keep everything secret from outsiders." I'd like to know the secrets.

Wednesday, June 17, 1959: Limberettes
We're signing our fun yearbook at school. Past heartthrob Sal wrote unromantically:

Good luck to a good kid.

Earl, Luke, and Phil wrote similarly. Paul was warmer:

Great luck in the future! I wish you were going to Schuyler.

I was surprised and happy that my team was in the yearbook:

Volleyball was enjoyed by many girls this year. There was a large turnout of teams after school for the play-offs, which ended with the Limberettes from Homeroom 202, captained by Angela Weiss, winning the Hackett championship.

Welshie at Patroon School deserves credit for teaching winning skills.

Thursday, June 18, 1959: Yearbook
I'm embarrassed to see my silly story in print:

Perils of Percival

Percival and his fifty brothers lived together in a small round house. It was cold and dark there most of the time. Suddenly a light appeared, and Percival saw an object, which was almost white with five slender projections. At the tip of each was a red circle. This large object scared Percival because it quickly picked up Percival's house, brothers and all, and carried it away from its cold, dark home. Our hero's home was set down in a cheery, warm place. The red-and-white object opened it and removed only Percival. This act greatly frightened him. Suddenly, he was dropped into a sea of liquid, golden in color. You see, Percy was a maraschino cherry!

Other honor students wrote seriously: *Theodore Roosevelt, Our Vanishing American Heritage, The Blessings of Freedom,* and *Reflection.* Even hilarious Craig stunned me with a serious, poetic essay: *A Symbol of Our Heritage* about "Old Glory," our flag. He praised "gallant men and courageous leaders who have fought so that posterity could enjoy freedom and security." He wrote, "With dictatorship, freedom and justice cannot prevail." I couldn't resist being goofy.

Friday, June 19, 1959: Awards and Prom
After tough exams, I felt happy about Sara's enthusiastic congratulations about my class day prizes: fifteen dollars for the highest overall grades and character ratings and five dollars for Latin. I said:

> Eva deserved her English prize! Neal won in math and cit ed, and Marcus won in science. I'm glad that scholarship letters for being on the honor roll all year went to Doreen, Eva, Julia, Tad, Marcus, Artie, Neal, Steve, Craig, Luke, Lon, and Phil. Our tulip queen got a letter and had perfect attendance. Sal never missed a day. It's unfair for Jewish holidays to count against perfect attendance when we get Christmas off. Artie wrote unromantically in my yearbook, "Spend your prize money wisely." So I bought a wooden tennis racket named for pro Doris Hart.

Sara chuckled. Wearing my white nylon semiformal, I went to the prom alone. I danced with handsome Paul four times, dancer Craig three times, and two others. A gang of us ate at Joe's where Paul treated me! I got home after one! It was a large charge!

Saturday, June 20, 1959: Fabulous
Tonight's party was a blast!! I danced with funny Craig, masculine Luke, cute Lon, handsome Artie, and three others! Artie held my hand and took me on a long, romantic walk in the moonlight!! After he talked about being a doctor, he smiled when I joked, "I have a boo-boo that needs treatment." I enjoyed sitting on Artie's lap in the back seat on the way home. Though he didn't kiss me, his romantic behavior made it one of my best nights!

Sunday, June 21, 1959: Picnic and Sister
The DeMolay picnic at Thatcher was full of laughs. After lunch, Craig took me on the Indian Ladder. We swam and played paddle tennis and shuffleboard. I adored riding home with Craig holding my hand in the back seat of a gorgeous red convertible with white upholstery and long fins. I had so much fun that I forgot to ask about DeMolay secrets. I overheard my parents mention Rowena being born dead nineteen years ago today. She might differ from me, like Mom and Sara. If she was the favorite, I might be worse off.

Monday, June 22, 1959: Grades and Camp
I laughed, thinking that the girl who wrote, "To the Brain," in my yearbook would cross it out if she knew my algebra exam was 86 percent. I don't know what I did wrong. With 98 percent as the lowest of the other four exam marks, I'm pleased with my average: 96.2 percent. Doreen and I like our camp jobs, helping arts and crafts counselor Mrs. R. The kids, age five to twelve, are cutting newspaper strips to combine with a flour-water paste for paper mache masks to paint and decorate.

Tuesday, June 23, 1959: Ambitions
My yearbook homeroom page contains thirty students' names and goals. Mom, always pushing teaching, said, "Two girls want to teach and a boy wants to be a professor."

I changed the subject. "Seven boys and a girl want to be doctors and two boys chose vet."

Mom responded, "Three girls share my interest in nursing."

I noted, "A girl choosing doctor probably won't get dates."

Sara asked, "Is that why four boys picked lawyer with Eva the only girl?"

I nodded. "Even though we must catch up with the Russians, only three boys each chose scientist and engineer."

Mom commented, "Angela, this girl shares your interest in interior decoration."

I said, "I listed 'field of art' because I like all art, including decorating houses."

Sara asked, "You know that Fern went to art school and I used to paint?"

I nodded.

Mom explained, "I dropped out because the close work caused eyestrain. I still want to paint."

I said, "You'd be a good nurse, teacher, or artist."

Smiling, Mom thanked me.

Wednesday, June 24, 1959: Forty-Two

Mom and I cooked a delicious rib steak birthday dinner for Sara, who said, "Angela, thank you for the great card and red gingham apron you made!" We played canasta on our front porch until dark around nine.

Despite chirping, "Pretty please," poor Tumba stayed inside to avoid escape. Though Sara got birthday attention, Dad behaved. Is he jealous because Mom and I love Sara's sense of humor and personality? I hope Grandma keeps paying Sara's rent.

Friday, June 26, 1959: Eva

Doreen, Eva, and I enjoyed the musical comedy *Say One for Me* with cute Debbie Reynolds, handsome Robert Wagner, and boring Bing Crosby. Afterwards, I said, "Eva, your yearbook composition, *The Paradox*, sounds as good as serious, grown-up writing. Like Doreen's piece, it was poetic and made me think, something I usually avoid." They laughed. "I hardly know what paradox means."

Doreen added, "Eva, I liked your idea of people copying the harmony of nature to get along better." After turning red, Eva thanked us, changed the subject away from herself, and got us giggling.

At home, Sara called the essay "brilliant."

After lovely descriptions of the sea, sun, and sky, Eva wrote:

> I realize how much nature resembles our troubled world. We seldom agree, but nature will compromise. Man is too proud. If we reach for that horizon beyond what seems to be the last, we, too, will reach the peace and compromise of nature.

Eva, who lives in the other high school's district, signed my yearbook:

> Good luck to a great kid and a wonderful friend. I'll miss you next year. Love, Eva

I wrote in her yearbook:

> Dear Eva, I love your sense of humor and high intelligence! I will miss you and hope we can stay in touch and get together! Love, Angela

Monday, June 29, 1959: The Moon

After the Center dance, I told Sara, "Rex danced perfectly with me and took me to The Moon for pizza."

Sara laughed. "Izzy-Kirk never took me to the moon."

Grinning, I replied, "In his homeroom, Rex won biggest flirt, class clown, best dressed, biggest talker, and best dancer! He has the personality for his ambition: fashion designer."

Wednesday, July 1, 1959: Talent

I shared with Sara about the third Tower of Talent in Menands:

> The rich Schine family and radio station WPTR put it on to benefit disabled kids at Variety Club's Camp Thatcher. Someone said that WPTR's 50,000 watts can be heard as far away as Boston! After seeing performers arrive in open convertibles, I swooned when Sam Cooke sang *You Send Me* and felt excited hearing Cathy Carr and the Impalas, Fabian, the Everly Brothers, and other favorites. I was glad that listener votes made cute Frankie Avalon

king of song! Connie Francis got the queen-of-song trophy again. Mitch Miller led the band. I loved every minute!

Monday, July 6, 1959: Nun and Fun
After seeing wonderful Audrey Hepburn in *The Nun's Story*, Tara said, "I'm ready to take vows as a nun."

I laughed and added, "She's so graceful and lovable!" At the Center, I was thrilled to dance and talk with Luke and smooth AHS senior Barney, who works at my camp. I'd love to date them. What a perfect evening!

I laughed when Tumba said, "I love summer," several times.

Monday, July 13, 1959: Tornado
Last night, Aunt Myrna called. "We had a freak tornado with winds of over forty miles an hour! Our house is safe, but some Gloversville homes were damaged." I dreamed that Albany, only forty miles away, had a tornado. I saw the scary, dark funnel approaching in the sky and felt strong winds before waking myself up. I was relieved it wasn't real.

Friday, July 17, 1959: Fears and Movies
As I worried that AHS will be too hard for me to win scholarships and that I'll be stuck at Albany State Teachers' College, Craig called and made me laugh. I was glad when he said, "We'll be in the same Latin and advanced English and history classes."
On the phone, I said to Eva:

What a great week of movies! Sara and I saw *This Earth Is Mine* with handsome Rock Hudson. Doreen and I saw excellent Elvis movies: *Loving You* and *King Creole*. Sara took me to first-rate revivals. *Stalag 17* made me realize how frightening being imprisoned must feel, especially by the Nazis in a World War II prisoner-of-war camp! Watching the drama *A Place in the Sun*, I wished for violet eyes after noticing Elizabeth Taylor's.

After a chuckle, Eva said that she also had been impressed by *Stalag 17*.

Angela Weiss

Sunday, July 19, 1959: Kurt
Driving southwest past pleasant rural greenery, the parents and I were happy to return to Young's Gap in the Catskills. Our dinner table for six included teen Kurt and his parents. In the nightclub with a small stage and medium-sized dance floor, Kurt and I talked at the long teen table and danced. Adults sat at round tables covered with white linen tablecloths. My picture postcard to Doreen included:

I miss Donald and hope for teen boys whose looks, dancing, and conversation are better than Kurt's. Hearing about his family's money and possessions was boring.

Tuesday, July 21, 1959: Distracted
During yesterday's rain, I won close ping-pong games with four boys. I felt strong after occasionally smashing the ball over the net, instead of into it. Today, I enjoyed swimming in the pool; playing shuffleboard, paddle squash, and canasta; and sending Tara a postcard:

What's new in Albany? I saw *The Al Jolson Story* with Al and Kurt, who bought me a Coke. As the only girl, I felt distracted in a good way. I hardly remember what the movie was about.

Love, Angela

In the nightclub, the female singer from NYC was good. I liked dancing with a new boy and our teen coordinator, a college junior.

Thursday, July 23, 1959: Competitors
While swimming, I appreciated Al and Kurt lifting me onto the raft. On a walk, Al put his arm around me and held my hand. As we watched a softball game, Al and Kurt each had his arm around me and competed. Kurt offered to buy me something to eat. Al asked, "Will you go steady with me?"

I replied, "No, thank you, but it's nice of you to ask." Playing ping-pong after dinner, we got in a real gone mood, laughing uncontrollably at the slightest thing. NYC boys tend to have good senses of humor. Rather than feel romantic, I enjoyed joking in a group. In the nightclub, I had fun dancing with a college man, eighteen, and Kurt, who bought me ice cream.

Friday, July 24, 1959: Fighting

I wrote to Eva:

> I hope you're having a fun summer! As I lay in the sun in my white bathing suit, three boys showed off and amused me. On a walk after dinner, Al and Howard actually fought over me, pushing and hitting each other to escort me and hold my hand. (Why don't Paul and Artie fight over me? Ha! Ha!) We got silly and laughed a lot. In the nightclub, sweet Al danced with me. Love, Angela

Sunday, July 26, 1959: No Kiss

Yesterday and today, I loved playing singles and doubles ping-pong with five boys and bowling with three. I was happy with my score of ninety-five, but not sixty-six. I enjoyed dancing with three boys and seeing a talented comedian and a singing duo in the nightclub. Howard's arm was around my chair. On a walk, Al held my hand and bought me ice cream. Today, I took pictures and exchanged addresses. I couldn't believe my eyes: Howard and Al hit and pushed each other to escort me on a lake walk before I left. Somehow, I ended up with Al, who begged for a good-bye kiss. I politely avoided it. Though he's fun, he'd need to become a talented intellectual for me to feel like kissing him. Dad drove us back to Albany before dark when oncoming headlights blind him. I was happy to see Sara, who laughed about the boys' fighting over me as the only girl.

Friday, July 31, 1959: Males and Lanyards

Reading Joe's letter, I wondered if we'll ever see each other again after last summer's romantic evening at Aunt Rhoda's party. A special delivery letter said that Al from Young's Gap is still thinking about me. Craig sent a card while vacationing with his family. I enjoyed a visit from Frankie and Carl. Dad said, "Even without pay, your camp job is good experience."

I replied, "While at Young's Gap, I didn't miss anything exciting. I'm lucky being in arts and crafts, rather than stuck with the same kids all day. Doreen and I prefer the cute eight-year-olds, who cooperate more than pre-teens."

Mom asked, "What are they making?"

I answered, "Lanyards with different braiding patterns and colors, like the one I made at camp."

Saturday, August 1, 1959: Lawyer

After Sara and I saw the movie *Anatomy of a Murder*, she said, "I love the Duke Ellington jazz music! Jimmy Stewart was convincing in portraying lawyer courtroom behavior during a real murder trial."

I said, "Maybe I should copy Craig and Eva and help people as a lawyer. It seems exciting." On the bus, Sara and I kidded with boys from school.

We laughed when Tumba's monologue included "Give me a kiss," before he flew to us.

Monday, August 3, 1959: Luke

At the Center, I danced with Frankie, Rex, and Luke, who took me out! We had sodas at Buddy's and cheesecake at a bakery. Triple dating with two cool couples was fun. Sara chuckled after I said, "Luke's after-shave lotion smelled so good that I was sniffing like a dog!"

Wednesday, August 5, 1959: Pecks

I told Sara, "Marsha's fun party included ping-pong, dancing, and talking. The cute twins she still likes were there. During kissing games, I pecked three nice boys, but no one I want to date."

Thursday, August 6, 1959: Don't Know

After Sara saw a movie alone, we saw her standing in the entry hall breathing hard. She exclaimed, "After I exited the New Scotland bus, a man followed me and grabbed my breasts from behind. I kicked him, fought him off, and ran home. Let's call the police." Her face was white and she seemed upset. Mom looked confused. Dad sounded mean, as if Sara made up the attack to get sympathy, maybe because her clothes weren't torn and she wasn't crying. Rooted to the spot, I didn't know what to say or do. She must have felt terrible not getting sympathy or help. She turned to me. "Angela, what do you think?"

I froze with three adults staring at me. Sara has never lied. I believed her, but Dad seemed so sure. Did he know something I didn't? I felt flustered and paralyzed. I wanted to say, "Don't look at me. I'm just a kid who doesn't understand this." Hearing myself say, "I don't know," I knew I'd made a terrible mistake. Cruelly doubting Sara added insult to injury. Who can blame her for packing her suitcase to leave?

Angela's photograph, left to right, of
Herm, Fern, Grandma C, and Sara.

Friday, August 7, 1959: Stuck
Dream:

> Riding in the Adirondacks at night, my parents and I suddenly saw a deer in the road. Blinded by our headlights, the deer seemed unable to move. We braked in time and turned off the lights until it ran off.

Last night, I felt like the deer, afraid to say or do anything. It was over my head, too grown-up. If I'd said something better, Sara wouldn't be leaving. I love her more than my parents, who are a big pain. Why didn't Mom stick up for her sister? Was Dad remembering that Uncle Jules put Sara in a mental hospital? Sara has always seemed stronger and saner than my parents. I'm so confused.

Saturday, August 8, 1959: Gone
Refusing to talk to any of us, Sara put her suitcases in a taxi and left. Mom said, "She must have taken a train to NYC." Sara always supported me when my parents picked on me, especially at family meetings. I let her down the one time she needed me.

Sunday, August 9, 1959: Silence
No one's talking about Sara. Dad looks happy, but Mom seems sad. I miss Sara already. It's scary being alone here without support. Is Sara in her old apartment? I prayed that she'll be all right.

Monday, August 10, 1959: Escape
I escaped to the Center dance. I felt happier talking to Aryeh, Luke, and Barney, but they didn't ask me to dance. After dancing with Frankie and a pal, Doreen and I went with them to the Boulevard for chocolate milk and cookies. I'm too upset to mention Sara, even to Doreen. I hope that Sara still loves me. When I grow up and get away from my parents, I'll visit her.

Tuesday, August 11, 1959: The Mostest
Tall, dark, handsome Barney works with the oldest camp boys. When he taught me how the different chess pieces move, I said, "The knight is the cutest." The evening staff party was a real

blast! Doreen, her date, Barney, and I ate, walked, talked, and danced. Having Barney's arm around me and holding hands were the mostest (*sic*)!

Wednesday, August 12, 1959: Crush
On the phone with Eva, I shared this:
> After camp, Barney swam with Doreen and me and drove us home. He called to talk for thirty minutes and ask me out. I'm excited because of my crush on him.

Friday, August 14, 1959: Last Day
Mrs. R said, "Angela, you did a fine job in arts and crafts. Thank you for your reliable attendance, cooperation, and help with the kids." Camp was good experience and fun. After we swam, Barney drove me to a pal's house. I enjoyed hearing bongos and drums played really well to jazz records. I tasted the boys' beer. Ugh! I'd never drink it. Joe's letter and Frankie's call didn't prevent my feeling awful about Sara, who's on my mind all the time at home.

Saturday, August 15, 1959: Missing Sara
Barney and I took the bus downtown to see *Holiday for Lovers* and *A Night to Remember*, about the Titanic sinking. His arm was around me, we held hands, and my head was on his shoulder. We kissed twice. I wanted to write or call Sara about exciting Barney and the interesting movies. I hope she's less upset with me than with my parents.

Sunday, August 16, 1959: New Jersey
When my parents and I drove on the Thruway past NYC, I wanted to find Sara. No one mentioned her. Since she left, Mom laughs less and looks worried. Our nice little Belmar vacation hotel includes meals. At the ping-pong table, I talked to several bus boys, including college students!

Tuesday, August 18, 1959: Asbury
Dad said, "Let's go four miles north to Asbury Park's boardwalk." The games and food resembled Atlantic City. We missed earning

enough Skee-Ball points for a prize. At Belmar beach, I talked with three boys from our hotel. In the evening, I joked and danced with four guys, including a drummer! It's heaven flirting and dancing with older guys.

Thursday, August 20, 1959: Surprised
I'm glad that the parents are having fun at the beach and pool with other old people. I'm surprised that they allow me to date older boys. I'm ashamed to introduce the overweight parents to boys. Mom's ugly clothes and loud voice embarrass me.

Friday, August 21, 1959: Ranger and Tonto
I squeezed this on large postcards to Eva and Doreen:
> Busboys Quinn and Vin, both twenty, are Belmar's Lone Ranger and Tonto. Tuesday, Quinn talked to me at the gorgeous beach, held my hand during an evening boardwalk stroll, played miniature golf with me, and kissed me goodnight. Wednesday, Vin took me to *Never Say Goodbye* with Rock Hudson. Thursday, after beach fun with Quinn, Vin danced with me in the evening. Did he talk about Quinn to find out my feelings? I just listened. Today, after enjoying the beach with both, I had a blast dancing with them and with a professional dancer, twenty-two! I'm lucky to be the only girl with older boys, a romantic dream come true!

Saturday, August 22, 1959: Hawaii
At the beach, Quinn said, "Hawaii, which has beautiful beaches, is now our 50ᵗʰ state!"

I said, "I love ocean swimming and beach tanning." The afternoon was a real ball: swimming in the pool with one boy and kidding with another. At night, the female singer and male comedian were good. I was excited, dancing and flirting with boys from fifteen to twenty-two! What a perfect vacation!

Sunday, August 23, 1959: Good-bye
I said good-bye to everyone and enjoyed kisses from the Lone Ranger and Tonto. Driving home, Dad said to Mom, "Hon, you

found an ideal hotel near the beach. Belmar's beautiful! I wish we didn't have to work tomorrow."

Mom replied, "It was a bargain. I'm glad we got rested up." At home, letters from Gil and Donald inspired images of dating them while visiting Sara.

Monday, August 24, 1959: Barney
When Barney called, I described my exciting vacation without mentioning boys. At the Center, we danced, held hands, and took a walk. His invitation to the ABG Fraternity weekend made me happy to go with a fun boy I like!

Tuesday, August 25, 1959: Plane Attack
I thanked Barney for driving me to the dentist. At the movies, I wished for Sara's opinion of complicated *North by Northwest* with blond Eva Marie Saint and suave James Mason. I felt scared when a plane tried to shoot adorable Cary Grant, mistaken for a spy, in an open field. Debbie Reynolds made the romantic comedy *It Started with a Kiss* fun.

Wednesday, August 26, 1959: Carol and Ramah
I enjoyed blond Carol Lynley in the movie version of *Blue Denim*. A perfect clothes model, she's often in my *Seventeen* monthly magazines. I read every word. Frankie called about his exciting Wisconsin summer at Ramah Jewish overnight camp. I've lost interest in Jewish activities, but I still pray to God at night.

Friday, August 28, 1959: Advice
I asked Doreen's advice about Barney:

> I like him, but it's not love. Today's party with two couples was fun because we weren't alone. I like kissing Barney goodnight. Yesterday at my house, when we played records and cards, I got annoyed when he pushed to be physical, especially in our cellar! Keeping his paws off my body was no fun.

After Doreen said she'd think about it, I thanked her and felt better.

Saturday, August 29, 1959: Hopes
After seeing Frank Sinatra in *Hole in the Head*, I've been singing its song *High Hopes*:

> Any time you're feeling bad, 'stead of feelin' sad, just remember that ram. Whoops, there goes a billion kilowatt dam.

With high hopes of talking to or seeing Sara soon, I smiled when Tumba repeatedly said, "Sara."

Sunday, August 30, 1959: Avoidance
Mom sounded worried and annoyed:

> Using Sara's number from information, I called. Though we used to laugh about it, it wasn't funny when Sara used her old trick before disconnecting: "I have to go. Someone's at the door." Sara pulled the same "I must leave" trick with her own mother and told your uncles before hanging up, "I'm late for an appointment."

Naturally, Sara's hurt and mad. We should have believed and supported her. Why didn't I help her before it was too late? I hope she doesn't stay angry at me.

Monday, August 31, 1959: Let's Dance
At the Center, Barney talked through the records and danced with me only once. Wanting to dance to every song, I felt frustrated that girls must wait for boys to ask.

Wednesday, September 2, 1959: Foreign
I liked my first foreign film: *Wild Strawberries* in Swedish with English subtitles. The movie seemed different. I'd like Sara's opinion. I bet she loves it.

Thursday, September 3, 1959: Disrespect
Barney was nice to drive me to the bowling alley to meet Doreen. I was satisfied bowling eighty-four. I liked her idea of chaperoning! At my house, the three of us played cards. After he left, Doreen and I shopped. While buying wool Bermuda shorts, a black blouse, navy satin heels for the dance, and black leather flats in size

7AAA, I said, "Barney made me uncomfortable by touching my knees under the table! I'm glad he left."

Her eyebrows went up. "Pretty nervy with me there!" I agreed that he wasn't respectful.

Saturday, September 5, 1959: Frat Dance
Saying nothing about my appearance, Barney probably disliked my hair, set in curls, and dress. I didn't mind wearing the navy nylon again to save money. With other couples, we took the chartered bus seven miles to the Hendrik Hudson Hotel in Troy where we danced. At Joe's, I had cheesecake, soda, and onion rings. Barney kissed me goodnight three times. He arranged everything well and showed his good sense of humor, so I had fun!

Monday, September 7, 1959: Skin to Touch
When Doreen asked about the White's Beach picnic, I reported:
> On the chartered bus, Barney held my hand. With his arm around me, I had a ball on a boat ride around the lake. When we stopped in the middle of the lake, Barney's pal played cards with a boy in another boat. I couldn't stop laughing when he stole the boy's oar for a few minutes. At the beach, we swam in the lake and, on the raft, caught flies and joked. After eating and playing cards on the beach, we watched a ball game. I wanted to dance more than once at the pavilion, but Barney wanted to walk in the grove. He kissed me a few times really well! On the bus home, his arm was around me and he ran his hands along my legs. "You have such smooth skin, the skin you love to touch." Though I liked his compliment, I didn't want him touching my legs. After cheesecake and ice cream at Joe's, we took a cab home and kissed goodnight.
> It was fun, except for being pawed!

We both giggled before Doreen said, "His ex must have let him do more."

She agreed when I said, "Older boys seem to expect to go farther."

Angela and Barney

Tuesday, September 8, 1959: Albany High
High school is exciting, so grown-up! I'm happy to have sophomore English and history with the smartest kids and good teachers. To avoid cutting up a frog in biology, I'm taking Spanish. Plane geometry seems more interesting than algebra. We need more time in gym to finish games. I'm laughing because changing into and out of our ugly bloomer uniforms takes almost the whole forty-five minutes.

Thursday, September 10, 1959: Latin and Ropes
Are all Latin teachers tiny, white-haired ladies, like Hackett's Miss W and AHS's Mrs. G? With twinkles in their eyes, they make Latin fun. Latin class is full of really smart kids! If I go to the big NYC Latin contest, I can call Sara. Barney found me at school, walked me part way home, and later called. As a senior, he knows the ropes. Amusing Craig also called.

Saturday, September 12, 1959: Scary
Sound asleep this morning, I felt my hair yanked hard. Waking myself after assuming a nightmare, I was shocked to see Mom standing over me pulling my hair. Her face looked furious, as if she hated me. When I tried to sit up, she came to her senses and let go of my hair. Without an explanation or apology, she left me shook up. If I tell Dad, he'll defend her, as usual, and not allow a door lock. I've overheard Aunt Myrna and Mom discuss the change of life. Does it make mothers crazy? It's bad enough that fat, strident Mom blabs, but now I can't trust her to act sane. I'm scared. I hope I can fall asleep.

Sunday, September 13, 1959: Mitch
Relieved to fall asleep last night, I was glad to awaken with all my hair. It was a treat that exciting dancer Mitch, also at AHS, called. Our romance petered out. I'd like Mitch more if he read books, like Frankie, who called twice.

Tuesday, September 15, 1959: Private
After she asked about Barney, Eva listened to me:

Almost daily, Barney calls or walks me home, carrying my
books. He seems confident and looks good. He makes me
laugh, which is important. I hope Barney avoids pressuring
me to go farther. The possibility of pregnancy scares me.
Do Schuyler guys seriously expect to have sex?
Eva said that male classmates seem to expect more than at
Hackett. I added:
It's unfair. Boys push to go all the way and look down
on girls who do. Word seems to get around after boys
brag. I'd hate to be gossiped about. I don't want a fast
reputation. Boys should be gentlemen and keep everything
private.
Eva agreed and said that gentlemen were *rara aves*. I laughed,
enjoying this Latin term for "rare birds."

Thursday, September 17, 1959: Disturbing
Getting pregnant would be awful. I'd never escape from home,
go to college, and get a good job. From novels, movies, and kids
at school, I understand that a boy may tell a girl, "I love you and
will be careful," before using a rubber incorrectly or using none.
An illegal abortion could kill her. I've heard that the rhythm
method fails so often that people joke about it. I feel sorry for
an AHS girl whom XEA sorority girls mentioned. She's raising a
baby alone after school expulsion for being pregnant. Why wasn't
her boyfriend expelled for getting her pregnant and for skipping
out without marrying her?

Friday, September 18, 1959: Surprise
Barney drove me to Marsha's house for Tara's surprise
fifteenth birthday party. I felt happy seeing sweet Tara totally
dumbfounded! Her mouth fell open and no words came out. Her
face got all red. She even had a tear in her eye. She deserved
the party! Though I loved talking to her and Doreen, the less
brainy boys at the party from our old crowd interested me less
than my male classmates at AHS. Barney's affectionate company,
dancing, and goodnight kiss made it fun.

Saturday, September 19, 1959: Charm

During the Year of History Parade, celebrating the 350th anniversary of Henry Hudson's discovery voyage up our river, Paul dazzled me for a half hour! His big brown eyes gazed into mine as if I'm the girl of his dreams. His wide smile and even white teeth put me in a trance. When Paul shook my hand goodbye and held on to it, I wished he attended AHS. I talked to Barney after the parade and attended Frankie's evening party with last night's crowd. I miss having good dance partners.

Sunday, September 20, 1959: Ailing and Times

I got nervous when Mom said, "Grandma doesn't feel well and agreed to move here from Saratoga. She has generously insisted on paying rent." Is Grandma ill about Sara? Dad's unlikely to feel jealous of Grandma. I spent the day trying to finish the Sunday New York Times for American history class. It's more detailed than Albany newspapers. I like the magazine. I've yet to finish a Times crossword puzzle. Remembering yesterday's record low for that date of thirty-two degrees, I'm sad that summer's over.

Sunday, September 27, 1959: Empty

We put Grandma and her suitcases in our car and returned to Albany. In Sara's old room, the long closet has only Grandma's few loose dresses, all black crepe. The skirts are almost down to her ankles. Because she speaks only Yiddish, I liked it better with Sara here.

Monday, September 28, 1959: Hands Off

I adore Indian summer! It was over eighty today. Eva called to ask about school and Barney. After a few comments about classes, I said:

> All last week, I saw Barney in school or talked to him on the phone. At a party Friday, dancing with him and his pal was fun. Barney kissed me goodnight a few times. Tonight at the Center, he seemed less attentive, maybe because I won't go farther. Movies and books show that, once a boy starts touching your body, one thing leads to another. If I got pregnant, I'm afraid the parents would kill me

or kick me out. How would I support a baby? Boys have it easier. Babies don't ruin their lives. No boy is worth giving up my future freedom.

I felt better hearing Eva share similar feelings and fears.

Tuesday, September 29, 1959: Adlai

I really go for my Greek classmate. Dominic's fun, smart, good in sports, and masculine-looking. He said, "I want to try out for a school play. Will you come watch me act?"

I replied, "I'd love to! Someone mentioned that you play classical piano. If you give recitals, I'd enjoy hearing you play. Your hands look strong, perfect for the piano."

He turned red, making me wonder what he imagined his hands touching. He smiled with dimples showing. "Now I'm motivated to practice harder to be good enough to play for you." A reader, Dominic talks so intelligently that I'd probably never get bored. After telling me all about Adlai Stevenson, who lost against President Eisenhower, he concluded, "Adlai's got to win next time. He'll make an outstanding President."

Thursday, October 1, 1959: Hilarious

At an evening lecture, Craig and I had a ball with Eva and Xavier, both at Schuyler High. These three bright, witty comedians kept me laughing. In the ladies' room, I said to Eva, "You look great! Are you slimmer?"

"Thank you! I've finally made my doctor happy by losing twenty pounds to improve my diabetes."

"Congratulations!" I gave her a hug.

"After no dates last year, I had to do something." We both chuckled.

I asked, "Have boys you like asked you out?"

We giggled after she said, "Are you kidding?"

Saturday, October 3, 1959: Fluid

Grandma is back from an overnight hospital stay to remove fluid from her lungs. Mom explained:

I just learned that Grandma had a mild stroke a few years ago. Fortunately, it didn't leave permanent damage. But she's almost eighty with high blood pressure. Refusing a hired caretaker, she wanted me to quit my job to take care of her, but we need my salary.

Grandma's so quiet that I don't mind her being here. She must make and eat her juices and food while we're gone. When we're home, she's in her room, maybe to avoid intruding. I have yet to hear Grandma or Mom say Sara's name during Yiddish conversations. They must discuss secrets because no one translates and includes me.

Sunday, October 4, 1959: His Ex

I have enjoyed talking to smooth Barney in school and would like more dates with him, but he sat with his ex at the synagogue. She's welcome to an ungentleman who blabs about what she lets him do. I'm glad kissing is all I've allowed. Why risk missing college? I'm determined to avoid my parents' struggle to make ends meet.

Monday, October 5, 1959: Flirtation

After XEA, I had fun flirting with five good-looking, smart AHS boys, including Luke, Lon, Rex, and smart, popular senior Parker from my Latin class! Though Barney never bored me, tonight was more exciting than any date with him. If I have to go farther than I want to date Barney, then I'm fine without him. I'm puzzled that other girls prefer the security of one boyfriend. How do they avoid feeling in a rut? My cramps are gone, so I'm okay having my period.

Saturday, October 10, 1959: Parker

We won the Troy High at AHS football game! A senior gave Marsha, Marie, Parker, and me rides home. After a Hot Shoppes soda, we laughed while riding around the city dropping people off. It was a blast! I'd love to date yearbook editor and Latin Club president Parker, who has light hair and blue eyes.

Monday, October 12, 1959: Atoning

On the Day of Atonement, I prayed for forgiveness for my unintentional mistake with Sara. I miss her love, support, conversation, and companionship. I wish I could relive that night and make it right. Life seems unfair when one blunder, like getting rattled for a second, ruins everything. I'm discouraged that Aunt Lila's 1952 autograph in my book was right:

Your future lies before you, like a drift of driven snow.

Be careful how you tread it, for every mark will show.

Wednesday, October 14, 1959: UN and Regret

Our class is writing guest editorials for a newspaper contest about the UN's fourteenth anniversary. My ten paragraphs include questions to make the point that no organization can perfectly solve all world problems. When Artie called to invite me to his party, I responded, "Thank you. I'd love to go, but I promised to attend another party." I felt sorry to turn him down. Not limiting myself to one boy or one crowd gets me invitations to more parties.

Saturday, October 17, 1959: Great Day

At the AHS football game, which we won, Marie and I had a blast with three boys, including Paul. He flashed his smile and made my heart flutter. Eva's party was the most, with ping-pong and lots of joking. I danced with expert Craig, thoughtful Dominic, and fascinating Paul, all more fun than Barney. I asked Paul, "Do you still play baseball?"

Smiling, he answered, "I want to go out for it each spring at school. I'm playing basketball now, but not well enough for varsity."

Hardly thinking straight as he looked into my eyes, I flirtatiously asked, "What other activities do you enjoy at school?"

He chuckled and gently squeezed my hand before replying, "I love art and want to join the art council. Next year, I hope to do art for the yearbook and newspaper. This year, my job leaves no time."

"I love art and had fun painting watercolors before getting busy with more homework at AHS. Do you want to be an artist when you grow up?"

"I'd rather keep it a hobby because it's hard to make it pay. I like math, so my goal is engineering." I admire Paul for working to help his family.

Sunday, October 18, 1959: Clothes

On a windy day at Beth's house, Grandma smiled at her two great-granddaughters and Beth's good-looking husband. I always enjoy these well-dressed cousins. Wearing the flower-printed dress I sewed got me thinking about how important clothes are. If I look my best, boys talk to and dance with me. When dressed badly, I've been a wallflower and missed dancing to the latest hits. I talk to friends to decide what to wear. I love socializing! Romance can always happen, not that I want to go steady.

Wednesday, October 21, 1959: Uneasy

Before the parents arrived home, Grandma, who's under five feet tall, came out of her room smiling. Her gray braid hung way down the back of her old-fashioned dress. I felt awkward without understanding her Yiddish. I'd be less uneasy if Grandma knew English. I smiled for a few minutes to avoid rudeness before pantomiming homework with my books and escaping to my room. She's home alone all day, so I'm trying to be friendlier and like her more. Mom says she's intelligent. She has always read a Yiddish newspaper. Dad has always seemed warmer than Grandma and Mom.

Saturday, October 24, 1959: Makeup

Eva, her date, and funny Xavier made seeing *The Best of Everything* and eating ice cream a lot of laughs. Joan Crawford, not my favorite actress, portrayed sad events in some women's lives. In the ladies' room, I said to Eva, "Your hair looks great and your eyes look bigger and bluer!"

"Thanks for noticing! I'm setting my hair every night and wearing eye shadow, eye liner, and mascara to darken my light lashes. It's a drag, but I'm dating." I joined her in laughing.

"My mother used to say, 'It hurts to be beautiful,' when she set my hair in fourth grade. That's when Paul chose me as his girlfriend." We both giggled.

"Do we either use cosmetics or become old maids?" We smiled.

"Probably. After wearing eye makeup while on the tulip queen court, I got attention from boys I liked. Why didn't I have the brains to keep it up?"

"I'm flattered that you think I know what I'm doing." We both laughed. Eva's date was pleasant, but less sharp than she. If smart Xavier were not very overweight with terrible acne, he might be more than a friend.

Monday, October 26, 1959: Yeats
I took Midol to prevent cramps from my period. At the Center, I enjoyed talking to Yeats, an intelligent junior, slightly taller than I, with dark hair and beautiful green eyes with long, curling lashes. I enjoyed looking into his eyes while listening to him talk about history, politics, and current events. I admire him, Eva, and Craig for planning to make the world a better place, as lawyers for people without power and money.

Wednesday, October 28, 1959: Luke
I called Eva with good news:

> Yesterday at lunch, Luke approached, smiled down at me, and said, "How about coming to the Alpha Beta Gamma Thanksgiving dance as my date?" I accepted! After wanting to date him for a year, I'm thrilled! He dances very well. It's feast or famine. Though I prefer Luke, I regretted declining expert dancer Rex's invite today to the same ABG dance. I hope he asks me out again. Maybe makeup really works.

Eva laughed and expressed happiness for me.

Thursday, October 29, 1959: Extracurricular Activities
After Luke called to talk, a tall junior wanted me to join USY at Temple Israel. USY boys, like Artie, seem better than most Young Judaea boys. But I'm in too many things, including Latin Club and Forum (current events club). My homeroom elected me Red Cross representative. I'm lucky to be invited to join the

Daughters of Minerva Literary Society, Theta Alpha, because I prefer Theta Alpha to Theta Sigma girls.

Friday, October 30, 1959: Eva's Activities

When Eva called, I asked about her activities. When she mentioned Future Teachers of America, Dramatics Club, a community service sorority, Red Cross, Science Society, the chorus, and the school newspaper, I laughed and said, "I thought that my four were too many! I need time for homework, chores, and dates."

Eva laughed. "What's a date?" I laughed before she continued, "Without an outside job, my mother would die of boredom without housework. Out of 200 kids, my Schuyler class has only twenty college entrance students. Low academic standards mean I can get by with less studying." We both chuckled.

I replied, "I wish you were in our class of 400. I find AHS difficult, especially because I need top grades for scholarships."

"Because my dad's been on disability since his work accident, I'll probably live at home and go to State."

"I can't wait to leave home."

Eva laughed. "It's too bad girls can't win athletic scholarships. As a complete klutz, I admire your athletic ability! Athletic boys can get away without top grades."

"It's unfair. Thanks for the compliment. As someone who can't act or carry a tune, I admire your acting talent and singing voice! I haven't heard of scholarships for those."

"Thank you! Plays, concerts, and other activities prevent boredom with school. I wish Schuyler had literary societies."

"The four AHS societies go back to the nineteenth century! My Alpha group started in 1878, nine years before Sigma. I wonder what girls wore and said back then."

Eva laughed. "I bet they talked about boys. What are the boys' societies?"

"Philadoxia and Philalogia both have good boys. Speaking of males, what's Paul up to? I miss both of you this year."

"Paul is homeroom veep and class treasurer. With so much charisma, he'll probably be class president next year."

"Does he have a girlfriend?"

"I don't think so, but girls swoon and fall at his feet." We both giggled.

Saturday, October 31, 1959: Jana
Julia's Halloween party was fun! Paul, handsome as a dashing pirate, smiled down at me and said, "Your little girl costume reminds me of how cute you always looked in your fourth-grade Brownie outfit."

Feeling my face get red, I smiled happily and said, "Thank you!"

"Through my brother's Schenectady friend, I have news about Jana."

I replied, "I've missed her!"

"After fifth grade, Jana moved to Schenectady. I lost track of her. She's now acing Niskayuna High where she was citizen of the month, impressive for a soph!" Taking my hand, he guided me to the couch. When he sat close, I was thrilled to feel his arm around my shoulders while he shared this article:

Jana has an outgoing, pleasing personality and is always willing to lend a helping hand. A reporter on our school paper, she's also an active member of Tri-H-Y, Debating Club, the chorus, and her church youth group. Jana enjoys bowling, skiing, and reading adventure books. She collects miniature figurines. In the entertainment line, Jana casts her vote for the new TV show *Hennessey*. She confesses to a weakness for pizza from Cornell's. She likes all her teachers (tactful!) and puts English and French at the top of her subject list. Jana is quite talented at writing. She has to be to correspond with five boys at the same time. Recently, she won an award in a national contest for her essay: *What Being a Good American Means to Me*. And you know the old saying, "It takes one to know one."

After mentioning my happiness about Jana's success, I thanked Paul for loaning me the article. I wish she attended AHS. Like Eva, Doreen, Tara, Marsha, and Julia, she's special.

Sunday, November 1, 1959: Gibberish and Dress
Today's rare hail storm reminded me of the last Albany hail in 1958 before Sara and I returned from NYC. Tumba flew

around, perched on our shoulders, and talked a blue streak. He said, "Sara," along with a lot of gibberish. Do other birds prefer certain people? Tumba likes Mom the least, even though she sometimes feeds him.

Mom said, "We don't have money for a new dress for every dance." I hope that Luke, whose clothes show good taste, didn't see my navy nylon at the last ABG dance. Always comfortable with Luke, I'm eager for our date!

Saturday, November 7, 1959: Shopping and Sara
I'm excited about my sophisticated black sheath dress (size 9), shoe boots (size 6½), 32B contour bra, and nail polish. While shopping, Mom looked worried and said, "I wonder what's happening with Sara." The lines between her eyebrows got deeper. I didn't know what to say. Mom must miss Sara. When I'm on my own, I hope that Sara will talk to me. She must know that I love her more than anyone else.

Sunday, November 8, 1959: Smart and Funny
Xavier has called me almost daily in recent weeks. I feel sorry for him. I'm attracted only to lean boys. He, Eva's date, Eva, and I had a good time seeing hilarious *Pillow Talk* with cute Doris Day and Rock Hudson. I laughed when Eva and Xavier cracked one joke after the next. Eva is funny but never mean. I'm glad that she's dating, despite her brains and glasses. Her wide blue eyes look pretty without glasses, but she said, "If I want to see the movie or anything, I'm stuck with these specs." I'm lucky to be far-sighted. I can see well without glasses.

Monday, November 9, 1959: Zeke
At the Center, I enjoyed dancing with Artie, rebellious Frankie, and Zeke, who took me to The Moon for pizza. Being the only girl with four boys was fun. Zeke's mysterious manner, dark hair and eyes, handsome face, and low voice intrigued me. About my height, smart Zeke gives classical piano recitals, like Dominic! I said, "I'd love to hear you play."

Tuesday, November 10, 1959: Red-Faced

I'm excited that my UN essay was on the editorial page of Albany's morning newspaper! Classmates clapped after hearing Mrs. E read it. I felt happy, but self-conscious. My face got hot. My okay photo was captioned:

Angela, who is taking a college preparatory course, hopes to study at Cornell or Syracuse University. Her favorite subject is world history. Her career goal is lawyer or interpreter.

I like these parts of my article the best:

The world would be worse with no UN. We might have a third world war. Without UNICEF, more undernourished and ill children would die. Newer nations, especially in Africa, wouldn't have self-government without the Trusteeship Council. Without UN loans, developing countries would have lower living standards with reduced industrialization, poorer transportation, and less education. UN action has improved situations in Iran, Greece, Kashmir, Indonesia, Korea, Hungary, and the Middle East. Germany, Algeria, the Far East, the Middle East, and disarmament are continuing problems. The more problems that we have solved, the more experience we shall have. With more experience, we are better equipped to settle new difficulties.

After discussing ways to help the UN, I ended with:

We cannot help matters by just sitting back passively in our armchairs and saying that everything will be solved in time. We cannot help by absolutely condemning the UN either. Action is what we need to further the world peace that we cherish so much. Support the United Nations!

The Times Union will publish four more essays this week. I'm lucky to win because the first two winners were upperclassmen.

Thursday, November 12, 1959: Famous

Mom sent my article to every relative on earth. Did Sara get one? Something tells me that it's useless to ask Mom for her address. What a fun evening! Luke called to tease me about being famous. I laughed when Craig phoned. "I don't know whether an important writer like you has time to talk to an ordinary mortal like me." I'm glad they don't seem envious, even though they submitted essays.

Wednesday, November 18, 1959: World Affairs
Mrs. E encouraged our class to attend the Albany World Affairs Council meeting. I felt grown-up listening to a panel of college professors discuss the UN anniversary. After the program, I laughed at the jokes of Craig, Eva, and Xavier.

Thursday, November 19, 1959: Shoes
One black shoe and one dark blue shoe on Mrs. E caused a double-take. I could hardly keep from laughing out loud. Craig, two rows away, noticed my attempts to control myself and mouthed, "What?" When Mrs. E turned to write on the board, I pointed to her shoes. Seeing the different colors, Craig silently cracked up and told other kids. Everyone was smiling. Craig mischievously tried to catch my eye to make me burst out laughing. My face felt hot and red. I tried to pay attention to the lecture, but the shoes were too hilarious. Hearing the bell ring, I breathed a sigh of relief.

Before I could escape to the hall, Mrs. E called Craig and me to her desk. "What's so funny?" I pointed to her shoes. We all had a good laugh. "I'm like an absent-minded professor," she joked. She must dress in the dark and rush to get her three sons off to school. We're lucky she has a sense of humor.

Saturday, November 21, 1959: Craig
When Craig called about homework and joked about school and classmates, I said, "You're so funny."

I felt happy to hear, "You're my best audience. You appreciate my jokes more than anyone else." I wish he hadn't added, "Is your aunt still here writing a book?"

I replied, "She had to return to NYC." Ashamed of how I let Sara down, I changed the subject.

Wednesday, November 25, 1959: Cooking

After lighting Sabbath candles and saying blessings on Fridays, we eat Mom's barley soup and roast chicken. In recent years, I've cooked weekday dinners so we can eat when the parents get home at six. I usually bake potatoes; broil hamburgers, steaks, or lamb chops; and prepare vegetables, such as celery, carrots, asparagus, and string beans. Tonight, after heating frozen peas and making a salad of lettuce, tomatoes, and cucumbers, I made my favorite: breaded veal cutlet. I melted margarine because butter isn't kosher with meat. After dipping the cutlets into flour, beaten eggs, and bread crumbs, I was frying them when the phone rang. Mom said, "Craig, Angela's cooking and can't talk now." When he called later, Mom said, "She's eating dinner." The third time he called, I was taking a bath. I hope he calls soon. I don't want to miss anything important.

Friday, November 27, 1959: Dennis

Eva and I met downtown to see *Hound Dog Man* with cute Fabian and pretty Carol Lynley. After joking around, we took different buses home. On Park Avenue, I took a shortcut across the dark parking lot. Suddenly, hands from behind grabbed my chest. I yelled, "Get away," fought to pull off the hands, and squirmed away. Out of the corner of my eye, I recognized Dennis, a younger Patroon School delinquent. As he slinked away, I ran the three blocks home at top speed. Looking back, I felt relieved not to see him. Catching my breath, I told myself to act calm and normal. If the parents find out, Dad will yell, blame me, and never let me out alone. I put on a good act, smiling and waving at Dad in his easy chair. He glanced up, smiled, and returned to his paper. Grandma was probably asleep. I was lucky to reach the bathroom without seeing Mom. I'll hide this paper in case she snoops in my diary. I'm mad at that jerk Dennis and glad to escape and keep him from getting what he wanted.

Sunday, November 29, 1959: ABG Dance and Summer Place

Doreen, who had nothing new to report, was happy that last night's dance was great:

Mom let me have my hair done. I loved Luke's corsage of six white roses, which matched the white rose outlines on my dress. At the downtown hotel and at Emmy's *Brauhaus* in the Helderberg Mountains, dancing with Luke was wonderful, including the scent of his after-shave lotion. Luke explained, "Emmy's resembles a German beer place with dark wood paneling, cuckoo clocks, photos, and knickknacks on the walls." The dirndl waitress uniforms (gathered skirts and tight, patterned weskits laced over white blouses with puffed sleeves) reminded me of the movie *Heidi*. When our waitress leaned over our long table to take orders, some boys seemed ready to put their hands down the front of her low-cut blouse. I was glad that Luke was a gentleman. To order beer, the boys showed fake draft cards, which Luke said they had bought to prove they're over eighteen. Beer tastes awful, so I don't mind that girls can't order it! No one drank too much or acted rowdy. Luke held my hand and had his arm around me.

I danced every dance with him, except for two with Rex who joked, "You should have come to this dance with me. Look how well we dance together." Rex's fast turns and exhilarating dips resembled Mitch's!

Today, *A Summer Place* was a terrific escape movie. Blond Troy Donahue and cute Sandra Dee played a young couple. Their parents, when young, had loved each other, but married other people. I liked the theme song.

Luke

Angela Weiss

Monday, November 30, 1959: Secret
The parents have shown no signs of knowing my secret. Telling friends is too risky. Word may get back through their parents. Did Dennis attack Albany Hospital nurses and Sara? The locations are only seven blocks apart. Though I'm mad that he wasn't punished, complaining will backfire. Was he retaliating for Patroon traffic court penalties, when I was a school officer?

Wednesday, December 2, 1959: Lon
Why does blue-eyed Lon call every week? He dresses well and is slim with blond hair. Since he gets good grades, is homework an excuse to call? Boys are hard to figure out. I wish he'd ask me out.

Thursday, December 3, 1959: Cloud Nine
I floated home after Craig's invite to the Jack Frost semiformal dance! Dad asked, "Is he Jewish?"

I answered no.

Mom said, "We don't want you dating non-Jews."

After my jaw dropped in amazement, I asked, "Why not? Ken took me to dances. Craig's a top student and school leader."

Dad said, "High school is the time to date only Jews. One thing leads to another. People marry high school sweethearts."

I replied, "It's one date. I'm not in love. I don't want to go steady." Tears of frustration filled my eyes. "You're so unfair! It's hard enough to get invited."

Mom said, "You're popular. Show interest and a nice Jewish boy will ask you."

I said to Dad, "Shouldn't you practice what you preach about discrimination?"

Mom answered, "Say what you want. You can date only Jewish boys."

I asked, "What if Protestant parents kept their daughter from dating a Jewish boy? You'd complain to the B'nai B'rith Anti-Defamation League."

Dad said, "That's different. Jews are a minority with a history of being discriminated against."

I felt like screaming, "Maybe hypocrites like you give Jews a bad name. You're wrong to make me miss this dance!" From Cloud Nine, I crashed to the ground.

Friday, December 4, 1959: Officially
It broke my heart to tell Craig no. He replied, "I'm officially Jewish: my mom's mother is Jewish."

But Mom said, "If he attends church, he's not Jewish." I'm embarrassed that Craig knows that my family is bigoted. I hate my parents for making me miss a major dance with an ideal date! Why work hard at chores, homework, and tests if I'm punished, like a bad kid? I can't believe it!

Saturday, December 5, 1959: Unchaperoned
At the Center, I played ping-pong and danced exclusively with Artie. When he invited me to an unchaperoned party, I said, "Thank you, Artie. I enjoy being with you, but my parents require chaperones." I'm all for chaperones to avoid make-out pressure, a bad reputation, and even pregnancy. Everyone gossips. I wish boys were satisfied getting experience with Green Street prostitutes.

Luke has said, "Guys with enough money go there Friday nights." My parents stupidly consider Craig risky.

Sunday, December 6, 1959: War
On the phone, Eva laughed when I said, "In the Cold War, I'm the good American; the parents are evil Russians."

Later, as Dad's friend, Karl Levine, left our house, I walked out with him. He said, "What's up?"

I said, "I need to get out of this house. I can't stand another two and a half years!"

He asked, "What happened?"

I answered, "I do all my homework and more than half the chores and house cleaning and get As on my tests. But my parents treated me like a juvenile delinquent with all Fs. I had to turn down my only invitation to one of two big AHS dances this year."

He asked, "Why?"

"I'm suddenly forced to date only Jews. Craig's family attends a Protestant church. My parents said no, even though Craig's officially Jewish. His mother's mother is Jewish."

He said, "Hmmm."

"Dad's always criticizing prejudice, yet he's discriminating against Christians. This fall, Mom went crazy, scaring me out of a deep sleep by yanking my hair. I need to escape."

"Can you live with your aunt in NYC?"

I shook my head no.

"How about your Gloversville relatives?"

"They'll side with my parents."

"Your parents would kill me if you stayed with us."

"I know. I'm ready to run away. If you think of anything, please let me know. Thanks for listening."

Wednesday, December 9, 1959: Hal

Cousin Hal is studying for a Ph.D. in political science at Columbia University. His letter left me excited:

Congratulations on your article in the Albany newspaper. I found it difficult to believe that it was not by a professional, so clearly and competently was it written. Not only were your ideas sound, they were expressed convincingly and in good English, something usually missing in writing by high school students.

I was especially interested since I am studying the UN in one of my courses. Perhaps I can let you write one of my papers. It will have to be just as good as the article and a good deal longer. My professor helped draft the UN Charter in 1945 at San Francisco.

I suppose you are now a celebrity at school; was there any strong reaction or letters to you or the editor concerning your views? Many people disagree with them, you know.

You should consider Barnard among your college choices. I have no doubt that you will be admitted, and it offers you much that Syracuse and Cornell do not. I was admitted to both and turned down a full tuition scholarship to Syracuse. If you are interested, we can discuss this further.

Keep up the good work. Regards to your mom and dad.
Love, Hal

I look up to him. I never thought of Barnard. I'm relieved and rewarded by my report card's straight As, but can I keep it up?

Thursday, December 10, 1959: Non-Celebrity

Laughing about the word celebrity, after thanking Hal for his letter, I added:

I'm not a celebrity. I don't know whether anyone has written to the editor about my article because homework keeps me too busy to check the paper. Our teacher hasn't mentioned anyone commenting about my ideas.

Saturday, December 12, 1959: Trojans

Eva, sympathetic about the Jewish-only rule, laughed after I said:

Last night's basketball game was frustrating. AHS lost. Jewish Parker was nearby, but talked to a pal, rather than me. Godlike seniors like him usually make me too nervous for conversation. Jewish Zeke sat behind me, but didn't ask me out again. Maybe he likes girls without eye makeup. The eye makeup may have backfired by attracting Jewish Victor. If he had Xavier's personality, I would have accepted a ride with him.

Eva wondered if Zeke had heard that I'm not fast.

I responded, "I bet you're right. Barney's blabbing may also be preventing Lon and Hank from dating me. Do Trojan rubbers in boys' wallets mean that they expect to go all the way?"

I giggled after Eva replied, "I bet most Trojans show wishful thinking. The wrappers I've glimpsed look tattered after years of disuse."

Sunday, December 13, 1959: Victor and Escape

When Doreen called, I said, "Redhead Victor called. A junior, he's taller than I with a nice physique. I'd feel more interested if he was well-read, creative, amusing, or special in some way. He may be pals with your JP."

She replied, "I understand how you feel. JP gets good grades and is musical but he doesn't make me laugh." After hanging up, I wondered if Karl Levine has talked to my jail keepers. There must be a way to escape.

Monday, December 21, 1959: Dreamy Eyes
The Center was a blast with four dance partners, including Artie and Victor, who held my hand and had his arm around me. He dances well and won half of our ping-pong games. Interesting tennis player Yeats also played ping-pong with me. I went into a trance while looking into his long-lashed, greenish eyes and hearing his leadership ideas. I was impressed that he's president of Key Club, a service organization, as well as Forum. Wondering if he's the rare popular Jewish boy interested in a non-fast girl wearing eye makeup, I smiled.

Friday, December 25, 1959: Hanukkah and Christmas
I called Eva to say, "Merry Christmas! Hanukkah started today. I can't remember its starting on Xmas before."

"Happy Hanukkah! I love being off school. I'm reading an interesting bestseller, *The House of Intellect* by Jacques Barzun."

"What do you like best about it?"

"It's irreverent."

I laughed and said, "It sounds good!" Later, I imagined hiding at Eva's house. Her parents don't know mine, but probably lack money to feed an extra person. I don't want to get them in trouble. Dad would call the police, who might follow me from school and arrest them. If Sara weren't angry, living with her would be perfect. There must be someplace to go. If only I could think of it...

Saturday, December 26, 1959: Sneaking and Babysitting
I told Mom, "I'm meeting Eva at the movie *Little Abner*," without mentioning Craig. I don't like sneaking around, but refuse to ruin my social life more than necessary. If someone reports back to the parents, I'll say, "We ran into Craig, who sat with us." He gave me a holiday gift: a tiny, adorable mink pin! Eva was

wonderful to help. I enjoyed being the audience of these two clever comedians. Yeats and Victor left phone messages while I was having fun babysitting for the cute eight- and five-year-old Franklin boys. Two dollars earned won't enable me to run away, so I'll save them for college.

Sunday, December 27, 1959: Ride
Victor, Yeats, and a pal took me for a ride, including Howard Johnson's ice cream. I had fun because Yeats is intelligent with a wry sense of humor. He enjoys golf and works on the yearbook. It was fun to practice a little Spanish together. Along with Artie, Luke, Craig, Dominic, Lon, Neal, Steve, Marcus, Tad, and Ken, Yeats is in Philologia literary society. Victor's not in either society.

Tuesday, December 29, 1959: Headquarters
Going south on the Thruway, I was a captive audience: three hours felt like ten. While driving, Mom nagged and asked nosey questions about boys. Dad, irritated at every little thing, seemed ready for a temper tantrum. I can't stand their annoying voices. Except for evergreens, the trees were bare of leaves. The lifeless winter landscape looked brown and gray. Ron and I enjoyed touring the UN glass-and-steel headquarters, which Le Corbusier, Niemeyer, and other architects designed over seven years ago. In the ladies' room, I was too chicken to skip out to Sara's apartment. I was afraid to confide in religious Ron, who might agree with my parents. Gil was fun on the phone.

Wednesday, December 30, 1959: No Kisses
I'm elated after an exciting NYC movie date with Donald, now a senior. After Howard Johnson's hamburgers, Donald made even the boring Money Museum amusing. I'm thrilled to do anything with him. During a long walk on Broadway, I felt like asking, "Will your parents adopt me and let me move in?" Why doesn't he kiss me? He's the opposite of fast Albany boys. New things to do and Donald's stimulating personality make Manhattan dates wonderful. Though Donald never mentions religion, we assume he's Jewish, like other Catskill vacationers. In Aunt Lila's

bathroom, I quickly scribbled and hid in my purse a UN picture postcard to mail to Craig:

> Thank you again for the mink holiday gift! I adore its soft, silky feel. You would have loved the hilarious movie I saw today: *The Mouse That Roared.* Peter Sellers played a female head of state and other roles. The tiny country declares war on the US to receive foreign aid. I hope we get picked for the March NYC Latin contest. Your best audience, Angela

Thursday, December 31, 1959: New Year

Victor danced with me and had his arm around me at his okay party, my only New Year's Eve invitation. Eye makeup hasn't motivated better Jewish boys to beat down our door. Has Barney gossiped that I'm prudish?

1960

Friday, January 1, 1960: New Year's Resolutions
Keep trying to escape from home. Until then, be nicer to Grandma.

Tuesday, January 5, 1960: Dreary
Last night, I went to sleep early and woke myself from a nightmare like the Rapunzel story:

> Locked in a tower by a witch and wizard, I looked out the window to see Craig. He tried to rescue me by climbing up my long brown hair. The witch threw a sharp boomerang, which chopped off my hair. Poor Craig fell and lay on the ground injured. Upset and crying, I couldn't reach him to help.

Tonight, I told Doreen, "Victor has called every day since his party. Has JP improved?"

She laughed. "We feel the same about JP and Victor. They're better than no one. These short days are dreary."

I agreed. "Winter's my least favorite season."

Wednesday, January 6, 1960: Partying
I had a fun fifteenth birthday party with Eva and Doreen eating dinner at our house. I love my gorgeous gifts, mostly from parents and relatives: a dress, perfume, jewelry, pajamas, robe, skirt, blouse, and ten dollars! In my room, the girls laughed when I said, "If I don't run away soon, I may miss every school dance until graduation. Guess what? Mom was planning a surprise birthday party Saturday."

Eva asked, "Is it on?"

I shook my head no. "When I found the guest list near the kitchen phone, Mom admitted she was about to invite everyone."

Eva smiled and said, "Were all the boys Jewish?"

I nodded and laughed. "I'd be happy with Luke, Hank, Lon, Parker, Artie, Yeats, Zeke, and even Myles and Mitch. The girls were perfect: you two, Tara, Marsha, and Julia."

Doreen smiled. "Were Victor, Rob, and Earl included?"

I giggled. "Yes! Doreen, you're smart! Mom picked only boys who don't interest me."

Doreen laughed. "Were Udeh, Oren, and Carl included?"

"You're right, except for Lewis instead of Oren. Three frogs would be fine if princely Craig, Dominic, and Paul were there. Mom's six would be no fun."

Doreen

Thursday, January 7, 1960: Fifteen
Victor called to sing *Happy Birthday* on the actual day. I'd love a summer birthday. Fifteen years ago, a huge blizzard slowed Dad's trip to Albany Hospital. Mom said, "Dad fainted after hearing that his wife was fine and his daughter was twenty-one inches long and eight pounds, six ounces." Was Dad nervous because Rowena was born dead?

Friday, January 8, 1960: Counting
On the phone, I told Doreen, "The warm day in the low forties cheered me while buying a bargain skirt-blouse-and-jacket suit with birthday money."
    "Where did you find it?"
    "Expensive Solomon's has a sale!"
    "I'll go tomorrow."
    "I'd shop with you, but I'll be at Columbia High." In thirty-one months, I'll be gone for good unless I escape sooner.

Saturday, January 9, 1960: Exhilaration
I rode with Luke's older brother and senior Parker to be timekeeper for a fun National Forensic League debate competition. Next time, I'll be a debater! At the Center, dancing with seven boys was exhilarating, including Artie, Victor, and Yeats, who took me to another girl's sweet sixteen party at Jack's Restaurant. Victor took me home and kissed me goodnight.

Wednesday, January 13, 1960: Let Go
At dinner, Dad said, "I've been fired. Stuck at the same low salary for years, I made my first request for a raise in over two years. My boss responded, 'Since you're dissatisfied with the pay, work elsewhere starting February 1. Business is bad. With the holidays over, we need fewer salesmen.' I replied that I needed a raise to support my family, including a daughter who will go to college. It didn't matter. He was looking for an excuse to let me go." My mouth dropped open in shock. The color seemed to leave Mom's face and she looked older a day after her forty-eighth birthday.

Finally, Mom said, "We'll manage. After I won the award for *The Brain*, my bosses requested an upgrade of my job to senior typist, which pays more. I'll ask if it will be approved soon. Angela can find a paying summer job. We'll cut back on expenses and vacations."

"Hon, thanks for your support! I'll try commissioned, door-to-door sales. It will pay more if I sell a lot."

Feeling sorry for Dad, I said, "I'll babysit more. You can reduce my allowance to twenty-five cents a week. With my birthday gifts, I won't need clothes for ages. I've stopped growing." I pictured wearing my old yellow net or navy nylon if a miracle occurs and a good Jewish boy invites me to a dance.

Using his old nickname for me, Dad said, "Dolly, I appreciate your help!" I'm not superstitious, but why did this happen on the thirteenth?

Friday, January 22, 1960: Waiting
On the phone, Tara said, "I see Ben in French and other classes. I wish he'd ask me out."

After I expressed sympathy and she asked how I was doing, I said, "Victor has called every day for a week. With little to say, I have gotten off the phone quickly without hurting his feelings." She agreed with my comment, "I love being a girl, except the drag of waiting for boys I prefer to rescue me from being stuck at home or with guys who don't interest me." I haven't told friends that Dad will start selling vacuum cleaners door-to-door next month. Dad has worked hard for years. Firing him seems unfair, just like forcing me to miss a big dance after I've worked so hard at school and chores.

Saturday, January 23, 1960: Steady
At our AHS basketball game, Victor held my hand. After dancing at the Center, we doubled with another couple for Calsolero's pizza. Victor gave me a chain with a good luck Canadian penny and a round medal with his Bar Mitzvah date, before asking, "Will you go steady with me?"

I replied, "Thank you. I'll think about it." I'm planning words to avoid dishonest encouragement and hurt feelings.

Monday, January 25, 1960: No and Blue Moon

After driving me home from school, Victor brought up going steady. I said, "Thank you for asking me. I don't believe in it, so I'll have to say no." I've known him only six weeks. I'm glad that he didn't seem upset. He asked for my picture, which I signed, "Yours, Angie."

Today, a classmate said, "I can't imagine the upcoming Blue Moon dance being better than the Jack Frost."

Her friend replied, "I swooned over Parker in his dark suit dancing as Jack Frost king." If I could date Craig, I might have enjoyed both big dances this year. I feel like giving up. The only thing that keeps me slaving away is picturing doing as I please when I have a good job after college.

Tuesday, January 26, 1960: Doreen and Victor

On the phone, Doreen was excited about Neal's invitation to the Blue Moon! She said, "He's on the student council, which sponsors the dance. My mother's letting me splurge on a new formal!"

I said, "That's wonderful! You deserve to go with someone you like! I'm really happy for you! What color dress do you prefer?"

"Maybe mint green. I might need your help in deciding on a dress."

"Doreen, I'd love to help with that or anything else!" When she asked about me, I shared about tonight's date with Victor at the Palace Theatre. "*The Story on Page One* was a good movie. He held my hand and had his arm around me. After we walked to Joe's for a snack, a cab took us home for goodnight kisses. Without the need for much conversation, I had a nice time."

Friday, January 29, 1960: Doubling and Donald

Victor and I cheered our basketball team to a win. Double-dating with Marie and her date for Calsolero's pizza was fun. Victor kissed me goodnight. I accepted his invite to see *The Gazebo*, a Debbie Reynolds movie, tomorrow. With my period here, I'm less grouchy and hoping the cramps won't worsen. Donald sent a wonderful letter. I love his writing. He'll attend Queens College near his apartment next year.

Tuesday, February 2, 1960: Laurels and Transformation

Though I'm relieved about my 98.3 percent average, I can't rest on my laurels. My six exam marks ranged from 100 percent in geometry and world history to 96 percent in health. With Dad's salary gone, I feel more pressure to earn scholarships. Talking to Eva on the phone, I said, "With no way to escape from the tyrants, maybe I should temporarily change into an ant to crawl away beyond their reach. This cool idea came from a story we read in English class about a guy who turned into a giant beetle."

"Was it Kafka's *The Metamorphosis*?"

"Yes. My ending will be happier. After gaining freedom, I'll convert back into myself and date any boy I want." We both giggled. "I love English. I can't wait to read Tolstoy's *Anna Karenina*!"

"I wish we had advanced classes. We're slogging through *Silas Marner*. On my own, I've read George Eliot's better novels: *Mill on the Floss, Middlemarch,* and *Daniel Deronda*."

"Wasn't George Eliot a woman?" I asked.

"She was brilliant and far ahead of her Victorian era!"

"I'm adding her novels to my reading list."

"Angela, I'll read *Anna* on my own while your class reads it."

"Great idea! You can explain any parts I don't get!" We both laughed.

Wednesday, February 3, 1960: Talk and Letter

I was surprised that Victor held my interest on the phone for almost an hour. Pen pal Joe sent a lively letter about his high school leadership activities in Bala Cynwyd near Philadelphia. In answer to my question, he wrote that his town's name is Welsh, like the original Quaker settlers. I wonder whether he's stuck dating only Jewish girls. I'm growing my hair long, hoping for more dates. Tumba said, "Be my Valentine," for the first time!

Friday, February 5, 1960: Punishment

Lighting the Sabbath candles got me thinking about God, whom I don't really understand. Is missing out on big dances my punishment for not standing up for Sara? Was she attacked as punishment for freeloading off Grandma? Maybe Dad lost his job because he was cruel to Sara and unfair to me about the Jack Frost. Mom's been mean to pull my hair and make me miss the Jack Frost. Though she's lost Sara, she seems to be getting off easier.

Saturday, February 6, 1960: A Blast
After I spent hours studying and doing chores, seven dance partners at the Center lifted my mood! My favorites included Piano Fingers (Zeke) and Dreamy Eyes (Yeats), who put his silver identification bracelet on my wrist and joked about going steady. We went to The Moon where Luke and Lon briefly flirted with me. Variety prevents boredom.

Sunday, February 7, 1960: Bowling and Rally
Did the cute, red-haired pinsetter help me get my top bowling scores ever: 115 and 111? Victor bowled well. The interfaith youth rally was fun with boys of all religions as dance partners. Godlike Parker talked to me until moving on after I became tongue-tied, as usual. Victor took me home.

Thursday, February 11, 1960: Stag
Eva phoned to say, "Doreen and I have been looking for a strategy to keep you sane for the next thirty months." We both laughed.

"I'm lucky to have such wonderful friends!"

"We can't be fairy godmothers for big dances, but you can spend time with Craig, Dominic, and Paul at movies, parties, school plays, concerts, and games, if you go stag or with us. We'll tell the boys that you'll be there."

Tears filled my eyes. "Eva, thank you! Your approach is perfect. I'll turn down boring dates and attend events alone or with you and Doreen. I'll enjoy the boys I prefer."

"After hearing the reason you missed the Jack Frost with Craig, non-Jewish boys may be afraid to call. Will your parents let you talk to them on the phone?"

"Yes! I have an extension phone! I can say that they called about homework."

Eva said, "I'll let them know that calling's okay. Craig, Doreen, and I are planning parties."

"I can't wait! You're so sweet to make things better for me! If I can help you with anything, please tell me. I'll thank Doreen, too. Your brilliant solution, yesterday's over-fifty temperature, and Valentine's Day coming have cheered me." We both giggled after I said, "I may even get through high school without men in white coats coming for me. Thank you so much!" I'm glad that parties, library books, and some school activities are free. My allowance should cover low-cost events. I'm lucky to have seen enough movies to skip them unless Dad earns money.

Saturday, February 13, 1960: Awful Day

After discovering that Grandma had died in her sleep, Mom collapsed and went to bed. I don't think she cried, but she was too upset to do anything. Dad was busy with funeral arrangements. When men came to take Grandma's body to Gloversville, I was afraid to see her dead and stayed in my room. Mom nodded yes when I asked, "Should I call my aunts and uncles?" Eager to talk to Sara, I found the number in Mom's address book. I worried about how to give the horrible news. When Sara answered the phone, I said, "This is Angela. I'm sorry. I have bad news. It's about Grandma."

Sara said, "All right."

I said, "She died in her sleep last night."

Without sounding upset, Sara said, "Thank you for telling me," and hung up before I could mention the funeral. The doctor brought Mom a sedative. Seeing her in bed all day was disconcerting (a word from the Scholastic Aptitude Test list). Mom and Grandma seemed indomitable (also on the SAT list). I don't understand death. How can Grandma walk around one day and be too weak to live the next day? What a shock! Calling relatives, I had to act grown-up today. I hope I did well.

Sunday, February 14, 1960: Bleak

Victor called to say, "Happy Valentine's Day!" After hearing about Grandma, he said, "I'm sorry." I'm less upset than Mom. My parents were silent on the drive to Gloversville. The pale gray sky was typical of our drab winter days. In the gloomy tan

Reformed synagogue with brown trim, we sat near my uncles and their families.

Mom commented on the medium-sized crowd: "These are my brothers' friends. Ma's friends have died."

Reciting *Woman of Valor*, the rabbi sounded good, especially the last line, "Wherever people gather, her deeds speak her praise." But it could describe any woman. Did the rabbi even know Grandma? She gave money to charity, but didn't go to the synagogue. I was disappointed that Sara was absent; I wanted so much to see her. Did Sara's silence make Grandma die sooner? After short prayers at the cemetery, they buried Grandma next to Grandpa's grave. The cold and wind made everyone hurry to cars and turn on heaters. Though it was well below freezing, we were lucky it wasn't below zero. I was glad to go to Uncle Abner's and Aunt Myrna's house for refreshments with relatives and their friends.

I overheard Mom say, "The doctor said that she died because fluid accumulated again in her lungs. Her heart failed." I felt better talking to Lydia and Ella in their pretty upstairs bedroom. They were sad because of good experiences with Grandma, who lived a block away until 1957. During the ride home, Mom probably thought that I was asleep in the back seat when she told Dad, "Ma had it tough with Pa's drinking, poker, and floozies. Without separate bedrooms, she would have had more pregnancies. Without abortions, she would have had nine kids." Surprised, I felt more sympathy for Grandma.

At home, I grinned when Tumba chirped, "Be my Valentine." I'm relieved that the funeral is over.

After saying the prayer, "Hear, O Israel, the Lord our God, the Lord is one," I fell asleep wondering if God made Grandma die to punish Sara for avoiding Grandma and to penalize Mom for acting mean.

Monday, February 15, 1960: Grown-Up
I'm sorry that all my grandparents are dead. I wish I'd been nicer to Grandma. Helping Mom and seeing Grandma buried made me feel older. My parents spend their time working and worrying about money. Knocking on doors in the cold, wind, and snow from

nine to six every day, Dad hasn't sold anything in two weeks. With homework and chores taking most of my time, I'm going to have as much fun as possible while I'm young, especially since people can unexpectedly disappear or die. I want to laugh and flirt and dance. I want to get to know smart, fun, interesting boys. If I can't be boy crazy forever, I'm going to enjoy it while I can.

Characters

Mother's Family

1875: Grandpa C born near Vilna (now in Lithuania); died 1946
1880: Grandma C born near Minsk (now in Belarus)
1898: they married
1900: they emigrated to NYC and later settled in Gloversville, NY
1903: Uncle Abner born
    Married Rosa
        1932: red-haired Beth born Gloversville
            Married
            1955: June born Long Island, NY
            1957: widowed and glamorous, remarried in Albany
            1958: Jill born Albany
    Divorced; 1944: married Myrna in Gloversville
        1946: Lydia born
        1949: Ella born
1905: Uncle Peter born
    Married Faith in Gloversville
        1927: Nick born
            Married
            1951: son born
            1953: son born
            1957: daughter born
1907: Uncle Isaac born; died 1946
1912: Angela's mom Fern born Gloversville
    1937: married Herm in Albany, NY
        1940: Rowena born and died Northville, NY
        1945: Angela born Albany
        7/3/54: parakeet Tumba arrived
1917: Aunt Sara born Gloversville
    1940: married George in Albany; divorced 1947
    1948: married Jules in Spring Valley, NY; divorced 1951
    1955-1959: loved Mort, NYC boyfriend

Father's Family

1876: Grandpa Weiss born in The Ukraine; died 1946
1878: Grandma W born in The Ukraine
1898: they married
1900: they emigrated to NYC
1901: Aunt Hannah born NYC
     Married Cal in NYC
        1928: Justine born NYC
           1950: married in NYC
           1953: son born NYC
           1958: daughter Angelina born NYC
1903: Aunt Rhoda born NYC
     1933: married Harvey in NYC
1908: Aunt Lila born NYC
     Married Bert in NYC
        1938: Hal born NYC
        1945: Ron born NYC
1911: Angela's dad Herm born NYC
     1937: married Fern in Albany, NY
        1940: Rowena born and died Northville, NY
        1945: Angela born Albany
        7/3/54: parakeet Tumba arrived

Males in Angela's Life

Name	First Mentioned	Description
Al	7/23/59	Catskill boy
Ari	3/28/57	Israeli medical student and Hebrew substitute teacher
Artie	2/2/57	Heartthrob
Aryeh	1/6/57	Classmate
Barney	1/26/58	Boyfriend
Ben	4/3/57	Tara's heartthrob
Billy	8/19/53	Ma Meade's delinquent grandson
Buddy	3/29/57	Crush nicknamed Rub a Dub, Dub, and Dubby
Carl	1/5/57	Naïve classmate
Craig	9/17/58	Date and class leader
Dennis	11/29/59	Patroon School delinquent
Dominic	9/29/59	Crush
Donald	7/20/58	Catskill romance and pen pal
Earl	10/26/58	Date
Edwin	12/27/56	Boyfriend
Francis	5/22/59	Classmate and nephew of Kirk Douglas
Frankie	1/1/57	Rabbi's son and date
George	11/9/53	Jana's boyfriend
Gil	6/22/58	NYC pen pal, Cousin Ron's friend
Hank	9/13/58	Intelligent crush
Howard	7/24/59	Catskill boy
Hy	2/16/58	Crush
JP	12/13/59	Doreen's date
Jimmy	7/13/55	Bully
Joe	8/17/58	Pen pal, cousin of Uncle Harvey
Karl	7/15/54	Angela's dad's friend

Ken	5/14/57	Classmate and date
Kurt	7/19/59	Unappealing Catskill boy
Lewis	2/2/57	Cute occasional dance partner
Lon	10/13/58	Crush
Luke	9/3/58	Crush and date
M&M	9/15/58	Nickname for Mitch and Myles
Marcus	2/3/56	First date and classmate
Mario	11/5/57	Handsome hoodlum
Mitch	5/18/57	Boyfriend
Myles	1/6/57	Sexy date and friend
Neal	10/26/57	Doreen's crush
Oren	4/15/57	Son of Levines, parents' friends
Parker	10/10/59	Godlike senior
Paul	11/9/53	Boyfriend and heartthrob
Phil	5/6/59	Homeroom president and date
Quinn	8/17/59	NJ date
Ray	11/3/57	Boyfriend
Rex	2/7/59	Occasional date and dance partner, nephew of Kirk Douglas
Rich	7/24/58	Catskill boy
Rob	1/27/57	Date
Sal	10/31/58	Hackett infatuation
Steve	9/9/58	Hackett boyfriend
Stu	1/10/59	Distant Gloversville cousin
Tad	3/12/50	Husband at age five and date
Tommy	1/7/52	Mayfield boyfriend
Ty	2/16/58	Acquaintance
Udeh	1/6/57	Classmate
Victor	12/11/59	Frequent date
Vin	8/18/59	NJ date
Wendell	7/9/51	Ma Meade's younger grandson
Will	4/23/58	Intense crush

Wolf	11/17/57	Tara's smooth date
Xavier	10/1/59	Platonic friend
Yeats	10/26/59	Date
Zeke	11/9/59	Date

Females in Angela's Life

Name	First Mentioned	Description
Anna	5/21/54	Classmate
Barbara	7/5/57	Classmate and campmate
Bea	7/24/55	Friend
Cara	7/8/55	Neighbor
Doreen	9/28/54	Close friend
Eva	12/13/58	Close friend
Evelyn	4/16/57	Angela's mom's friend
Froggy	7/11/57	Campmate
Gina	4/29/54	Bully
Hilda	4/29/54	Bully
Irene	3/21/57	Blond classmate and campmate
Jana	11/9/53	Best friend, fourth grade
Julia	10/29/55	Friend and party hostess
Lil	2/16/58	Daydream rival
Ma Meade	8/18/53	Colonie business owner
Marie	11/1/58	Classmate
Marsha	10/13/54	Close friend
Naomi	11/23/57	Ray's past girlfriend
Pam	10/29/57	Campaign manager and classmate
Robin	4/16/57	Daughter of Levines, parents' friends
Rose	2/16/58	Daydream rival
Tara	10/14/51	Close friend

Acknowledgements and Permissions

Though real people and events inspired the author, *Boy Crazy* is a work of historical fiction, which grew out of the author's childhood diary. Photos of real people are included to create an authentic 1950s ambience; however, the actions, dialogue, and qualities of the characters are creations of the author's imagination.

The author is grateful to the friends and cousin who inspired the characters Doreen, Tara, Craig, Marcus, Hal, Paul, and Artie and who approved the use of photos, writings, and memories. The cover photo shows Artie and Angela at a February 1959 dance.

The author thanks the executor/beneficiary son of the cousin who inspired the character Beth for approval of the use of the photo under June 9, 1957.

The Director of Communication of the Albany Public Schools consulted their attorney, who confirmed that group and individual class and yearbook photos are in the public domain and thus may be used in this book. Examples are the photos under January 7, 1952, June 9, 1957, September 18, 1957, May 8, 1958, September 3, 1958, December 2, 1958, March 18, 1959, and January 6, 1960.

The Niskayuna High School newspaper excerpt under October 31, 1959, is in the public domain.

Grateful acknowledgement for permission to include the photo under October 23, 1953, is made to Susan Graham, Special Collections Librarian, University of Maryland Baltimore County, owner of the papers of photographer Mildred Grossman.

The author is the copyright holder of all childhood drawings and paintings, which she created during the 1950s.

As mentioned under December 7, 1956, the relatives (both deceased) who inspired the characters Aunt Rhoda and Uncle Harvey kindly gave the author the diary, which the author photographed for the book cover.

The author's family members paid unknown photographers, whose names are missing from the author's originals, for the photos under March 5, 1950, June 24, 1955, and August 21, 1957, of Angela (based on the author) and under January 13, 1957, and May 27, 1953 (taken around 1927), of the author's deceased aunt, who inspired the character Sara. The age of the photos makes it likely that the photographers are deceased. All efforts to identify the copyright holders have been unsuccessful.

As beneficiary of deceased relatives who took the snapshots, the author is the copyright holder of the other photographs.

The author thanks the Mensa Writers' Group for years of invaluable feedback, which helped improve the book. Special appreciation goes to Alan, Sherre, Ed, Will, Ken, Erica, Michelle, and Bill.

The author is grateful to Kevin for photo editing help and to Sherre for cover design assistance!

Last but by no means least, the author is exceptionally thankful for generous Bela's encouragement, enjoyment and appreciation of the book, specific advice, professional marketing contributions, and invaluable editing and proofreading! He has been the masculine incarnation of Clio, the Muse!

Angela Weiss was a staff writer/graphic artist of in-house books, instructional manuals, research study reports, web pages, and promotional materials. She has ghostwritten biographies and edited books and articles. **Boy Crazy** is based on her childhood diaries. Still boy crazy, Angela appreciates life in Los Angeles, where she enjoys intellectual, cultural, outdoor, and athletic pursuits, especially dancing.